RUMPELED

CINDERMAMA BOOK 2

INES JOHNSON

THOSE JOHNSON GIRLS

Edited by Dragonfly Editing
Cover design by Yocla Designs

Manufactured in the United States of America
First Edition March 2016

To my daddy, JJ "Badd Finger" Johnson, without whom, this book would have been mute.

Now, put the book down or you'll be sorry...

...I'm telling you, Daddy, if you turn the page you won't see me as your sweet little Sparkles anymore...

1

———

"It's not you, it's me."

Guy Rumpel had said those words to countless women throughout the course of his life, as he crawled out of their bed, left them behind a backstage curtain, or walked out of a bathroom stall while they were still straightening their skirts.

The difference today was that he hadn't fucked the woman sitting before him. This woman wanted to get down and dirty out in public, with thousands cheering her every dip, drop, and twerk. Frankie Benjamins sat across from Guy in his spacious office, looking for an angle to get into the music industry.

"I want it to be you." Frankie uncrossed and then re-crossed her shapely legs, giving Guy a complete Sharon Stone view of her wares.

Worse than the porn industry, the music industry was a cesspool of debauchery, depravity, dissipation, and degeneracy, and Guy was its charmed prince. He stood over six feet tall, with the dark, thick locks of a Mediterranean prince, dressed in a tailored suit. Outside the window, the platinum towers of Manhattan rose into the sky like staff notes.

"Everybody knows you're the best talent scout in the business."

"A and R," Guy corrected her. And he *had* been the best talent scout in the business. Past tense. But he didn't correct her on that.

Frankie raised her painted-on eyebrows in incomprehension.

"It stands for Artist and Repertoire. It means I not only find talent, I produce and manage my finds, including their image, their sound, and their careers."

Frankie had an image. Guy was getting an eyeful of it as her lush silicone breasts spilled over her top. Her fat-injected ass barely fit in the chair. She tapped her acrylic nails on his desk and tossed her purple tresses over her shoulder. She had an image, but she had no sound. Her voice came out like a crooning crow's.

"Are you telling me you don't want to manage my assets?" Frankie Benjamins had a third of male American television viewers fawning over her assets. She was one of the top reality stars on the Music Now Network's hit show, *Sex and R&B: Miami*. Her ass-twerking escapades as the side chick of legendary rapper, Sammie Q, had pulled her out of the strip clubs and into the spotlight.

The problem was that it wasn't enough light for Guy to bring her onto his roster at Badd Finger Records. He was looking for a new sound, not a phat ass. So, while Frankie held a good portion of the male population by the balls, Guy didn't feel a twinge in his pants.

"*You* came to me," she reminded him.

Guy narrowed his dark, gray eyes, as he looked Frankie over one more time to be sure. He squinted at her, well not exactly at her, more like just in front of her. Past the garish color of her hair were the pale, flaxen specks of light surrounding her person. When he'd first spotted Frankie twerking on the pole of a gentleman's club, he'd thought he'd seen the vibrant yellow of a canary coming off her sweaty, bouncing size D's. But looking at her today, her aura touched nowhere near the brightness of a lemon. Guy couldn't afford to make another mistake.

"We're just not right for each other," Guy said. More words he'd used to end dalliances with women he'd slept with. But in this case, the words were true.

In days long past, Guy could spot a would-be starlet buried under the dark rags of a street urchin, the thin strips exposing a stripper, or the expensive cloth that swaddled a socialite. It was his gift. It ran in his family. His mother's people were descendants of Gypsies who had the Sight. Many of them saw auras and used their visions to predict the future. Others only saw the golden aura of their true love.

Guy was able to spot talent. More than that, he had the unique ability to hone that talent, spinning the dim shades of yellow of a person's aura until it was solid gold. But these days, his vision was failing him.

Frankie wasn't the canary in the coal mines he'd thought he'd seen all those months ago. She was more like a speck of dust that had burned itself out with a short life of hard living. She stood now and rounded Guy's massive oak desk. Guy tried to hold in his sigh. He knew where her six-inch stilettos were heading.

"Are you sure we can't work together?" she purred. "I'm a lot of fun to work with, especially with all the late nights that I would dedicate to my... music."

She ran one of her taloned fingers down his chest. It

didn't have the desired effect she was hoping for. "Unfortunately for you," he said, "I think with the head on my shoulders."

Frankie's eyes went from seductive to sinister in a quarter note. "Let me be clear; if you give me a record deal, I will fuck you better than any bitch has ever fucked you. I will let you put it anywhere and at any time you want, so long as you make me a star."

They stared each other off. Guy encountered countless hopefuls on a daily basis who offered him the same trade—a fuck for fame. They thought that was all it took; a few thrusts and then they were stars. But it wasn't that simple. Guy was the one who'd have to work his ass off for the pale talent who offered their bodies for his brand of polishing. More and more, over the years, it had left him drained and depleted.

"The truth is, Frankie, you need someone who can give you the attention a bright star like you needs."

Her eyes perked from sinister to solicitous.

"You know that my top artist is Agave, and her sophomore—that means second—album is coming out in a matter of weeks. I just won't be able to spare you any attention, and I doubt you'd want to wait for months before my schedule opens up again..." He let the sentence trail off, hoping she would pick up the beat.

"You're right," Frankie straightened and stepped away from him. "I'm hot right now. I can't wait around for you."

"I understand."

"It's your loss."

"It definitely is."

Guy watched her ass cheeks trade space in her tight skirt; one went up while the other sank down. As Frankie sashayed her bitter lemon body out of his office door, Guy sat back in his leather chair. He closed his eyes and pinched the bridge of his nose. Another headache was coming on.

His throat was suddenly parched. He reached for his soda, only to find two empty bottles on his desk. He pushed the button to call his personal assistant.

"Maya, can you bring me a cold soda?"

"Of course, Mr. Rumpel."

A moment later, Maya walked into his office with a bottle, condensation running down the sides. Maya had a cute face, but she wore a formless dress that made her shape look like a box. When she'd first come on board, Guy had assumed she'd dressed that way to keep men away from her. But soon, he realized she was one of those women who had no clue that she was attractive, and spent more time on her work than on her looks.

"Mr. Calloway called while you were in your... *meeting*." Maya said meeting with a slight air of distaste. She had had her fair share of run-ins with wannabes trying to curry favor with her boss. "He'd like for you to stop by his office when you have a chance."

"Why didn't you tell me that when he called?"

"You were in with Ms. Benjamin. I didn't want to disturb you."

Guy had dumped a pile of work on Maya's desk earlier this morning, a stack of one-hit-wonders and non-starting artists he would be breaking up with. He'd given Maya the honors of delivering the news to the castoffs. He knew payback when he saw it. He growled at her, which she ignored, and then shot out of his chair and headed out of his office, bypassing Maya's outstretched hand with the soda.

He stepped out into the hall and then paused. The way to his boss' office was littered with a string of hopefuls looking to audition for an upcoming showcase. He knew the people standing in the halls were desperate for a shot, and would take any angle they could get.

Guy looked at them and blinked rapidly, his vision going blurry. They were all a haze of pale yellows. He saw a pasty, butter-hued girl in a mini-skirt, shorter than the span of her hands. She wore heels as high as her feet were long. She shimmied her curve-less hips in the approximation of a twerk she could've only learned watching Disney stars gone wild. There was also a lively, saffron group of boys, but Guy loathed boy bands, and kept going.

He made his way to the end of the hall without incident and paused outside of JJ's office. The door was open, as it always was. Inside, he saw JJ Calloway, CEO of Badd Finger Records. The large bear of a man stood over six feet tall and half as broad. His brown skin matched the mahogany of the furniture in the room. Gray speckled his dark hair, but above that, Guy saw the bright sparks of amber that remained from JJ's time as a 60's R&B singer turned record mogul.

JJ had his hand outstretched toward a man who was his opposite in every way. The man was short and thin. Blonde hair topped the thin man's head, with an aura that barely reached the pale shade of the inside of a vanilla bean.

The pale man looked up at Guy as he made his way towards the door. "There's the man! What up, bruh?"

Guy plastered on a fake smile. "What's good, T-Dawg?"

Guy didn't miss the irony of two white guys appropriating African-American slang. Guy's father was white, but his mother's ancestry could be traced back to Moorish Spain, which was how he accounted for his golden-brown skin and thick locks of hair. T-Dawg, on the other hand, was paler than porcelain.

T-Dawg was on Badd Finger's rap label. The 'T' stood for Theodore, which was given to him by his socialite mother. The 'Dawg' was appropriated by Theodore when he met Andy Jepson of the television show, *U.S. Icon*. Andy, who called everyone "dawg", had the misfortune of calling Theodore T-Dawg and Theodore ran away with the name.

Guy had spotted T-Dawg while on stage at a socialite charity event. To this day, Guy swore it was the expensive alcohol and the enthused applause of the upper-crust crowd—none of whom knew the first thing about urban music—that had convinced Guy to sign the milquetoast talent. The boy had been a one-hit wonder who'd never risen back into the top fifty charts.

Guy shook his head as he watched T-Dawg walk out of the room. "You renewed his contract?" he turned to JJ.

"His mother bought herself a seat on my board of directors after we signed her baby boy. I don't really have much of a choice anymore."

Guy grimaced, guilt rolling across his handsome features. There had been a series of duds that Guy had sworn would be the next big thing, only to have the artist hit once and then be done. Or worse, not chart at all. With the music industry undergoing so many changes in this new, digital, streaming world, the traditional brick and mortar record companies were feeling the heat.

"Guy, we need to talk."

Those were never good words. Guy turned his back and closed the door to JJ's office.

"You've been on this road with me for a while, son."

"Yes, I have." After the door clicked shut, Guy took a seat at JJ's right hand. "Since the days when this company was nearly forgotten, I helped bring it back into the spotlight."

"But you've been slipping this past year. There was a time when everything you touched turned to gold."

That was over a year ago, before Guy'd been cursed. "In the time I've been here, I've brought in more than half of the talent that tops the charts. I've produced over a dozen gold records."

"That's the Guy that I want." JJ snapped his fingers, the sound bounced off the gold records decorating the walls of the office. "The Guy with the golden touch. We can't afford any more failures. We need chart toppers if this company doesn't want to go back into the darkness and be forgotten again."

"Agave's second album is expected to go platinum."

"That's another thing I wanted to speak with you about." JJ balled his big hand into a fist. "I hear there may be trouble in paradise?"

"No," Guy avoided eye contact. "She and I are better than ever."

"You know how I feel about producers dating artists."

In his heyday, Guy had developed a bit of a reputation, often using the studio as a place to coax more than musical high notes from his artists. But that was long ago. The truth was Guy hadn't had much of a sex life in a longer time than he was willing to admit, not ever since a certain woman stormed out of his life.

"It's different between me and Agave."

JJ nodded, never taking his eyes off Guy. His deep gaze reminded Guy of his clairvoyant aunt, Gale. "Make sure and keep her happy. We can't afford to lose her. And you need to get out there and scout for some fresh meat."

"I won't let you down." Guy reached out his hand to his mentor and they shook on it.

Heading back to his office, Guy was able to skirt any

hopefuls. But crossing the threshold, he felt suddenly fatigued.

"I'm headed home for the day," he said to Maya.

"You're not going home tonight. The construction on your loft started this afternoon. I've reserved a room for you at the Waldorf Astoria."

"Fine, and would you set up a meeting for me with Agave—"

"Agave is waiting in your office."

Guy turned to face his current star. She came up and gave Guy a wet kiss on the mouth. Guy held her toned body to him, needing to hold on to something familiar and true for a moment. Agave was svelte. There wasn't an ounce of fat or jiggle on her body. She looked as though she'd been cut from marble, but she felt warm and pliant in Guy's arms.

"Hey, baby," she said, as she ran one hand down his chest. "Rough day?"

Guy nodded as he led her into his office, away from onlookers in the hall, and closed the door. "I'm fine. What can I do for my number one girl?"

"Guy, we need to talk."

Dread filled Guy's stomach, his fingers and toes went numb. "You know those are my five least favorite words."

Agave didn't take a seat. She stood, her hands folding and twisting. It brought to Guy's mind the first time he'd seen her singing during a slam poetry contest. She'd been nervous but her star had burned brightly before his eyes. It had shone somewhere between butterscotch and Dijon. He'd spent a year polishing her rough edges until the rare gem that she was shined through. Today she looked dim, like the sun on an overcast day.

Finally she looked up, at him. "It's not you," she began, "it's me."

"Correction, *those* are my five least favorite words."

"I want to go somewhere."

Guy felt warm under his collar. He reached for the soda Maya had left for him earlier and downed it in two gulps. The sugar rush went straight to the top and he felt light-headed.

"I know I have some appearances coming up, but Caroline's feeling neglected. I want to take her on a trip somewhere special and romantic, just for a couple of weeks.

"Agave, you can't disappear with your girlfriend for a couple of weeks. Not when your next album is dropping in another month."

"Guy, I've done everything you've ever asked of me, including this ruse of being your fake girlfriend to hide my... private life. I need you to make this happen for me. Once the album drops and the tour starts, I'm not going to have any time to see her and we need this time. You know how I feel about her. Please?"

Guy sighed again. Agave was the hottest pop star on the charts. Women wanted to be her and men wanted to fuck her. To keep that going, Guy and Agave pretended to be in a hot and heavy relationship. He was her beard, but he got something out of it, too. They didn't broadcast their romantic ties, but it was common knowledge in the industry. That way, no one asked either of them questions about what did or didn't go on in their bedrooms. Everyone just assumed. And that was fine by them.

"Come on, Guy."

"I'll make a deal with you," he said. "Let me see if I can move some things around for—"

She squeed. The clouds moved away from her person

and her star burned brighter with the love she felt for Carolyn. Guy envied them that. Love made every one brighter.

"You should take some time off," Agave said. "Go get yourself laid."

"I can't deal with a relationship right now."

"I didn't say a relationship, I said laid."

Guy didn't respond. Though Agave was his beard, she didn't know all of his secrets. Watching her brighten because of the love she'd found shined a light on a fact that Guy had been avoiding for some time. He could no longer handle his problem alone. He needed the help of a loved one. So, after shifting around Agave's schedule to accommodate her love life, he called Maya, hoping to cause a shift in his own.

"Maya, I need you to book me a flight home."

2

———

"This is so stressful. You are so lucky no one ever asked you to marry them, Midori."

Midori Miller gritted her teeth so hard she heard her molars grind. Catching her client's eyes in the reflection of the full-length mirror, Midori used her tongue to poke each corner inside of her mouth up into a simulation of a smile. But it didn't matter.

Phancy Jenning's eyes weren't on Midori. They were on her own size two waist, not down near her calves where Midori knelt. So, Midori dropped the facade of a smile and turned back to the lace in her hands. She'd rather pay more attention to it. The smile she offered the fabric didn't need an inner push.

Phancy's wedding gown was a thing of beauty. The bodice was a low scoop neck that showed off the woman's breasts. The fine lace at the shoulders was so light and airy that it fluttered like the wings of a butterfly. The lace material then wrapped around the torso in an intricate fashion that had taken Midori days to effect. And then the material fluttered out once more until it reached the ground in a crescendo. Phancy looked breathtaking in the gown.

From the front.

The back was another story; a story Midori was trying to alter.

"Sometimes, I envy you," Phancy continued. "Dropping out of modeling when you did. I wish I could eat what I wanted and gain ten pounds." Phancy dropped her gaze down to where Midori knelt, hemming the dress. "Or more."

Midori wore a simple, black sheath dress that fell to her knees. The dress was cinched at the waist to accentuate the curves that—contrary to current opinion—Midori was not ashamed of. And her long black tresses were pulled up in a bun so that she could work without obstruction.

Midori picked up her sharp scissors from the floor. It took everything in her to aim for the fabric and not Phancy's bony ankles. Luckily, Midori's breeding kicked in. Though they were in a New York City hotel room at the moment, both Midori and Phancy were Southern Belles. Each highly trained in the art of etiquette, manners, and cutting down a rival without breaking a nail.

"Well, I've been too busy running a business to bother with men," Midori said. "It's made me truly value the dollar, having to earn it myself and not rely on my daddy or another man."

"God, I couldn't imagine not having a man for a week, much less a decade," said Phancy.

The lace caught in Midori's nail. She carefully extricated her finger, lest she damage the delicate fabric.

When they'd first met, Midori had thought that maybe she'd found a kindred spirit in Phancy—someone else who'd been ostracized because of her odd features, which the fashion industry deemed beautiful. There was a time when exotic-looking models of mixed heritage were all the rage. Midori, whose mother was Japanese and her father African-American; and Phancy, whose mother was originally from Thailand, and her father also African-American by way of Kenya, were once the toast of the New York and Paris fashion scene.

Midori had entered that world, lured there by the beautiful clothes, the sparkling accessories, and the eccentric people who appreciated her unusual looks and unique sense of style. When she met Phancy, a girl of mixed heritage similar to her own, Midori had thought she'd found a soul sister.

She'd been wrong.

Lavender eyes twinkled down at Midori. There was a fake smile on Phancy's face to match her contacts. Unnatural eye color was in this season. If it was a trend, Phancy was right on top of it. Anything to get a leg up—even if that meant putting her legs up in the air.

"You have no idea how much work it is to stay on top," said Phancy.

Phancy stepped off the stool, giving Midori a good look at her Jimmy Chu's.

God, when's the last time she'd had on a new pair of high quality heels? Much of her designer wear was over a decade old; from the last time she'd walked a runway. And contrary to current opinion, she could still fit into... all of the shirts. Her hips had spread a bit in the past ten years. Phancy's hips were as narrow and flat as ever, which was why Midori was having trouble fitting her wedding dress.

Midori designed clothes for real women, with real

curves, bumps and humps. Phancy, her fake name and fake eyes included, was a caricature of what the fashion world considered a real woman. She had size D breasts—thank-you, silicone. Size two hips. Size eight feet and age twelve hips. No grown woman had a twelve year old's hips. Grown women grew up.

This was one of the reasons Midori didn't regret her decision to leave the runway. She'd been signed at sixteen, right after her last growth spurt. The year before, she still had the same body she'd had at twelve. She'd stood just under six feet tall with small boobs, a small waist, and no hips. All that changed just before her sixteenth birthday when her breasts developed and her hips hit a bump in the road. A bump the guys on the street called out to, but the guys in the fashion world pursed their lips at and tried to hide.

Midori pursed her lips now as she stood looking at the excess fabric at Phancy's backside. She'd designed the dress to be a waterfall, but because it had nothing to fall *from* on Phancy, it hung like a straight curtain. "I'm going to have to let it out a bit."

Phancy whirled around, nearly knocking Midori back. Midori pulled the shearing edge of the scissors away, more concerned with nicking the lace of the dress than Phancy's skin.

"What are you talking about? I haven't gained an ounce." Phancy gripped the back of the gown, her smug face shifting into a look of horror.

Midori's eyes rose to Phancy's, her memory clicking into place. Phancy was the type of person whose bark and bite were equally treacherous. But she was also the type who could dish it out but couldn't take it. Midori was tempted to play against the other woman's insecurities, but she didn't have the time nor the energy to play these childish games. She had grown woman things to do.

"The dress looks fantastic in the front, but the back isn't falling the way it was designed to because you lack... the extra assets." It was Midori's signature style, accentuating a woman's humps and bumps, not hiding them.

"Well, of course it's not gonna fall that way," Phancy brushed at her backside as though to flatten it farther.

Though the world of modeling dabbled from time to time in the ethnic and exotic, those were not the standards of beauty. Midori had been raised proud of both her parents' heritages. Phancy—

"I'm not some African bush mama."

—had not.

You'd think, as black women, they would stick together. But in the world of modeling, where ethnic faces were few and far between, and the jobs even fewer, Midori and Phancy had been pitted against each other as two of the only women of color walking the runway.

Midori watched Phancy flatten the back of the dress once more. It threw her whole design off. Phancy had had all of her bridesmaid's gowns designed by an up-and-coming designer out of Milan. But she'd reached out to Midori for this gown. When Midori asked her why, Phancy told her it was because she'd seen another gown Midori had designed.

Last year, Midori had made a gown for Pumpkin Tavares, now Pumpkin Charmayne, the wife of a reformed playboy, and now Mayor of her hometown in Louisiana. That dress had gotten Midori an increased, and more monied, clientele. But Pumpkin's wedding was small potatoes in comparison to the grandness and attendance of Phancy's. The people who would see Phancy in Midori's dress were ones who mattered in the fashion world. Midori's hands shook as she grasped the scissors at the thought. Then an idea struck her.

"It's a shame," Midori began, opening and closing the scissors. "The derrière is in this year. Have you seen the Kardashians? And who's that pop singer everyone is swearing had ass implants?"

With the seed planted, Midori gathered the fabric. She opened the shears, and—

Phancy grabbed the fabric out Midori's hands. "You know... I don't want you taking any of the fabric away. If you snip in the wrong place it could ruin the whole dress. Why don't you just add some padding to fill in the back?"

"Excellent idea." Midori closed the scissors. "I should've thought of that."

"Well, you're just a seamstress. I had to guide you on the whole design."

Before Midori could talk herself into keeping her mouth shut, the door to the hotel room opened.

"Phancy pants? You in there?"

Phancy shrieked. "William, don't come in here. I'm in my wedding dress. You can't see me." She hopped down from the stool and shut herself in the bathroom.

Through the door came a belly with a shiny belt buckle that had, of all things, a dollar sign gleaming at the straining clasp. William J. Mason, III was from old money, and he'd laid new money on top of it. Ignoring Phancy's protests, he came into the room like he owned it. He probably did.

Mason surveyed the room. His eyes landed on Midori. Then they spent an inordinate amount of time roving over

Midori's breasts and hips, giving her body parts tons of unwanted attention.

Midori gathered up her fabric, allowing it to drape in front of her body to obstruct his view. "Phancy, if you'll just take off the dress I can finish the rest of the alterations tonight."

Midori heard a muffled cry from behind the door.

"She's a little dramatic," said her fiancé. His leer now on Midori's thighs. Midori had worn a knee length skirt to allow her free movement while making her alterations. She now wished she'd opted for long slacks... and a floor length fur coat.

This wasn't the first committed man who looked at her as a temporary plaything while the missus was preoccupied. Midori gathered her tools, keeping the scissors clenched in hand and in clear view.

"Maybe you could come back later," said Mason. "We could do a fitting with my tux?"

"Sorry," Midori placed the fabric in her garment bag. "I only do women's clothing."

Mason frowned, as if he didn't understand. Then, as if on cue, a light went off in his eyes. "There's a woman I know who needs a fitting. She's my mistress and she needs some new lingerie. She's in room 846. Perhaps you could pay us a visit later on tonight."

Midori's stomach turned. Less at his offer—she'd heard worse during her days at after parties and model castings. Her stomach clenched at his assumption that she was the kind of girl who would take such an offer. She and Phancy were far from friends, but it was evident that they were working together. Plus, Phancy was in the next room for god's sake.

Men with money, with power, thought they could take

whatever they wanted. That anyone they deemed beneath them would just fall at their feet, follow behind, or be thankful for their crumbs. Well, he had the wrong one today.

Midori would never be anyone's plaything again. She wouldn't keep anyone's secret or be their secret. She was a legitimate businesswoman who'd made her own way on her talent, and didn't rest on her back. Midori opened her mouth to tell Mr. Belt Buckle all of that when the door to the bathroom opened.

"The dress is in there, Midori. Wait until we leave before you bring it out. And make the last alterations here before having the front desk bring it to my room. I don't want you to take it back to your dingy hotel. Lord knows I don't want my dress to get bed bugs. Come on, Wills, take me out to dinner. Don't you think it's so sweet that he didn't have a bachelor party his final night as a single man. He wanted to spend it with me."

Midori looked over at Mason. He still had his eyes on her breasts.

Phancy snapped her fingers in front of his nose. The older man blinked, his eyes going strangely glassy. Then he gave Phancy a dopey grin. They rubbed noses, grinning like school children.

"That's my Willy Wonka," Phancy cooed.

Midori laid a hand on her stomach in an effort to keep the contents steady.

"Take as long as you need," Phancy said. "I'll be sleeping in his room." She pulled Mason out the door and he followed like a puppet on her string.

Midori locked the door behind them. She felt oddly drained. Then she remembered she always felt drained when she worked with Phancy on the runway and in shoots. The woman seemed to have that effect on people. Midori shook it off and got to work on the dress, intent on getting out of there before Mason had a chance to come back.

She put the final touches on the gown that was now hanging on a mannequin. When she was finished, she rose and surveyed her work. Phancy would look like a million bucks in it, which was probably what she was getting, once the divorce was final.

Midori straightened and backed away from her creation. The dress was as near to perfection as it was ever going to get. The gown was fit for royalty. It looked at home in this expensive suite in the Waldorf Astoria. Midori shook her head to realize the dress would be spending the night alone in this room, which cost more than a month of groceries. But that was the way of the wealthy.

She was ready to call it a night and head back to her hotel room near the bus station. She looked and smelled like a wreck. She decided to take advantage of the hot water and sweet smelling soap, and jumped in the shower to wash away the day. The water on her skin felt good. It washed away her time with Phancy and the encounter with her distasteful, soon-to-be-ex-husband fiancé.

Midori was wrapping a towel around herself when she heard the door jiggle. She looked at the clock. It wasn't even midnight yet. Was he back already? And she was standing in the middle of the room in a towel. She eyed her shears, which were across the room.

She could scream. But that would alert the hotel staff, who might alert the media, who were surrounding the hotel because of all the celebrities and socialites staying for the wedding. And how would that look? Fledgling designer seduces groom before wedding day. That wasn't the kind of exposure Midori wanted for her business.

The door opened. A large figure loomed in the dim light.

How the hell was she gonna get out of this?

3

Guy fought a monster headache without the benefit of having imbibed any alcohol. The bright lights and boisterous sounds of New York City at night roiled through his body like vodka over rocks. Surviving the unwanted advances of a sexually aggressive stripper who was out of touch with reality, and the pressures of trying to keep up a hot and heavy relationship with a closeted lesbian, left Guy with a stiff neck instead of a stiff cock.

Escaping to a hotel room where no one could bother him would be a welcome relief. After a peaceful night's sleep, he would escape the incessant throb of the city for a trip down south where things moved at a slower, quieter pace.

Guy grimaced as a room service attendant rolled a cart of unfinished, roasted vegetables down the hall. The asparagus lay limp, untouched. A speared stalk of broccoli wilted over the tines of a fork.

His stomach grumbled, but not for any of the green fare on the cart. He hungered for something sweet and decadent on his tongue. A lush chocolate cake to assuage his throbbing head. A velvety slice of cheesecake to ease its way down his stiff throat.

Guy's fingers went numb with anticipation of the treat. It took him a second to fish the room key card from his pocket. The first swipe netted him a red light. He tried it again, with the same result.

The young woman at the concierge desk had been a mess with a large wedding party trying to check in. The hotel had been booked solid, even though Guy had a reservation. It had taken a bribe to get the concierge to get the key he now held in his hand. She'd recognized him; it was New York after all. She was a budding songstress, of course. Guy had slipped her his business card in order to secure his room. He had to remind himself to put the chain lock on the door or face a midnight visitor with hopes of sweetening a potential record deal.

After a third swipe, the key card failed again. Guy shut his eyes. The last thing he wanted to do was go back down and face the budding songstress who'd had a thick Jersey drawl and a straw colored aura. He sent up a prayer and tried once more. This time it worked.

Guy stepped inside, closing the door behind him. The light was already on, which was odd. His first order of business was to reach the phone to place his room service order. Before he could reach the desk where the phone lay, he caught a flash of white from the corner of his eye.

In the middle of the room was a mannequin in a wedding dress. Guy nearly laughed at the absurdity of it. Was this some kind of joke?

While Guy's tired brain tried to puzzle that one out, another flash of movement caught his eye. He turned his head. Standing to the left of the mannequin was a woman dressed in only a towel. All the anticipation of dessert slumped out of him.

Guy had his fair share of groupies, desperate women and men trying to slip him a CD. Models and video girls sneaking back stage or into his hotel room. Even would-be child stars coming up to his table in restaurants. But he was not in the mood for it tonight. He did not have the time or disposition to deal with a groupie or wannabe starlit after the day he'd had. He just wanted a moment of peace where he had to focus on no one but himself.

The woman made a movement towards him. Guy assumed it was to drop the towel and show her wares. He held up his hands in a stop motion and shut his eyes.

"Look," he began, "I'll make a deal with you. Whatever you're selling, pushing, or promoting, just leave it on the desk and I'll look at it or listen to it in the morning."

He heard a shuffle, which indicated she'd moved. When he didn't hear her belt out a tune or make a sexual suggestion, he decided he'd better chance a look. Not because he was interested, because he wasn't.

Guy tentatively lifted an eyelid. Then he wrenched them both open in utter shock.

A tall drink of a woman was standing before him. She had honeyed skin that was the color of piecrust just out of the oven. Her eyes, the color of caramel drizzled on top of a warm brownie, slanted in an exotic way. She had plump, strawberry red lips that didn't look artificially injected. The towel was pressed down on her chest, not buoyed, which would indicate a lack of silicone. The towel was still pulled tightly around her body, but Guy could make out the humps and bumps of her body. Her mouth was agape, but no sounds came from her lips to try to impress or seduce him. Most shocking of all, she had a pair of scissors in one hand, and they were pointed at his chest.

Guy dropped his hands. "What the hell is this?"

"Get out of my room," she snarled, waving the sharp shears at him.

"Are you studying to be an actress? Because this is feeling pretty damned real. I could probably get you on as an extra—"

"I said out." She waved the shears again.

Guy took a step back, utterly confused. How would she get what she wanted from him if he wasn't in the room?

"What are you?" She waved the shears again. "Some friend of the groom's? All of you guys are the same, thinking women want you for your money or your connections or whatever."

Guy cocked his head. Yeah, that was what women typically wanted him for. What was this particular woman's game? Guy looked down at the keycard clutched in his hand. "You sneak into my room, with this bawdy wedding dress, right after I—"

"Bawdy!" The scissors lowered, but her chin rose sky high.

He looked into her eyes. The deep hazel brown contrast made her skin shimmer with more honey, or was that gold?

"I'll have you know, this is top of the line, quality lace." She reached out and ran a hand gently over the fabric.

Guy looked over at the dress. Then back at her. She looked more interested in the dress than in him.

Guy was an excellent read of people. He could make anyone a star, had made a great many people stars, people who would never have reached the altitude without his guidance and golden touch. He could always tell what people wanted, and he could see how to help them achieve it. He was more a talent magician than talent scout.

But this woman, he couldn't quite get a read on. It was as though a cloud surrounded her aura, as though she were shielding herself. Guy focused, and stared just in front of her person. A single ray of golden-yellow broke over her shoulder, but he blinked, and it was gone.

She had the height and posture of a model, but she had to be in her mid or late twenties, too old to enter that arena. She didn't strike him as a singer either, not with that husky voice. He would've guessed actress by her indignant performance, but the way she looked at the dress instead of carrying on with a performance gave him pause.

Guy was intrigued. "Tell me what you want from me?"

She tore her gaze from the dress. Her grip retightened around the handle of the scissors. "I told you, I want you to get out of my room."

"Your room?"

She nodded.

"Where's your key card?"

She flinched. "Well, it's not exactly *my* room. It's the dress' room."

"Oh," Guy backed away. "The dress booked the room." She was a crazy.

She frowned at his retreat. "The bride. She got the room for the dress."

Now she was looking at Guy as though he was the one talking crazy.

"There's a wedding happening here tomorrow," she said. "The bride booked the room so we could do the last minute alterations."

"The bride?"

"The bride is my client. I thought you might be one of the groom's guests?"

Guy shrugged. He had no idea who was in the wedding party. He looked at the dress. Then down at the shears in her hands. On the floor was a case with measuring tape and materials. "So, you're a seamstress?"

Her eyes blazed once more. "No, I'm a designer. I designed this dress."

"Oh. It's... nice."

Another fire in those hazel eyes.

"Look, I'm sorry." Guy put his hands back up. "I don't know anything about fashion."

"This dress is more than nice. It's a masterpiece."

She stood there in a towel and detailed the technicalities of her craftsmanship on the garment. It all went over Guy's head. He studied her again. Her long legs. The purple paint on her toenails. The way the corners of her eyes tilted up like a secret smile. As she spoke about the dress another ray of golden-yellow broke from her person. Guy focused on the ray. It looked pure and golden, but the moment she stopped talking and turned back to him, it blinked away again.

Guy cursed under his breath. He was seeing things now. His gifts only lent themselves to the performing arts. He had no understanding of fashion. There was no reason he should see any light around this designer. The curse must be getting worse.

The tiredness returned to his shoulders. "I guess the hotel mixed up the rooms."

"No," she put down the scissors. "We were just using this room as a fitting room. I'm supposed to have checked out by now. I was just getting freshened up before leaving. Just let me get dressed and I'll get out of your way."

She ducked into the bathroom.

Guy sat down on the bed, his appetite suddenly gone. He massaged the place where his neck and shoulder connected, and tried to ease the stiff ache. He could deny it no longer. His Sight was failing him. He was well and truly cursed.

For the last year, he'd taken on more than one artist he'd thought was a deep shade of yellow. Rather than admit he'd stepped on a banana peel, Guy had worked twice, sometimes four times, as hard to get the duds onto the bottom of the charts.

The numbness returned to Guy's fingers and his head began to throb once more. He wondered if the constant headaches and numbing were more aspects of the curse. His fingers and toes weren't his only appendages that were constantly numb.

Guy didn't have time to sink any farther into his woe-is-me. The designer reemerged only five minutes later. He was stunned at the quickness.

"That was a fast change." He stood, remembering his manners when a lady entered the room. He'd spent so much time around women who acted anything but the genteel lady, his knees creaked as he straightened them for this one.

"Occupational hazard," she said.

She was dressed in a simple black dress, but the belt at the waist showed off her hourglass figure. Guy's fingertips and toes warmed as he regarded her curves.

She bent down to gather the rest of the fabric and her scissors into her case. Then she stood and put the wedding dress in a garment bag. Guy watched as she loaded the garment bag, her case, and the mannequin into her arms.

"Let me help you with that." He'd been standing still,

watching her body swish around in the confines of the dress.

"No, no. I've got it."

"Seriously, I can—"

"I'm good," she insisted. "I've been doing this for years without any help. I can handle it." And, as though to illustrate her point, she headed for the door, arms full, back straight. Her long legs carried her forth with grace and ease.

Guy dashed ahead. The least he could do was get the door for her. "You going to your room?"

"I don't have a room. I'm gonna drop the dress off and head home."

"You're not staying for the wedding?"

"I don't do weddings." She crossed the threshold into the hall.

"I didn't catch your name," Guy called after her.

"Why would you need it?" She paused, looking over her shoulder, her arms loaded with her wares.

Guy caught a glimpse of her rounded ass under the contours of her dress. It was heart-shaped. "Want to be able to say I met the famous dress designer before she blew up."

She didn't smile at that. "Name's Midori. Midori Miller." She turned and continued down the hall without waiting for his name.

Upon her retreat, Guy checked her aura again. He saw a ray of the brightest gold shine through, and this time it stayed after he blinked. Even if it were a mirage, a trick of the curse, Guy drank it in. It had been so long since he'd seen real, golden talent. He felt the tiniest kick in his pants. But then Midori turned the corner, and the ray, the woman, and his erection were gone.

4

———

idori stepped off the Megabus and onto the pavement. She rolled her neck and stretched her arms. Her nostrils flared at a foul stench. She cringed when she realized her nose was in the vicinity of her armpits and the smell was coming from there. The shower from the hotel in New York was a long ago memory. She needed another, and soon.

Midori grabbed her small piece of luggage. It was vintage Louis Vuitton—a gift she'd liberated from backstage during her modeling days. The wheel had cracked, so she had to be careful how fast she went. The zipper was worn around the edges from years of over packing. The grip on the handle was loose. But no one ever noticed that the wheel was falling off, or that the sides were bursting at the seams, or that the suitcase was close to falling out of Midori's hands. They only noticed the stylish woman who carried the iconic pattern that broadcasted elitism, and branded her worthy of a moment's attention.

That was all Midori needed in most cases—a moment. In that moment, she could look at a woman and know how to dress her to bring out her best self. Midori was a genius at hiding imperfections and showcasing assets. She pulled the twice-hemmed collar of her jacket up to hide the puffiness of her eyes, regripped her luggage, and headed out of the bus terminal to her car.

The wheels of her suitcase had traveled over a carpeted airport walkway two days ago when she went up to New York. Midori had flown up to the city with the wedding dress, splitting the fare between four nearly maxed out credit cards. But now that the garment was delivered and tailored to perfection, she could simply squeeze herself into a bus seat. The bus cost a fraction of the airfare, but took four times as long to return her home.

As Midori stepped out of the bus terminal, she stepped directly into the glare of the setting sun. She raised her hand to shield her eyes and ducked into the shadows at the side of the building. From the shadows, she was able to spot her car in the parking lot. It was a 1982 BMW, originally her father's. The outside of the vehicle gleamed as bright as the day it was purchased. Midori slid onto the pristine leather seats. She shoved the key into the ignition, said a little prayer, and then cranked over the ignition. By the grace of the gods, it only took two tries before the car shuddered to life.

Midori's car rumbled down the streets of Saint Anne's Parish as the sun trailed behind her like an annoying, younger sibling. It was long past midday and the sun's tenure was nearly loose, but the disk hung big and bright in the sky, clinging to clouds as though they were monkey bars. The night-light of the moon appeared above the sun, announcing that it was time for it to go inside for the night. Darkness fell around the streets, and Midori finally let go of the stress of the last two days.

Phancy's check would put her back above water, but there was still more work to do if Midori hoped to stay afloat. There was always more work to do.

Midori pulled up to the white mansion with columns. It looked like a plantation; only she knew it was built in the last century, to look like an old southern home. When she rang the doorbell she expected a butler or maid to answer, but no.

"You're back already?" Malika "Pumpkin" Charmayne pulled the great door wide.

She was dressed in jeans and a T-shirt with bare feet, but the jeans were the fitted pair the two women had bought together a few months ago, and the t-shirt was a pattern that suited her honey-brown skin tone. Midori had made Pumpkin change her style to accommodate being a mayor's wife, and all of the appearances and charity functions that went with the role. She helped nudge Pumpkin with small changes that enhanced who the woman was at her core.

Pumpkin was a curvy girl like Midori. Pumpkin's height gave her an hourglass figure that lent itself to the easy breezy wrap dress, the V-neck top, and the pencil skirt. With these three additions to her wardrobe, Mrs. Charmayne was now camera ready with anything she pulled from her closet. Pumpkin's transformation proved Midori's point that finding your brand of style didn't have to be a complete overhaul, just a few minor tweaks.

"I thought the wedding was today?" Pumpkin ushered Midori inside the dark foyer and closed the door behind her. "Here, let me help you with that." Pumpkin reached for Midori's case.

"No worries, I can handle it."

Pumpkin ignored Midori and took the case from her

hands. "Why didn't you stay for the wedding? I thought she was one of your best friends?"

Midori wanted to warn Pumpkin about the weak clasp on the suitcase, but the other woman seemed to instinctively know, and handled the case with care. She had to remember, like herself, Pumpkin came from humble beginnings.

"Phancy doesn't have friends, more like frenemies. And I don't do weddings."

"Says the wedding dress designer." Pumpkin turned and led Midori down the hall towards the light in what Midori knew was the family room.

"I thread the needle." Midori fell in line behind her. "I don't buy into the fairytale."

Pumpkin stopped walking, and turned to face Midori with a quizzical look. "I got a fairytale."

"The mayor's one of a kind. And I'm not looking for a prince."

"I said the same thing a year ago."

"Well, there aren't any more like him, so I think I'm good."

Before Pumpkin could launch another argument, a blur of dark hair crashed into Midori.

"Mama!"

"Hey, precious girl." Midori wrapped her arms around her ten-year old daughter, Kimmei.

Kimmei was tall for her age. Her head came up to Midori's breasts, leaving Midori's face nestling in a bush of silky curls. Kimmei had her mother's angular face, with high cheekbones and large, catlike eyes. But Kimmei's nose was more aquiline and her lips were thin like her father's.

"Did you have a good time?" Midori asked.

"Yeah," Kimmei bounced on her toes. The child was

nearly incapable of standing still. "Seth was teaching me *Magic the Gathering.*"

Midori peered behind her daughter to see Pumpkin's nine-year-old son come out of the family room. His eyes were fixed on Kimmei in clear adoration. "You were teaching her magic tricks, Seth?"

"Not magic tricks," he said. "It's a strategy game."

Midori nodded. Her eyes connected with Seth's. He had dark intelligent eyes. Midori knew Seth had a crush on Kimmei, and Kimmei was likely as oblivious as any adolescent girl would be.

"And then we wrote a song together," said Seth. "It's about two dragons. You wanna hear it? But not from me. Kimmei sings it really nice."

Without being asked to, Kimmei took center stage. The foyer had been dark a moment ago, but the light from the family room seemed to have migrated out into the hall where they all stood, and centered on Kimmei. The little girl loved the spotlight and never shied away from attention. Midori looked around to see if she was disturbing anyone, but everyone just beamed at Kimmei as always.

Midori marveled at the tenor of her daughter's voice, so like her grandfather's. Midori's father had been an opera singer. He'd traveled the world singing. Audiences were astounded by the tall, slight black man with his baritone voice. On a stop in Japan, he'd met and fallen in love with Midori's mother.

When Kimmei finished her song, Midori and Pumpkin applauded as was expected. Seth clapped the loudest.

"That was a really inventive song, Seth."

"Thanks, Ms. Midori," Seth smiled shyly, his eyes still on Kimmei.

"How did everything go in New York, mama? Did your

dress get in the newspapers? Are your clothes going to be in a fashion show?"

"Everything went well, precious girl. The bride loved the dress." That was mostly true. An article of clothing was more apt to get Phancy's love than another living soul. "She's famous, so she will probably be in the fashion section of the newspapers wearing the dress."

As for her own fashion show, Midori had no interest in being near a runway again in her lifetime, and that went for her dresses too. Midori was a boutique dressmaker, catering to one individual at a time. The runway and retail corralled everyone into looking the same.

"I want to be famous," Kimmei twirled in the light of the family room. "I want to have people take my picture and ask for my autograph."

"I want your autograph, Kimmei," said Seth.

Midori's instincts were to reach for her child and pull her close to her where she stood in the dimly lit foyer. She knew that fame cast a harsh light on those who sought it.

"Midori, my dear."

Midori turned into another ray of sunshine. Gale Charmayne came from the opposite hallway. The older woman was dressed in her gypsy chic finest; a burst of colors that Midori would never have paired, but it worked on Gale. "It's good to see you, Gale."

"You, too, dear. You're just in time. Dinner's almost ready."

"Oh, no, no," Midori backed away, farther into the foyer. "I don't want to impose."

"It wouldn't be an imposition at all. Cooking is my love language."

"But I'm a mess." Midori squeezed her arms into her body to stay the stench of her travels.

"This place has a million bedrooms," Pumpkin placed her hand on Midori's shoulder, halting her retreat. "Take a shower. You probably have a change of clothes in your suitcase."

"But you all have already taken care of my child for two days. I don't want to take advantage of you."

Gale laughed and pulled Midori into a hug. The few steps forward brought Midori a step closer to the light cast by the family room. Midori was startled and stiff at first, but then her body melted into Gale's warmth. How long had it been since she'd been held?

"Someone can only take advantage of another if they let them," Gale said, as she pulled away from Midori.

Gale held Midori's gaze. Midori felt as though those light gray eyes were seeing into her past, shining a light on all of her disappointments and hurts. Midori felt that way whenever she encountered Gale Charmayne, but the older woman never pried, never cajoled. She'd never once asked Midori to tell her life's story. Every encounter seemed to be a study in patience, and Midori felt that her time was running out.

"Why don't you just stay the night?" offered Gale. "That way, you can sample some of my rum punch."

Midori opened her mouth to protest. She'd already spent so much time away from home and her business. She had a mess to clean up in her bedroom, a stack of bills in her office, and a mound of work she needed to sew in her shop.

She didn't even have a chance to weave together a valid protest. Gale held both of her hands in her own. Pumpkin still had a hand resting lightly on her shoulder. Midori had felt heavy walking into this house, but now she felt light. So much so, that she just wanted to sit down and let Gale fill her belly with food and her spirit with liquor. She wanted to chat with Pumpkin about the handsome man that she'd bumped into on her way out of the hotel room's shower.

And that's exactly what she did. Midori allowed the women to pull her out of the dark foyer and into the light of the family room.

5

———

*G*uy's head pounded as he left the airport terminal. After the dressmaker left without making any requests of him, he had received the expected knock at the door that was the female concierge come to deliver her performance. Thankfully, he'd placed the chain on the door and her off-key pleas fell on deaf ears. Unfortunately, Guy's ears later tuned out his wake up call and he missed his early morning flight. The next seat that Maya could get him on was in the evening.

It was the dead of night as he stepped through the sliding glass doors of the airport and into the Louisiana night. Even though Guy had slept through most of the morning, and then slept again on the plane, fatigue plagued his body. Looking up at the night sky, the stars looked like diffused puddles. He had to blink a couple of times to bring them into sharp focus, but they still looked hazy.

Guy sighed. He couldn't get to his Aunt Gale soon enough, to get this curse lifted, or rebuked, or whatever the hell was necessary to restore his full, working Sight and get his body back to normal.

And then, as though his worn body and foggy vision weren't enough, the roar of some jerk's muscle car made his eardrums throb.

"Hey, aren't you that guy from that boy band?"

Guy scowled at his cousin, Manny Charmayne, through the rolled down passenger window of his Mustang. Manny revved his engine louder with a cheeky grin on his face. His cousin knew how much Guy detested boy bands. Men weren't meant to dance in sync, in matching clothes. "Keep talking, Mayor. Just remember, I know all your dirty, little secrets."

"You're the only dirty secret I know." Manny got out of the car and embraced him. "It's good to see you. It's been too long."

"I was just here for your wedding."

Guy saw the flash of gold on Manny's left hand. His cousin looked happy, happier than he'd ever seen him. That didn't surprise Guy. Growing up in the Charmayne family, he was surrounded by happy couples who made each other stronger. Mostly.

"Why is it that I get the honor of your presence? Not that I'm complaining." Manny asked, as they both climbed into the car. "You're not going to stay with your sister?"

"It's a weekend when her husband's actually in town." Guy said the word husband as though it were a flat note. "You know how I feel about that guy."

Manny nodded his head to the broken tune. "Yeah, the same way I do."

Guy's twin sister, Beau, had married a man the family thought was all wrong for her. It was the only wedding ceremony that had ever been rained on, but Beau insisted that Phillip was her One, and no Charmayne had ever been wrong before.

"Speaking of better halves..." Manny hedged.

Guy knew where this conversation was going. For a while, he and Manny had been the oldest, unmarried males in the family, the oldest unmarried *people* in the family. Manny had nearly given up hope that he'd find his One, which was right when he'd 'seen' Pumpkin.

Years earlier, Guy had begun to suspect that it wouldn't happen for him; at least not in the traditional Charmayne sense. His Sight allowed him to see the gifts and talents of others. His skills and passion for music allowed him to hone the subpar talent of wannabes. But he'd never been able to see love.

Every woman he'd ever seen gold around, or polished until her own personal gold shone through, had been more interested in using him as a stepping-stone, rather than staying with him for the long haul. He'd spun his fair share of stories to the lackluster wannabes, for a roll in the hay. One such romp had left him in his present condition, a condition which no vibrant woman would put up with for too long.

"You've been dating your artist, what's her name? Sugar?"

"Agave." Guy squirmed in his seat as Manny fished for information.

"It's been a year hasn't it? That's the longest I've ever known you to be in a relationship. It must be serious."

Guy shrugged. Manny knew him better than most. They'd grown up together and were close, even though they'd lived the last decade apart. When they were younger, they both had been very popular with the ladies. Manny, with his dark looks, light eyes, and charm. Guy didn't get the Charmayne light eyes, but he did get his fair helping of good looks and charm.

"I was hoping to meet this woman who can hold your attention, but you didn't bring her to my wedding."

"She was busy." Agave had been off patching things up with her girlfriend, after a video shoot where she was shaking her practically naked ass in a group of similarly scantily clad men.

"You could've brought her this weekend," Manny said.

That was the one thing he couldn't do. The Charmaynes were not only an insightful bunch, they were also nosey. And they knew Guy well. They'd see that the relationship he had with Agave was a complete ruse in under five minutes. And then, worse, they'd start asking the question Guy didn't want to answer: why was he pretending?

"Well, she's obviously making you happy. You're getting a dad bod."

Guy looked down at his torso. True, his six-pack was more of a two-pack these days, but it had nothing to do with Agave. All the stress he was under was causing him to miss meals, then binge on fast foods, and drink sugary, caffeine-loaded sodas like they were water. His schedule kept him so busy that he hadn't seen the inside of a gym in over a year.

Guy had taken on so many mediocre artists in the past year and a half, and then had spent an inordinate amount of time polishing their lackluster talent until it had a semblance of gold. He'd earned the record company a number of gold albums with this hard work, but it had taken its toll on him.

When they pulled up to the house, all the lights were off.

"Looks like everyone's asleep," Manny said, as he grabbed his briefcase. "I've been in meetings all day. Why don't you just take your old room and we'll talk some more in the morning."

Guy had been eager to speak to his aunt, but disappointment clashed with fatigue and he knew he wouldn't be able to hold a coherent conversation before the sun came up. He climbed the steps to his old room. The lights were off and he was thankful for that. He knew the room by heart. He placed his suitcase against the wall and undressed.

When he slid into the bed, he noticed how warm it was. Then he noticed how fleshy it was. He reached out his arm and met a warm body.

Guy sprang from the bed and reached for the light. He blinked. And then blinked again. There was a woman in his childhood bed. She was looking at him with the same shock. The recognition dawned in their eyes at the same time.

"You," they said in unison.

"What are you?" she demanded. "Some type of creepy, bedroom stalker? You sneak into girls' bedrooms, trying to get lucky?"

"This is my bedroom," Guy insisted.

"First, your hotel room. Now, your bedroom. How'd you even find me?"

"I wasn't looking for you."

Guy looked at her. She wasn't in a towel tonight. This time she was in her bra and panties. Guy wanted to pinch her ass to see if it was real—the dream, not her ass—because this had to be a dream. He'd gone from blurry visions to clear hallucinations.

She grabbed a pillow. It didn't hide her curves that well. He snapped his gaze to her eyes, mostly so she wouldn't grab the sheet to cover the rest of her. But she wasn't the one who needed the coverage at the moment.

Holy shit, he needed to grab a sheet. When was the last time that happened? He knew better than to get too excited.

Well, more excited than his southern region apparently was.

He looked at her again, his glance accusatory this time. He wasn't hallucinating. There it was: shards of golden-yellow cutting through the haze. There was true gold surrounding this woman. But she looked like she was ready to bolt. More than anything, Guy wanted her to stay, just so he could stare at her -at the gold surrounding her- not at her body. Well, yes, at her body, too.

"This is the second time I've found you without clothes on, in my room," he said. "If anyone's stalking, it's you stalking me."

"I don't even know who you are."

Guy looked at her in disbelief. Something in his gut told him she wasn't lying. Charmaynes always trusted their gut.

She put her hands to her temples and rubbed. The pillow fell away revealing the angles and planes of her torso. "What the hell did Gale put in that punch?"

"Gale's rum punch? How much did you have?"

"Two glasses... and a half."

Guy chuckled. "You should be on your back."

Her hands jerked away from her eyes, but she didn't cover her body. She just glared at him. "I've had a really bad day. Yesterday, I had to deal with a client from hell. And then this guy keeps showing up in my room."

"My room," he corrected. "Both times."

She looked at him skeptically.

"I'll prove it. On the wall over there." Guy chucked his chin in the direction of the wall. "There are pencil marks. My aunt, Manny's mother, would measure my height each summer I stayed here. The marks stop at seventeen, when she died."

She turned and looked at the wall, giving Guy more

access to the curves of her ass. He felt another twinge in his boxers. His erection still hadn't gone down. He was almost tempted to do something about it, but he knew better than to get his hopes up.

"You're Manny's cousin?"

"Guillaume Rumpel. Everyone calls me Guy."

"Midori Miller."

"Yeah, I remember. What are you doing in my childhood bedroom, Midori?"

"Pumpkin, Manny's wife, she's an acquaintance—well, a friend, I guess. We were having dinner and then I had some of Gale's punch—"

"Say no more," Guy laughed. Many men had fallen to Auntie Gale's rum punch.

"So, you're a Charmayne?"

"Guilty. On my mother's side."

"I ask because you're staring at me. You looking for some sorta golden aura, because I can save you time. Trust me, I'm not The One."

"Oh, I see gold."

Midori's eyebrows rose.

"Not that kind of gold. That's not how the Sight works with me. I'm an A&R Executive. A talent scout."

"Oh." The oh sounded entirely unimpressed. "For, like, actors?"

"Music."

Midori shrugged. Guy had never had anyone shrug at his title before. He was tempted to pull out his dossier of solid gold records and chart-topping singers.

"I don't sing," she said. "I sew."

She seemed so comfortable in her body. That couldn't be the whole story.

"You used to model?" he asked.

"A long time ago," her tone was cautious. "How'd you know?"

"You're half naked and completely unselfconscious about it."

She looked down at her partial nudity and shrugged again. "That's not true." But she didn't bother to cover herself. "I'm not a model any more. I make clothes now."

"Did you make Pumpkin's wedding dress?"

"Yeah."

"Why didn't I see you at the wedding?"

"I don't do weddings."

"Why are you here tonight?"

"I decided to stay the night because..." She looked around the room as though she was just noticing where she was. "I just needed a break from my life."

"I know what you mean. I need the same kind of break."

"Is that why we keep ending up in the same bedroom?" She grinned, and then immediately sobered. "I didn't mean..." She motioned to his shorts.

He wondered if she could tell that he was aroused? He wasn't at full mast, but Guy was having all kinds of inappropriate thoughts of Midori's head thrown back in ecstasy. His eyes roamed her breasts, wondering what her skin would taste like.

Damn, it had been long since he'd tasted warm, wet woman. But the risk of a failure was too much to tempt his tongue.

"Aunt Gale would say we're in the same karass," he said. "It's an Egyptian boat that carries souls who undergo a journey together, because they have a shared purpose."

"I can't imagine what purpose we would share."

"I know a lot of people. Maybe I can hook you up with some fashion houses in New York."

Now she grabbed the blanket off the bed and covered herself. "I'm not looking for a hook up." Then she blanched at the sexual innuendo. "When people offer to help, they usually want something in return. And. I. Just. Can't."

"I understand what you mean. I make deals with people all the time. But the other person usually winds up taking more. I give so much of myself, they reap the benefits, and I'm left exhausted and... empty."

They stared at each other for a moment. Neither speaking or moving.

Midori broke the gaze and the silence. "Why are we pouring our hearts out to one another? We're complete strangers."

"No, we're not. We're on the same karass."

She smiled. "Listen, I'm sorry. I didn't know this was your room. I just took the first empty one. I'll find another."

"No, I'll go. You don't know where you're going. I do." Guy shoved into his clothes and grabbed his suitcase. "See you in the morning?"

She nodded, pulling the blanket up to her chest. He looked back again before he closed the door. She'd laid her torso down on the mattress, her dark hair spread out across the pillow. She offered him a small smile before he turned the light out.

Guy closed the door behind him. As the door clicked closed, he noticed his dick was still semi-hard and he was no longer tired.

6

Midori rolled over on the bed after the door closed. From the brief encounter, Guy Rumpel's scent saturated the pillow. Or maybe it had smelled this way for years and his presence tonight added a fresh layer.

His natural smell was that of essential oils. It reminded her of bay leaves, warm and meaty, sweet and spicy. Having spent so much time around chemical-based perfume fragrances, she appreciated the smell of the earthy, oil scent. She inhaled deeply, her tongue rubbing against her inner lip asking to be let out for a taste.

Midori clamped her mouth shut.

She hadn't had a reaction like this to a man in... God, she couldn't remember the last time. What was it about this guy? He had the dark Mediterranean looks of his cousin Manny, but with darker eyes and lighter skin. Those dark, gray eyes had tried to penetrate Midori's tough exterior and get at the heart of her. She'd nearly let him in when he told her he saw gold.

But she hadn't let him in. He wasn't the first man to tell

her she was talented, different, or special. Her heart had pounded in her chest at his praise. She'd felt the familiar fluttering in her stomach, then the usual shortness of breath. Her palms began to sweat and the numbness rained down her legs.

When he mentioned her modeling career, the memories of standing and being judged and prodded had her belly churning acid. Those old pressures settled around her like a heavy fog. She remembered the hope of go-sees, where one designer would tell her she was perfect but would never call her for a show, while another would point out her flaws, dismiss her, then call her back for another round of the same. It was during that time that she'd begun dissociating from her body.

Guy's eyes had roamed her body and Midori had fought to stay in the present and not dissociate. He was a talent agent for singers, she told herself. He had nothing to do with the cruel, judgmental fashion world that cast her up high one day, and flung her down hard the next.

Midori rolled over, determined to let these thoughts go, and sleep. Instead, she caught another whiff of Guy's scent and her eyes opened wide.

He'd offered to help her, to introduce her to some people in New York. Midori knew plenty of people in New York. She preferred life here in Saint Anne's, where she didn't face the capricious judgment of New York and Paris. She worked one-on-one with clients, giving them exactly what they wanted or pushing them towards the style they needed.

She'd taken many a housewife out of yoga pants of colorful prints meant to distract, and put them into high-waisted skirts with solid colors meant to attract. She'd refitted prim society misses in cocktail dresses with streamlined blazers as they left ballrooms and entered board-rooms. All while the runways continued to send messages to those mothers to get on the treadmill if they ever hoped to be stylish again. The department stores told those misses they needed to spend thousands of dollars to look like everyone else. Working one-on-one, Midori was able to show the everyday woman, from the schoolteacher to the mayor's wife, how to enhance her own unique beauty. Though there *were* times when she wished she could reach more than one woman at a time, but life in the slow lane of Saint Anne's kept the numbness away.

Midori's phone rang, breaking her mental reverie. She knew better than to answer this late at night. It could only mean one thing. But she knew he'd keep calling until she answered.

"It's late, Michel."

"Bon, you are awake."

Midori clamped down on the shudder that began at her cheek where her cellphone rested. She'd always been a sucker for accents, and Michel's French brogue had done her in ten years ago. But not tonight.

"Dor?"

She crossed her arms over her chest as he rolled his R's. Ten years ago, she'd loved that pet name, believing it was his way of saying j't adore. Now it sounded too much like door, which was how Michel treated her for the duration of their relationship.

"I'm trying to sleep because it's late," she said. "What do you want?"

"Were you up working, cherie? I want to know how it went in New York?"

His soft tone wasn't fooling her. It had when she was a twenty year old girl, but she was a grown woman now.

"All right, Dor. You don't have to tell me, but I want you to know that you're not alone. I'm here if you want someone to listen to you."

It wasn't true. Midori was alone. Always alone. And truthfully, she preferred it that way. Friends could smile in your face and then stab you in the back. Love made you stupid and blind, so blind that everyone else saw the lies but you. "We don't have anything to discuss."

"We have something to discuss. We have a daughter."

"You wanna see your daughter?"

"Yes. I want to come and see you."

"If you want to see *your daughter*, you can come and see *her*. You don't need to see me."

He huffed, just like she knew he would. Michel had no interest in spending time with their daughter. He only wanted to get Midori alone in a bedroom, or living room, or a laundry room.

"I'll see when I can get over there. It's high season here in Paris," was his non-committal answer. "Listen Dor, what do you need—"

"I don't need anything from you." Michel's kindness always came at a price, and Midori was too broke to pay for it. "We're fine."

"I'll put a check in the mail."

Midori almost caved. The money could really help. Midori didn't lack clients, but she had a habit of buying the most expensive fabrics for the women she served. The fabrics would often eat into her profits. Everything from Michel always cost her so much more. The money from Phancy's dress would tide her over for a while, and then she had clients lined up. Small town clients, but they were enough to pay her bills. Just enough.

"I want to help you, Dor. You never let anyone help you."

He wanted the door to her heart to open to him again, but it was closed. "Why don't you take care of your own life, starting with your wife." Midori hung up the phone instead of waiting for his retort.

Michel had been her first love, and she'd fallen hard. He'd been an up and coming designer in Paris ten years ago, and she'd been cast to walk his debut show. After the show, he'd coaxed her into showing him her own designs. He'd gushed over them, calling her talented, different, and special. He hadn't needed to flatter her to get her into bed, but it hadn't hurt. Michel had taken some of her drawings and gained interest in them with the fashion house where he designed. He wanted her to work for him. He wanted to bring her into the fashion design world. All of her dreams were coming true.

She'd believed that what she and Michel had was real. She'd already been ready to leave the modeling world when she found out she was pregnant. When she told him, he'd recoiled.

Midori still remembered the feeling. Her stomach churned even now at the memory of the look on his face. Then her absolute devastation to learn the man she'd planned to spend the rest of her life with, the man she'd given her body, mind, and soul to, had betrayed her by hiding his wedding ring.

Worse, it wasn't Michel who told her about the hidden band. It had been Phancy. Phancy pretending to be concerned, pretending to be her friend, all the while it had been the best entertainment for the entire modeling world, and Midori hadn't known she was the star.

Midori'd slunk back to the states with her tail between

her legs and a baby in her belly. She'd reached high and touched her dreams. She'd been a top model, she'd been in love, and she'd nearly become a fashion designer for a house in Paris. But it all came crashing down around her. It had been a painful experience, one Midori never planned to live through again.

That world of spotlights and runways wasn't for her. This world—the real world, with real people who walked in the sunlight on the streets or under the fluorescent lighting of an office building—this is where she belonged and this is where she would stay.

*M*idori opened her eyes to the bright light of day. A scratching sound at the door woke her, and her pounding head refused to let her go back to sleep. The scratching sounded again. Midori knew the gentle inquiry couldn't be Kimmei who would've burst into the room unannounced. She wondered if it was Guy.

She brushed her hand through her hair only to have it tangle. Then she chastised herself. What was she doing grooming for this stranger?

"Midori? You decent?" Pumpkin poked her head in the door with a smile.

"How are you standing? You had as much of that devil juice as I did."

Pumpkin came in with a steaming mug. "I've brought you the remedy."

The remedy was a foul smelling concoction, but Midori drank, and the room stopped spinning.

"How did you sleep?" Pumpkin took a seat on the bed.

Midori took a second to swallow the brew. It loosened her tongue. "I had a midnight visitor."

Pumpkin looked around the room in confusion, and then she winced. "Oh, no! This is the room Guy stays in when he's here. Manny just told me he got in late last night. I'm so sorry."

"It's fine. He was a gentleman about it." Midori stared into her steaming mug, feigning disinterest. "How well do you know him?"

"He and Manny are really close, but I've only met him once, at the wedding. He's some big shot in New York. Why? What happened between you two?"

"Nothing happened."

Perhaps it was the way she said *nothing*, accenting each syllable in the word. Pumpkin's eyebrows rose and a matching grin lifted up her lips. "He came to the wedding without a date. Doesn't look like he's found his One."

"I'm no one's One." Midori brought the warm mug close to her heart and shuffled her body back towards the headboard.

Pumpkin scratched at her jaw, but she didn't say anything.

"Besides," said Midori, "if he's a talent scout, I'm sure he has women falling over him all the time." So, even if she wanted to date him—which she didn't—she would not play side-piece or secret-trick ever again.

Pumpkin shrugged and raised her palms. "He's a Charmayne. You know they all believe in happily-ever-after, with only one true love."

"I can't think about *ever after*." Midori waved the thought off. "I'm too busy with *right now*."

"Speaking of now, what are you doing Sunday night? Manny's throwing a gala to get new business interest in the parish; mainly manufacturers. But there's also a department store he's trying to get them to build here. Gunston Fashions. Have you ever heard of the chain?"

Midori not only knew the chain, she knew the man. She'd worked for Lorne Gunston when he was still just a designer. In the last decade, he'd blown up enough to have his own chain of department stores. And she knew that he'd probably remember her from her days in fashion, or more likely her dramatic exit.

"It could be a really good contact for you," said Pumpkin.

Pumpkin couldn't see the anxiety creeping up her spine. Midori twisted the half empty mug in her hands. "Business is good. In fact, I'm a bit overloaded."

"I know business is booming, which is why I thought this would be the next step for you. Getting your designs in stores across the country."

It was true, Midori had always dreamed of seeing her designs in stores other than her own, seeing her name on the tag of an article of clothing hanging on a rack and then off a woman's back. She would design her line to fit every woman's shape and size. Most designers only thought in single digits.

No sooner did these thoughts come into her head than the anxiety returned. Midori knew she could cater to her parish clientele and a few celebrities here and there, but could she face the fair-weather judgment of the gatekeepers of that industry again?

"I'll think about it," Midori said noncommittally.

"Well, for now, get yourself dressed. Gale's making a non-alcoholic breakfast." Pumpkin rose from the bed and headed for the door.

Midori shook her head, happy to see that it didn't make

her dizzy any longer. "I've imposed on your family too much."

"Midori, you *are* family." Pumpkin offered her a genuine smile that Midori couldn't help but return.

As Pumpkin shut the door, the anxiety left Midori and was replaced by warmth. She took another sip of Gale's concoction and it warmed the rest of her through.

7

Guy's head didn't pound, it rang like it was a gong and someone had banged it. He rolled over on the mattress, but felt like he was on a capsizing boat. He rolled the other way with the same result, only the ringing in his ears got louder. When he righted himself, he realized the ringing didn't stop. He peeled one eye open to see that lights were flashing.

His cell phone.

He scooped up the device, not bothering to look at the screen. It was the weekend, he was on vacation, and he refused to deal with work. This was the one place where he could put himself first. The one place he could get a little TLC, instead of busting his ass trying to produce rockstars out of rocks.

He hit "decline" and rolled onto his stomach. His head seemed to settle for a while, but then his phone rang again. This time Guy reached for the power button and pushed it until the phone was dead.

The ringing stopped. But then his head began to pound. This time, the pounding came from the door.

"I hope you're decent, but it doesn't matter if you're not because I'm coming in."

Guy wanted to groan, but he wound up chuckling at that familiar and welcome voice. He turned to the radiant face of his aunt, Galinda, who came in in a flurry of green and black fabric, bearing a steaming mug. Guy accepted the mug of tea and a kiss on the cheek. Earthy spices wafted to his nose.

After the first sip he asked, "If this gets on you, won't you melt?"

"Try it and I'll get you, my pretty, and your little dog too."

Guy chuckled again as he downed the tea. His head instantly cleared, and his spirits lifted.

"What are you doing in this bedroom?" Gale asked.

"My bedroom was taken by a lovely, young dress designer."

"Oh, you've met Midori. She's a nice girl. Beautiful. Smart. Talented. A lovely golden aura."

Gale was forever playing matchmaker, but she only did it with people outside of the family. Love was not a subject a Charmayne failed, even those who didn't have the Sight. Their relationships always worked out. There wasn't one divorce on record. But he knew that at the core of the glances and facial expressions Gale made at him, she, along with the rest of his family, was worried about him. He was now, officially, the longest running bachelor in the family history.

"You see her gold clearly?" Guy set the mug down. "I saw it for a second."

Gale leaned forward, her gray eyes twinkling. "You saw a golden aura around Midori Miller? The fashion designer?"

Guy scratched at his temple. "She must be very talented. I don't usually see anyone besides entertainers."

Gale tipped her head back with a chuckle. Guy's finger left his temple and rubbed at his chin as he watched his aunt in confusion.

She smiled as she returned her attention to him. "You and I see on different spectrums, dear. I see straight from the heart. Your Sight has always been lower."

Guy grimaced. Gale was the aunt who told him about the birds and the bees before his father got around to it. But Gale didn't use euphemisms likes avians and insects.

"I mean in the gut," she clarified with a swat to his arm. "Where their dreams and passions lay."

"She's talented," Guy agreed. "I've seen her work. I've never *seen* a clothing designer before. But she's also foggy."

Gale took his cheek and turned his head from side to side. "You're looking a little cloudy these days, yourself."

Guy pulled the sheets around himself. This was why he'd been avoiding his family. They saw more than most.

"Why won't you tell me what's wrong, Guillaume? I might be able to help."

Guy sighed, too tired to put up a fight. It was time to get help before this problem of his got any worse. "You've dealt with curses before haven't you, auntie?"

"Sure, why? You think you've been cursed?" Gale peered down at his heart. "I don't see any malady."

"That's because it's... a bit lower."

"Ah," Gale tilted her head and stared down at Guy's covered lap.

Just yesterday, Guy had had a half-naked stripper proposition him. Last night he'd slid into bed with a nearly naked woman, but it was his aunt who turned his ears red.

"You should probably go to an M.D. for something like that, dear."

That was saying a lot, if Gale advised he go to a medical doctor. She thought the lot of them were mostly useless. "I have been. They can't find anything wrong with my equipment."

"And so you think someone's put a hex of some kind on you?" Gale squinted as though searching for a mark around his person.

The problem had started after he'd spurned a young wannabe singer. She was a beautiful thing, but her aura was near coal. And the truth was Guy knew there was no amount of polishing that would get her singing talents to shine. No auto-tuning or army of background singers could help a voice like hers. Guy didn't tell her any of this until the next morning when she'd awakened him with a god-awful rendition of "Lady Marmalade."

When Guy broke the news about his inability to help her, it hadn't gone well. She stood in his hotel room and said a string of words that could only be referred to as dark magic. Guy had initially laughed it off, until he went out searching for a good time that weekend. And then the next weekend. And then the next month. No matter how up for a good time his companions were, Guy couldn't get it up to join them.

Doctors had run tests, to no avail. And now it seemed his aura-seeing aunt had no answers for him either. His last hope was to find the woman who'd cursed him, but he had no idea who she was... having never actually gotten her name.

"It looks like there's too much sugar in your life," said Gale when she straightened and refocused her gaze on his face.

Guy smiled at his aunt's sensing of Agave, but his star wasn't his problem.

"But that's nothing that a little love can't fix," Gale continued. "True love is the cure for just about any problem."

"Right now, auntie, I just need a break from all of my problems."

"Well, I've got the remedy for that." She patted his leg and headed for the door. "Come down to breakfast. I'm making veggie hash, straight out of the garden."

Guy hurried to get dressed. It had been ages since he'd had a home-cooked meal, and Gale was by far the best cook in the family. She had a way with herbs in both teas and food.

Before he left the room, he reached for his phone again. Six missed calls and four voicemails from various artists. A string of emails about potentials, most of who didn't have a lick of talent, or had mediocre talent at best. Guy shut his phone off again.

As he made his way down, he heard a sound as though a songbird had dipped its toe into the sultry pond. It didn't sound like it was coming from a radio. It sounded crisp, bright, like an early spring morning. It reminded him of his childhood and listening to the records his aunt, Manny's mother, used to play when he spent summers here. She loved jazz, and singers like Nina Simone and Bessie Smith.

Guy stepped into the kitchen. Gale smiled at him over a crackling pan of peppers and potatoes. She motioned her head toward the patio.

Guy saw his cousin sitting in a chair, his wife perched on his lap. A little boy leaned against Manny's side, his face in rapture. Guy turned his attention to the source of the song.

And there she was. A tiny package with gangly limbs

and a mop of curls sprouting from her head. Guy watched her throat vibrate as her voice trilled out a high note. It pierced his heart.

She ended the note to loud applause. The clapping should've hurt Guy's still throbbing head, but he was too light headed at hearing the girl's perfectly pitched song.

As though sensing his presence, the little girl turned to him. The first thing Guy noticed was that there wasn't an ounce of ego on her face. It was as though she reflected the joy of those who were listening, instead of inhaling their praise.

The second thing Guy noticed was the familiarity of her features. Set in a round face were a pair of cat eyes. Her skin was the color of a sandy beach on a summer's day. Her tiny lips, which had let loose such a big sound, had a small smile as she regarded Guy.

And then, finally, Guy saw it: a gold so pure, so bright that he had to look away. This was not a trick of the light. This was real, pure, golden talent. If he doubted his eyes, his ears had already co-signed the fact that this little girl had talent.

"Hey, Uncle Guy." Seth, Manny's new step-son, jumped up and dashed over to Guy, tugging him farther onto the kitchen patio. "Have you met Kimmei? She's my friend. Did you like our song? We wrote it together."

"Yeah, Seth. I liked her song very much." Guy smiled at Pumpkin and his cousin. "Morning Cuz, Mrs. Cuz."

They both grinned up at him from their cocoon of marital bliss.

Guy turned back to the little girl and extended his hand. "Kimmy?"

"It's okay, Kimmei," said Seth. "He's not a stranger. He's my new uncle, since my mom married Manny."

Kimmei took his hand. Guy felt that spark that he got when he knew an artist had that special thing that would make them a star. The little girl was the brightest gold he'd ever seen in his life.

"You have a beautiful voice, Kimmy."

"It's Kim-mei," she corrected him, her voice small now that she was delivering pleasantries instead of belting out high notes. "It's Japanese. And thank you, Mr. Guy."

And she had Southern manners, if she knew to put a Mister in front of his first name. Guy had been in a big northern city too long to have that please him so. "Do you like to sing, Kimmei?"

"I love to sing. When I grow up I'm going to be a famous singer like my grandpa."

"Your grandpa?"

She nodded. "He was an opera singer. I don't like opera all that much, but I do like jazz and musicals."

"Sing the one about the greasepaint," said Seth.

Without any guile, the little girl belted out a perfectly pitched rendition of Nina Simone's "Feeling Good" from "The Roar of the Greasepaint" as though she knew the meaning of joy. And she nailed the ending crescendo without a tremor.

"Kimmei? How would you like to be a famous singer right now, before you're all grown up? I'm an A&R executive."

She looked confused.

"A talent agent," he tried again. "I can make you a star, Kimmei. What do you say?"

"That would be cool," she grinned. "But I'll have to ask my mom first."

"Your mom?"

She nodded, pointing over his shoulder.

Guy looked over his shoulder and saw another beautiful face surrounded by gold. Although there were storm clouds hovering around Midori's shoulders.

8

The sight of Guy kneeling in front of her daughter, with his hand outstretched, his wide smile and his dark gray eyes, brought to mind the image of a lion toying with a fawn, a cat toying with a mouse, the devil toying with an angel. The image mimicked the first time Midori met Michel. He'd looked at her the same way. Not at her, but through her, to see how much he could get out of her and her talent.

Adrenaline rushed through Midori at the thought that her cub would come to danger at the hands of this predator. That Kimmei would experience the same roller coaster as her mother had. That her baby would be taken up high only to be dashed down low.

Midori was set to leap into the fray. But Guy straightened with a smile and she got a close look at what was actually in his eyes. It wasn't predatory. It was full of wonder and joy. It stopped Midori in her tracks. She became caught in the glow radiating off his face. It warmed her through. She wanted to curl it around her shoulders, pick up a needle and thread, and create something to adorn it.

"Midori, you remember I told you about my nephew, the talent agent."

Midori turned at the sound of Gale's voice, breaking the trance.

"I'm an A&R rep, auntie." Guy focused on Midori. "It means Artist and Repertoire."

Midori recoiled at the French term.

"I scout talent," Guy continued. "But I also develop the artist, oversee the recording sessions, and then market the artist and the album. Your daughter... her voice... It's unlike anything I've ever heard."

Kimmei came over to her mother, beaming. For a moment, Midori allowed her parental pride to override her fears. She knew her daughter had talent. The singing gene had skipped over Midori and landed firmly on her daughter, twofold.

"Mama, Mr. Guy said he could make me a star."

Midori ran her hand over her child's cherubic face. She had a flash of Kimmei as a little baby, smiling brightly, trustingly, up at her. Then Midori saw her daughter's face in a blaring spotlight, all eyes on her, judging her. Midori saw that beautiful, confident smile of Kimmei's quiver at the first line of criticism. She saw it break as the rug, inevitably, was pulled out from under her daughter.

"I could help take her to the next level—"

Midori glared up at Guy and clutched Kimmei to her. "She's not going to any level. She's just a child. Besides, she has school on Monday."

"It's summer break, mommy."

Midori winced that she'd forgotten. She peered around the group. All eyes were on her. Gale watching her intently. Manny confused. Pumpkin with a question mark on her brow. Seth looked adoringly at Kimmei. Midori's eyes landed back on Guy. He had the same contemplative look in his eyes. They seemed more black than gray today, likely because he saw the bottom line of dollar signs in Kimmei. Midori straightened her back, ready to defend her daughter.

Guy put up his hands. "I can understand if this is all too much. But what I'm offering is to make your daughter's dreams come true."

Midori had had the same offer once: the career of her dreams, the man of her dreams, the life of her dreams. None of it had been true, and when it all came crashing down around her, she'd hit the ground hard. There was still a bruise on her knees, and scars on her heart. The world up high, where the stars lived, was cruel. She would not allow her daughter to fall like that. Kimmei was going to have a normal life, not some life on a thin, unstable, ever-changing cloud.

"Thank you, but no thank you, Mr. Rumpel—"

"It's Guy."

In exchange for his name, Midori gave him a tight smile. "Kimmei's just a kid, and she's going to stay that way for as long as I can help it."

Guy studied her, likely looking for a chink in her armor. "Perhaps we can make a deal? Make this a win-win-win." The wave of his hand encompassed Midori, Kimmei and himself. "Come to New York, on me. While Kimmei works with me on a demo, I can introduce you to some people in the fashion industry and—"

"I don't need your money or your connections. I know people in the fashion industry. Ex-model, remember? I know what it's like to be a child thrust into the spotlight. To be in the adult world without understanding the rules and the games being played. I'm not going to do that to my own child."

"Hey, hey now." Pumpkin's calm voice came between them as she left her husband's lap.

Midori assumed she'd go to stand beside Guy and take his side. She blinked when Pumpkin came to stand beside her. Midori's heart skipped a beat at the unexpected show of solidarity.

"Maybe we should save this discussion for another day," Pumpkin suggested.

"Like I told you last night," Midori spoke to Guy, ignoring the three pair of adult eyebrows that rose at her words. "When people offer to help, they usually want something in return. And I just can't."

Guy's face sobered at her words, an apology in the crinkle at his lips. "I'm sorry, Midori. I'm sorry if I was being pushy. It's just not often that I see real, unmistakable talent." He looked down at Kimmei. "I still mean it, Kimmei. You have an extraordinary talent. Not everyone has what you do."

"Thank you," Kimmei offered him a small smile before stepping into her mother's side with a quivering lip.

"Pumpkin, Gale, thank you so much for all of your help these past couple of days. We'll get out of your hair now."

Pumpkin reached up and squeezed Midori's shoulder. "You don't have to go. Stay and have breakfast."

Midori shook her head. "I need to get back to the real world. Can't avoid it forever."

"We loved having you," said Gale. "Both of you. You should make it a habit."

Midori looked at the sincere faces of Gale and Pumpkin. She almost relented, but anxiety crept down her spine, and made her feet itch to move backward. "Another time," she told both women and then headed out of the house.

It was a silent retreat. Until they got inside the car.

"Mommy, why I can't I be a star?" Kimmei whined.

"Not now, sweetie. Maybe when you're older." *Hopefully never.*

Hopefully, Kimmei would never step onto a stage. She'd go on to be a music teacher, marry a local boy, and never have to deal with the glare of the spotlight. Or be seduced by men with light eyes, rumbling voices, and thousand-watt smiles.

Midori pulled up to her storefront home. Kimmei stomped up the stairs in a tantrum, but Midori didn't have the energy to admonish the child today. There was a stack of bills on the floor under the mail slot. There were unfinished pieces that she needed to work on for her local clients. This was a good life, a safe life, a *predictable* life. Midori set her suitcase down and prepared to get to work.

Her shop wasn't open, and still had her "on vacation" sign in the window, yet there was a knock at the door. Midori saw a woman's silhouette in the entryway. She recognized the shapely figure and unlocked the door, the closed sign swished in the cool morning air.

"Mrs. Garcia, what are you doing here so early?"

"I've been waiting for you to return home for days. I wanted to talk to you about my dress for the gala this weekend."

Midori spied the garment bag cradled in her arm. Mrs. Garcia took the dress out of the bag.

"Midori, I just don't know about this."

Mrs. Garcia was pear-shaped. She had more going on downstairs than on the upper levels. Midori had made her a solid white dress that hugged her curves below and had blue epaulettes at the shoulders.

"Mrs. Garcia, trust me. These colors brighten you up. We talked about taking small steps to an even better you. It's a step, not a leap."

"I do like the color. And you've somehow managed to slim my waist more than any diet I've ever been on. You'll be there, won't you? At the mayor's gala. I hear he's bringing in all manner of top industry professionals from across the country to bring more business into the parish. I hear there's going to be some big department store coming as well."

"Big events aren't really my thing. But you're going to do great. You'll come and tell me about it after."

After a bit more coaxing, Midori was able to get Mrs. Garcia, garment bag in hand, out the door.

She turned back to the stack of bills and papers that she'd piled on the desk. On top of the stack of mail was the *New York Times*. Phancy's wedding was yesterday's news. The bride probably hadn't made it into the Style section so early.

Midori grabbed and opened to the fashion pages. Her heart sped up in her chest. There on the front page of the Fashion section was Phancy in her wedding gown. Midori's wedding gown, that she'd lovingly stitched for weeks. It photographed beautifully; the detail work of the lace was clear in the gleaming photo. The headline read 'Phancy Wows at Wedding'.

But then Midori's heart skipped a beat and came to a dead stop. Phancy had taken credit for the gown. She'd told the papers that it was her innovative design, her idea for the lace, her inspiration for the fall at the back. Midori's name was nowhere to be found. But another name did come up in the article.

Gunston Fashions was working on a deal with Phancy to start her own line of clothing. Gunston himself had been at the wedding, and was quoted to say that he was looking for innovative designers like Phancy to rewrite the rules of the fashion industry.

The edges of the paper crinkled in Midori's hand. It shouldn't bother her. Midori didn't want the notoriety. She didn't want the fame. She abhorred the spotlight.

She pulled the pages taut and looked again at the photo of her dress. The dress she'd worked damned hard on. She'd gone over budget with that lace. She'd spent more hours than she'd budgeted to make that fall just perfect. She'd literally bled from all the needlework.

But what could she do about it? This just confirmed her belief that she was not cut out for the main stage. Every time she'd reached for something higher, she'd fallen down. And there was always someone like Phancy to rip the rug out from under her. Midori tossed the paper down. The pages fluttered out.

The spotlight was one thing, credit was another.

9

————

"I can't believe I let you talk me into coming to this." Guy looked around the ballroom. He'd spent much of his youth at this stuffy country club. Tonight, it was done up in shades of black and white. On the wall hung pictures; spacious lots of real estate in the parish that were up for grabs. In between those hung portraits of the smiling faces of the citizens of Saint Anne's Parish, with their sleeves rolled up, ready for a day of hard work.

Manny had outdone himself. His cousin had already made his rounds to each and every potential investor and businessperson. Guy had watched Manny schmooze the gathered business and industry professionals, using that Charmayne charm to bring more opportunity into the city to help uplift his constituents, just as Guy would work with his talent to make them shine as brightly as possible. It looked like everyone was on board to bring their money and their businesses into the parish.

Not too long ago, Manny had been traipsing around the globe doing the odd charity event here, the humanitarian mission there, but now he'd stuck down his roots and was making a meaningful and lasting difference in this small part of the world. He looked happier and more content than Guy had ever seen him. That was likely due to the love he'd found. Just like the force was strong with the Skywalkers, the pull to matrimony was strong with the Charmaynes.

Guy felt a tug in his own heart. He rolled his shoulders in the tuxedo he'd borrowed from Manny. The vest was tight over his abdomen, so he'd left it unbuttoned and kept the jacket closed. When he got back to New York, he'd have to find the time to get back into the gym.

Guy turned his attention to the entertainment. The singer's voice rang out a deep amber to Guy's ears, but appeared a passable chiffon to his eyes. He wasn't sure which to believe. He certainly wasn't going to approach her. He didn't want to take another chance on his faulty Sight and wind up putting in more work with another lemon. Guy pinched the corners of his eyes together.

"You still feeling worn out?" Manny asked, as they made their way around the room. They hadn't had much of a chance for a one-on-one, but Guy had told him that he was feeling burned out.

"I feel fine," Guy assured his cousin. "Great, actually."

He felt better than he had in weeks—no, months. It was due to the TLC he was getting from his family. Gale's herbal tea had flushed out his system and cleared his head. Then his aunt filled his belly with succulent foods from the family gardens. He'd rested in the family room on that full belly until Seth woke him later in the day for a game of chess. And though the kid pummeled him, Guy had had a great time. But the best part of his time at home remained hearing the songbird who'd slipped out of his grasp. He hadn't given up on signing Kimmei. He just needed to find an angle to get her mother to make a deal with him.

"Well, hold onto that feeling," said Manny. "Because here comes your sister."

Guy frowned. His sister, Beau, was his favorite person in the world, and not just because they'd come into this world together. He and Beau shared that twin connection: if he hurt, then she hurt. That was another thing the curse was interfering with. His connection to his ever-upbeat sister had frayed along with his Sight, and he hadn't been able to rely on her bubbling energy to get him through his bleak days.

This last year was the most time they'd spent apart. He had his own issues that he couldn't quite share with her. She had her hands full with a set of twin toddlers of her own, plus she ran a business, and she was constantly cleaning up the messes that her useless husband made.

Guy turned in the direction of Manny's gaze. His sister had her dark hair pulled up in a pretty style. There was a huge smile on her face, but Guy saw the dark circles under her eyes. It looked like she still wasn't sleeping well. Behind her, in her shadow, he spied the reason why.

"Gee-Gee!"

"Hey, Beau-Beau." Guy pulled his sister into a warm embrace. She felt slight in his arms. Guy's eyes landed an accusatory glare on her husband who slunk up behind her. Wasn't the lazy bastard at least able to put food on the table? "Phillip."

"Guy," Philip stayed back. "Manny."

"Phillip." Manny's tone was no more cordial than Guy's.

Neither man made a move to shake Philip's hand. Phillip didn't come close enough to offer. Instead, they formed a circle around Beau.

"Why didn't you come and stay with us?" she said. "You

know we have plenty of room. And the twins would love to see their uncle."

"Bring them over to Charmayne House in the morning," Guy said. "We'll make a day of it with Seth and Gale." He knew Phillip would decline the invitation. The man spent as little time around the tight-knit, opinionated, overbearing Charmayne bunch as he could.

"Ah, I should've known that's why you're over there. Gale's feeding you." Beau pinched Guy's side. "Wow, you're packing it on, brother. Did some woman finally catch your eye? Did you *see* someone?"

Behind her, Phillip rolled his eyes. He'd never put any stock in the magical side of his wife's family. Not even though Beau insisted she'd *seen* her husband in her dreams before she met him, and that was how she knew he was her One.

"Did he tell you anything?" Beau turned her attention to Manny.

"As far as I know he's still *dating* his artist." Manny used air quotes around the word dating.

Beau scrunched her nose as though she smelled a rat. "That's all for publicity. It's clear to see there's nothing between them. He's hiding something."

"Or someone."

The two of them now stood on either side of Guy, analyzing him from both corners.

"But why wouldn't he tell us?" Beau mused.

"Do you think he's ashamed of her?" said Manny.

"Maybe it's a *him*?"

"Well, there was that time at camp where I caught him—"

"All right," Guy held up his hands to stop the downward spiral of their picking on him. "That's enough."

Beau and Manny had loved to tease him ever since they were kids, mainly because Guy wasn't easy to rile up. He was the cool head amongst them, where Manny was the daydreamer and Beau the hopeless romantic.

He knew he'd have to tell them the truth. They'd annoy it out of him otherwise. "I'm not seeing anyone..." Guy began, but then he stopped himself in the lie.

He felt the ray of warmth before he raised his head and saw her with his own eyes. Her light called to him like a whisper in the ear and then a brush across the lips. He swallowed audibly as he took Midori Miller in.

A knot of disappointment coursed through him when he saw that her lush hair was pulled back in tight bun instead of fanned out around her shoulders. But the disappointment ran its course as his eyes slid down the long slope of her bare neck. His gaze clung to the surface of her collarbones and then the caps of her shoulders, before falling down the waves of fabric that washed over the upsurge of her curves. The dress was a modified kimono in a flowering pattern of red and white with a large structured bow at the back. All those details went mute for Guy as he saw the bright rays of gold reaching out from Midori's gut, the shards of light entwining her torso.

"Did I mention I invited Midori?" Manny glanced at Guy from the corner of his eyes, a smirk on his face.

Guy tried to tear his eyes away from the woman, but failed miserably. He knew he wasn't hallucinating these colors. She was the real deal. He'd seen her work, and assumed that what she wore tonight was another creation of hers.

"There's a department store that I'm trying to get to come to the parish," Manny continued. "I think she's worked with the owner in the past. I didn't think she'd make it. Midori doesn't seem to like crowds."

"Oh," was Guy's response as he watched Midori's body move like a slow moving river in that dress. She appeared to glide across the floor, her hips swaying in a push and pull fashion. Guy felt suddenly parched, like he'd been in a desert for years and she was a fresh drink of water. And then he registered the silence. His cousin and his sister were staring at him with knowing gazes. "It's not like that. Midori's just... very talented."

Beau nodded. "I can see her talents from here."

"I'm not interested in her like that." Guy suddenly felt twelve years old. Next, in an effort to put a stop to the schoolyard teasing of these two bullies, he would insist that Midori had cooties. "I'm interested in her kid."

Beau grimaced again, as though she smelled another dead rodent. At his other side, Manny chuckled. Phillip still stood apart, ignoring them all.

"That little girl has a golden voice," Guy said. "I want to sign her, but her mother refuses. I'm trying to figure out an angle—"

"Is that what the kids are calling it these days?"

But Guy had stopped paying attention to his sister. There were clouds creeping down Midori's back. He saw them descend in real time. Before he knew it, his feet were moving towards her.

10

Walking had been a key skill in her job a decade ago, but her movements now were short and jerky, like a quickstep, instead of long and graceful like a waltz. The wide obi at Midori's back felt like a hundred tiny laces pulling her spine taut, like a too-small corset. She could bring air into her chest, but it wasn't making its way down her spine. She made her way across the floor.

In the midst of her promenade across the ballroom, the singer up on the main stage hit a high note. Midori winced at the shrill note as the woman ended the song. Her ten-year old could hold a note better than that woman. Kimmei had no fear of the spotlight. The little girl would march center stage, grab the mic, and belt out a perfectly pitched tune. All the while, Midori would be standing in a corner, an anxious mess until it was all over and her daughter was back safely in her arms, where no one could hurt her feelings.

Midori took a deep breath and a definitive step forward. She found herself behind Lorne Gunston. She took another

deep breath and prepared to grab the metaphorical microphone away from the small crowd gathered around him.

"Excuse me, Mr. Gunston!"

The entire party jumped at Midori's belted out greeting.
In fact, a few of the wait staff stopped mid-stride, their trays
of champagne sloshing. Midori took a step back as Gunston
turned around to peer at her.

Lorne Gunston was dressed in a mash up of eras. His
crisp white Victorian Bard's shirt lay underneath a 50's
motorcycle jacket. He wore leather pants and cowboy boots.
But somehow, it all worked together on his tall, slim figure.

Just as she eyed Gunston's sense of style, he surveyed
hers. "I love it." He took a turn around the fabric clinging to
her figure. "It's Madame Butterfly meets... Jessica Rabbit."

Not exactly what Midori had been going for. She got the
M. Butterfly reference, but Jessica Rabbit?

"Curves are in this season, especially ass-curve."
Gunston cocked his head as he took in Midori's wares.

Midori held still out of the old habit of being on
display as a model. Her body had not been her own during
those days. She was a blank canvas for the designer, a
lump of clay for the photographer. But then she remembered she was the designer in this instance, she'd formed
her own image with this gown. But not just this gown.
Midori stepped out of her shell, out of the corner. She
channeled her daughter and smiled brightly at her
audience.

"Hello, Mr. Gunston," she said at an appropriate,
conversational tone. "My name's Midori Miller and—"

"Midori? Midori? Why do I know that name?"

Midori hesitated. Her spirit crept back one step,
preparing to shield itself.

"Ohhhh..." Gunston drew that single syllable out, back

to a decade past. "I remember you. You used to... *work* for Michel Chevalier."

It took everything inside of Midori to halt her backward motion. "I work for myself now. In fact, I just finished working with Phancy Jennings."

"That wedding dress was stupendous. Who knew that Capital B with her itch had any actual talent?"

Midori straightened her back in her kimono. "Well, actually I—"

But Gunston looked past her, and then he moved past her. "Guy Rumpel? What the hell are you doing in this podunk town?"

Midori inhaled to find some patience for this ADD artist. The spicy smell of bay leaves traveled over her tongue and awakened her taste buds. She looked over her shoulder. Guy's eyes were on her and not Gunston. Midori felt her skin flush under his gaze.

Guy's eyes took their time turning their attention from her to Gunston. "This is where I grew up. Lots of talent comes out of Saint Anne's Parish. Talent like Midori Miller here. Have you seen her work?"

Gunston's eyelined eyebrows rose. "No, but apparently you have. I see you've been busy since your time in Paris, Ms. Miller."

Midori's spirit couldn't rally under the glare of that kind of attention. It had taken this one mistake in her life, a mistake she didn't even know she'd been making, to derail her future. She'd come to Saint Anne's, a place where no one knew anything about her past as an unwitting mistress, all in an effort to escape it. But here it was, shining brightly in her face once more.

She began to turn away, but Guy blocked her path. For the briefest of seconds, she had the urge to lean against his chest and rest for a moment, to let him take away some of her load before she had to stand up straight and wrap her pride and her dignity tighter about her shoulders.

But she couldn't have leaned on Guy. His arms were crossed over his chest. He wasn't looking at her. His steely gaze was on Gunston and it was not pleased.

"Midori happens to be the most talented designer I've ever met," Guy said. "We bumped into each other a few days ago when she was finishing up a wedding dress for another client. Who was that again?"

Midori blinked up at those steely eyes. They softened as they gazed down at her. Midori searched for her voice. "Phancy Jennings."

"You did Jennings' dress?" said Gunston. "I should've known that bitch didn't have the talent to design that dress herself."

And that should've been the end of it. Midori got credit, not only for the wedding dress but her Kimono gown as well. As far as she was concerned, she was done. She nodded her thanks at Guy. She hadn't needed him to come to her rescue, but it had made things go both faster and smoother. That was the thing with men in power, they listened to each other before they'd listen to a woman making the same statement.

But it didn't matter. Now she could go home, slip into something more comfortable than a kimono gown, and get back to work on the Randolph wedding dress.

"Midori, you made it." Mrs. Garcia came up to Midori with her arms open.

The older woman looked like a stunner in the dress Midori designed for her. Beside her, Midori also saw Pumpkin, in another Midori Miller creation. Pumpkin's honey-brown skin glowed in her golden, princess cut dress that hugged her hourglass figure like a glove. From across the room, Midori spied the mayor, whose eyes were glued to his wife's form.

Mrs. Garcia released Midori and did a twirl. "You were right. My dress is a hit."

Beside her, Gunston's eyebrows rose even higher. "You designed the dress for the Senator's wife?"

"And the mayor's wife," Mrs. Garcia pointed at Pumpkin. "Midori makes magic with a needle and thread. I had no idea that such a small change, to break me out of my comfort zone, would make such a big deal. My husband loves the dress. We're probably leaving early." The woman embraced Midori again before giving her a wink and then disappearing into the crowd.

"Mr. Gunston, I see you've met our town treasure, Midori Miller." Pumpkin stepped into the role of mayor's wife. "Nearly half of the women in the town wear her designs. You'd be a fool not to offer her a rack or two in your store when it opens in the parish."

Gunston tapped his finger against his lip, his ruffled cuffs falling out of his leather jacket. "I'm thinking she might need to be in more stores than just this backwoods parish."

Midori saw Pumpkin's smile go tight. Gunston didn't notice, or ignored it.

"Do you realize that size eight and above is the first to sell out in my stores?" Gunston addressed no one in particular. "The plus sized market is untapped gold. And I think you might be just the designer to help me reap it in." Gunston eyed Midori again. "I'd love to see more of your work. You have a line of course?"

"A line?" said Midori.

"I'm leaving here on a red eye for Milan. But I'll be back

in New York in just a few weeks. I'm looking for something fresh and new for our stores. Something that will fit the masses."

"In your stores?" Midori parroted.

Gunston pulled a card out of his pocket. "Call my secretary. She'll put you on the schedule."

Midori stood stiffly, her fingers too numb to reach for the piece of paper. It was Pumpkin who took the card before Gunston walked away without a farewell.

Pumpkin rolled her eyes. "He's a character, but he's just offered you your dream." She held up the card as though it were the golden ticket. "You just got the offer to be sold in stores. Isn't that a designer's dream?"

Midori didn't reach for the card. She could only stare at the embossed letters. Gunston's name was written in a Victorian font, but his contact details were written in the newspaper Times font. "I don't have a line. I don't even have the designs to make a line. I don't have the fabric even if I get an idea."

"How long would it take to make some dresses?"

Midori blinked at the sound of Guy's voice. She hadn't forgotten he was there. How could she? His eyes had never left her. He'd been looking at her in that way that Gale often did, not at her but just before her, like he saw something in her that she couldn't see for herself.

"Don't they make dresses in one day on Project Runway?" asked Pumpkin.

Midori turned away from Guy and frowned at her friend. "It would take weeks."

"He said he would be away for weeks," said Pumpkin.

Midori shook her head. "I don't have the fabric, and then I'd have to make another trip to New York in the middle of the summer. My bank account can't swing that."

"Isn't that interesting," said Guy. "It takes me about a couple of weeks to cut a demo for new talent. And the development deal for a new artist has a lot of zeros on the check."

"Aren't your offices in New York?" asked Pumpkin, her face full of faux innocence.

"Would you believe they are? And I'd have to house my new artist and her manager. Just wish I had a deal with an amazing artist and her talented mother."

Midori stared between the two of them. "Did you just set that up?"

Pumpkin sighed. "Did we just pull your talent out of thin air and get someone with the ability to showcase it on a grander scale to gush over it? Not even this family is that powerful." She cast a side-glance to Guy. "I don't think?"

"This isn't a trick, Midori," said Guy. "It's a business deal. You have something I need to do my job, and I have something you need to get your job done. There's no hidden cost. It's an even trade—where we both get what we want." His eyes were warm again. They didn't leer. They didn't look just before her. He looked right at her.

Midori wrapped her arms around her bare shoulders. "Fame is fickle. I don't want Kimmei to be in that world."

"I wouldn't let anything happen to her. Trust me."

Those two words should've sent Midori running the other way. She had no plans to trust another man who offered her a favor. But something in Guy's eyes gave her pause.

"What did your client just say about breaking out of her comfort zones?" he said. "Taking a small step to a better you. How is what I do any different from what you do? You take what's already there and improve upon it. You do it with clothes, I do it with voices. You don't hurt people. You make them better."

Midori pulled her top lip into her mouth. She looked over at Pumpkin, who offered her no help. In fact, Pumpkin had moved to stand on Guy's side.

"Kimmei has actual talent," he said. "I don't have to polish her, I just have to guide her. Do you know how long it's been since I only had to guide someone and they didn't use me?"

Midori thought back to their conversation in the bedroom, the second time they'd met. Guy Rumpel knew what it was like to be used. She'd seen the same wariness in his eyes the first time they'd met in a bedroom.

Midori took a tentative step out of herself. "Oh…" she gulped. "Okay."

"Really?" Guy blinked. Clearly, he'd expected more of a fight. "I mean, okay. So we have a deal?"

He stuck out his hand. Midori hesitated for just a moment before placing her hand in his. The moment they touched, they jerked apart. Guy clenched and unclenched his fist. Midori rubbed her palm, her fingers were no longer numb.

"Sparks?" Pumpkin smiled between them before turning on her heel and joining her husband.

11

———

idori gripped Kimmei's hand tightly as they navigated the crunch of Times Square. In the past, she'd scoffed at the parents who put their children on those doggie leashes as they went out for a stroll. Today, she wished she had an adolescent-sized Bjorn carrier when an oversized Elmo came at them, armed with a friendly grin and paws wide open.

"Omigosh, mommy! Have you ever seen buildings so tall?"

Kimmei's head tilted so far back, Midori thought the child would fall backwards. Midori had to admit the city was much changed since the decade she'd catwalked these streets. It was a much more family-friendly atmosphere, with clean streets and chain restaurants. But she still kept her child close, knowing first hand that looks could be deceiving.

Guy Rumpel had promised Midori the moon to get her to sign Kimmei to a development deal. He'd returned to New York no sooner than they made a verbal deal the night of the gala. Midori hadn't heard from him since. Guy had sent them their plane tickets but no other details.

They walked up to the doors of Badd Finger Records with their suitcases in tow. The company was a study of silver and gold. The sides of the building were steel, and the top was crowned in gold. Inside, gold records decorated the walls. Midori didn't follow popular music so she didn't know any of the artists who'd struck gold, but she did recognize one name. Guy Rumpel's name was listed as producer on many of the gold disks.

"Am I gonna have a gold record like that?" Kimmei bounced on her toes.

In the lobby was a group of people, adults and children alike. Midori made her way around the mob to the front desk. "Excuse me?"

The receptionist held up a blood red talon as she spoke terse one-word answers into the phone at her ear. When she hung up the phone, she barely spared Midori a glance. "All potentials sign in here," she slapped a clipboard down on the desk.

Midori looked at the sheet of scrawled names: Trixi Blue, Bronx Sage, Indigo Moonblood. What were these? Names or nail polish colors?

Midori slid the clipboard back across the desk. "We're here to see Guy Rumpel."

The receptionist rolled her eyes and her neck. Though she was sitting down, she somehow managed to look down on Midori with an air of superiority. "Do you have an appointment?"

"Um... well, no. But we're here to sign a development deal with Mr. Rumpel."

"Of course you are. And so are all the other potentials."

She pointed her red claw at the crowd standing before a conference room door.

The door opened and the crowd moved quickly inside like a stampede. Midori and Kimmei were caught up in the motion, and before they knew it, the conference room doors closed behind them.

The room was filled with children, from what looked like ages eight to sixteen, and their parents. Most of the older children were on handheld devices, alongside their mothers, who were either chatting with each other or sending calculated glances around the room. Many of the older women held the strain of false smiles on their faces, or they, too, turned away from their children and spoke directly into their phones.

In the corner, one particular tween girl was throwing what could only be called a toddler's tantrum. The girl couldn't be more than twelve, but she had on eye shadow and blush. On her feet were kitten heels, and a too-short skirt clung to her boxy hips. Midori was sure the child's neck was straining from the amount of tracks sewn atop her head.

Midori didn't even let Kimmei put on lip-gloss, insisting that if the child's lips were chapped that she get a glass of water. Both Midori and Kimmei looked out of place in jeans, blazers, and boots. Midori had made their blazers herself. Both of the blazers had a huge lotus flower sewn onto the back and lapels. She was perfectly willing to let her daughter mimic a businesswoman, but not a streetwalker.

The moms and their young charges looked them both up and down, as though they were way out of their league. Kimmei didn't notice. She marched up to a girl her age and introduced herself.

The girl frowned her candy-apple red lips at Kimmei. "If

you don't do something about that accent, you'll never make it in this business." The little girl looked over at her mother and they both turned away and snickered.

Midori pulled Kimmei away from the toxic duo. People often thought it odd when Midori opened her mouth. She was a walking contradiction. She had Asian features with golden brown skin, and a Southern drawl. Kimmei's skin tone was lighter than Midori's due to her French heritage, but she had her mother's facial features and drawling accent.

Midori walked back to the door, preparing to leave this circus for good. Another young woman stood at the doors looking down at a clipboard. "There's no in and out."

"I think we're in the wrong place. We don't belong here."

The woman raised her eyes from her papers and looked Midori and Kimmei up and down. "Yes, I think you're right. Nursery rhyme recordings are a few doors down."

The room erupted into snickers. Midori felt the sweat trickle across her brow. Her heart rate kicked up in time to the laughter. Her numb fingers clutched Kimmei into her side. This had been a mistake. But it wasn't too late. They had their return ticket. They could board the flight and be back home before bedtime.

Midori marched them out of the room and down the hall. She nearly collided with another young woman holding a clipboard.

"Excuse me, are you Ms. Miller?"

Midori nearly walked past her, but this woman wasn't looking down at her papers. She looked straight at Midori and Kimmei with a bright smile. "I'm Midori Miller."

The woman breathed a huge sigh of relief. "I'm Mr. Rumpel's assistant. I've been looking for you. You somehow got past your driver at the airport."

"Driver?"

"Of course," she looked down and gave Kimmei a big smile. "Mr. Rumpel arranged to have a car take the two of you to your hotel. When the driver missed you, I was hoping you'd show up here."

Now that Midori thought of it, she had seen a man in a suit and chauffeur's cap holding a sign with the name 'Miller' in the airport, but she never once thought it could be for her.

"Cute jackets, by the way." The woman steered Kimmei and her back to the building's exit. "Mr. Rumpel is sorry he can't be here to greet you personally. He's caught up with another artist."

Guy's assistant, Maya she told them her name was, led Midori and Kimmei out the door and into a town car. Kimmei oohed and ahhed, and then oohed and ahhed some more when they pulled up to the Waldorf Astoria hotel.

They walked inside and were led up the elevator and into a spacious two-bedroom suite. Unlike the room Midori had fitted Phancy in a couple of weeks ago, there was a living room with a wide-screen TV as big as her couch back home. Beneath the television was an iPod system. With one push of a button Nina Simone crooned to them. Upon further investigation, they saw that a whole jazz and Broadway musicals collection was loaded, including the opera album her father had recorded.

Midori left Kimmei to the music and went to investigate the small office that sat between the two bedrooms. When she stepped inside, she gasped. Just behind the door, she found a mannequin. It was top of the line. There was a note on the mannequin's body. It said *Make her shine ~Guy.*

Midori reached out to touch the note. Her fingers

warmed on the cool parchment, a tingle raced up and down her spine as she reread Guy's words. The cramped feeling of that conference room left her, in this small work place Guy had made available to her.

The phone on the desk rang. Midori walked over and lifted the receiver to her ear.

"Midori?" Guy's deep voice sent a wave of heat across her belly.

"H-hey. Hi."

"Good, you made it." He sounded genuinely pleased. "I'm sorry I'm not there to greet you both. I'm dealing with a particularly needy client."

She could imagine what he had to deal with, after experiencing the crowd in the conference room.

"But I wanted to make sure the two of you were settled and have everything you need."

"The suite is great," she said. "All of the music, and then the mannequin. It's too much. I can't keep it."

"Okay, fine, when you're done you can throw it out."

"I'm not going to throw it out! It's worth more than I make in months."

"Then you should keep it." He paused, and she heard the smile in his voice. "There're no strings attached to it, Midori. Well, there might be thread draped over it," he chuckled.

Midori's eyes danced over the note. "Were you in my bedroom again? There's a note here from you."

He laughed, a hearty sound that made it all the way down to curl her toes. "No, I wasn't in your bedroom. I, unlike you, have manners, and I don't go into strangers' bedrooms."

Despite herself, Midori called up the vision of him standing in the doorway of his childhood bedroom while she lay in his bed. There was an attraction between them, she wouldn't deny it. But he'd walked away from it. With slow and heavy footsteps, but they'd carried him away just the same.

"Listen, I'm sorry, but I've gotta go," he said through the receiver. "I'll see you guys tomorrow."

"Yeah, tomorrow."

Midori hung up the phone. Outside the window, the New York City skyline glowed back at her, full of light and full of life. Midori tucked the note from Guy into her pocket and went back into the other room, to join her daughter who was now belting out "Feelin Good." Midori decided to join in.

12

Guy cradled the phone in his hand. He pressed the hard plastic against his chin, remembering the sound of the velvety voice that furrowed through just seconds before. She'd said in their first meeting that she had no singing talent. He wondered if Midori told the truth on that front, because he'd love to coax a few high notes out of her.

It had been awhile since he'd held this much attention on, or attraction to, a woman. Midori Miller was the first woman in a long time to stir his wayward hormones into action, even if it was just a few quick salutes. It must be her natural glow calling to his senses. Or could it be something more? What had Gale said about true love being strong enough to break any curse?

"Mr. Rumpel, you're needed on set."

Guy turned to the production assistant and cleared his mind of the errant thoughts of the dress designer. He'd long stopped believing that he'd see a true love glow like the rest of his family. He'd settle for a stiff cock that lasted longer than a song at this point in his life.

Before heading back onto the set, he made a pit stop at the craft services table. His hand reached immediately for a glazed donut, but paused. A long weekend of home cooked meals straight out of the garden had cleansed his palette. The sugar didn't seem as attractive to him now. He reached for a banana and a hot tea and headed back to the set. He was feeling light, optimistic, even excited. He downed the banana in three bites and took a sip of the warm tea. But then he frowned when he spotted his current artist.

Althea Bentley stood still in the middle of the set, with wardrobe personnel fussing around her. Her aura shone a muted chartreuse, which was odd, because just two days ago she'd burned bright, after they cut a remix of her hit song... which was steadily making its way up to the top of the charts. Her voice was amazing and the radio DJ's were eager to put her music in their rotations. Her first single sold 100K, the second 300K. She was so close to the 500K that would net them a gold record. But radio play was no longer enough. Guy needed to get Althea's music in the sight of the Video Jocks, which is why he was standing on a set instead of greeting Midori and his newest, solid gold starlet.

"How's my star?" he called from behind the wardrobe stylists.

"Guy, I don't know about this dress." Althea sauntered over to him. It was more like waddled over to him.

The dress wardrobe had stuffed her into was at least two sizes too small. Guy knew the dress was the height of today's fashion, with its neon bright colors and cut-outs. But on Althea, a former background singer for a number of R&B divas in the 80's and 90's, the dress made her look like a sausage bursting from its casing.

Guy took another sip of the herbal tea as he surveyed

this problem. Two stylists stood in front and behind her, shaking their heads in dismay at the fit of the designer dress.

"There's nothing we can do, Mr. Rumpel," one frowned.

"Designers don't make dresses for plus-sized women," the other grimaced.

Althea's light dimmed another lumen under their scrutiny. Guy set down his tea mug and approached, ready to work his magic.

"It's not the dress that people come to see." Guy tilted Althea's chin up. "It's that voice that makes them all come onto the dance floor."

Althea gave him a tentative smile. He saw her yellow pulse a small spark in the light of his praise.

"So, that's what we're going to showcase." Guy turned to the production assistant. "Bring in the background dancers."

Lithe dancers surrounded Althea, hiding her figure and the ill-fitting dress. Guy instructed the crew to shoot Althea from the shoulder blades up in low lighting. The effect hid the dress and Althea's excess curves. The video highlighted what mattered: the music.

In his pocket, Guy felt the vibration of his phone. Checking the caller ID, he stepped off the set and swiped right.

"How's my star?"

"She is great." There was brightness in Agave's voice that Guy hadn't heard since he'd first met her in that lesbian bar during an open mic night.

"It sounds like a little TLC is agreeing with you."

"Yes, especially the L part."

In the background, Guy heard a trickle of feminine laughter that he could only assume was Caroline.

"I wrote something," said Agave, "and I wanted you to hear it."

Guy pressed the phone to his ear and drowned out the playback from Althea's shoot. For the last album, Agave had been blocked as a lyricist most of the time, and they'd brought in outside songwriters. The song she sang to him now came out of a voice that rang with pure love. The voice that sang the song brightened the dimly lit corner of the set where Guy stood. Agave's voice hadn't rung this pure in their year of studio sessions.

"What do you think?" she said after the last note.

"I think that's your first single."

Guy heard a muffled sound on the other end of the line. Agave must've turned to tell Caroline.

"We'll need to change the pronouns," he said after the excited squeeing calmed down. Agave had clearly been singing about her love for another woman. But it would be easy to cover up that fact with a strike of the pen.

"Of course, of course." She spoke quietly, as though she had turned away from Caroline and was now cupping the receiver with her hand.

For the last two years, since Agave had been his artist, it hadn't been hard to hide her sexuality. When he found her, she was only recently out and was still finding her footing, both creatively as well as sexually. She'd had a string of lovers, but all were discreet and none of the affairs lasted longer than a month or two. Caroline was an entirely different story. Caroline was out and proud. She did not appreciate being shoved back into the closet by the woman she loved.

"We'll tweak whatever you think is best," said Agave. "I'll send you the lyrics and you can work your magic."

"That's my girl. I need you to get back as soon as possible so we can get that on the album before it drops."

"Wait—no. You promised me until the weekend. We're having such a good time, Guy. Please."

Guy couldn't deny that the time off with the woman she loved was doing wonders for Agave. "All right, but first thing Monday morning, you're in the studio."

"Yes, sir."

"Don't let me keep you from whatever it is you two are doing."

"You need to go out and do a little of what we're doing, yourself."

"Yeah, I'll get on that."

They clicked off, to the sound of more feminine giggles. Guy put his phone away and turned back to the shoot. The director had moved Althea farther into the background, while the young dancers in skin-tight outfits twirled around her. It looked as though the shoot was going really well. But in the dim lighting, Althea's light looked as though it had dimmed a few shades down the spectrum. Guy decided he'd give her the rest of the week off. The time off had worked for him, it was working for Agave; maybe it would work for Althea, too.

They wrapped the production a short while later, and Guy sent his artist home with instructions to rest up in preparation for next week's shoot. He made a note to hire even more dancers to surround her for the next video.

13

Midori was awakened by an energetic Kimmei singing at the top of her lungs and twirling between the furniture. Midori had been the same when she'd booked her first modeling gig and was put on a plane from Louisiana to New York. It had been the dead of winter and she'd been booked for a swimsuit catalog, as next season's swimwear was shot in the preceding winter months to be ready for the spring and summer magazines.

At the ripe age of seventeen Midori had stood on the top of a skyscraper, freezing her nipples off in a tiny bikini while a photographer frowned at the extra insulation in her ass. The photographer, his assistant, and the designer openly discussed how much they loved her exotic eyes, but not her wide nose. How her slim waist and toned belly caught the light, but then took a wrong turn at her fat ass.

Modeling had been Midori's dream, and she'd determined she wasn't going to let these three ruin it. She shut out the negativity, and twisted and contorted her body every way they asked. Her fingertips and toes went numb in the chill air. Sweat soaked her brow as she squeezed her ass cheeks together and tilted up her nose.

In the next photo shoot, her eyes were too exotic and her waist too thin. In the next, her feet too big, her hands too small, her mouth too full, her neck too short. It never ended. She was never skinny enough, tall enough, round enough, flat enough, pale enough, or dark enough.

She learned quickly that a compliment given one moment would be taken away in a different instance. She watched her friends turn to drugs to try to improve their bodies, but mainly to alter their depressed moods. Midori never took that route. Instead, she drowned the voices and shut out the judgmental eyes in order to defend her esteem. With each passing walk down a runway or flash of a lens, the numbness increased from the outside in.

Today, Midori stood in a suite at the top of the Waldorf Astoria, clothed in a bathrobe, her hair disheveled and a few extra pounds on her fat ass. She stood again at the precipice of her dreams, her very own line in stores. She hadn't dared to dream it again after Michel. She never dared to reach so high again.

Midori stretched her fingers up to the sun shining in through her window. The gold rays stretched across her hand, warming her fingertips through. Was this what Guy saw when he looked at her? A light ray of warmth coming off her skin like a chiffon wrap? Or maybe he saw it radiate around her head like an Elizabethan ruff? How much of her did it cover, and how tightly did it fit her form?

As Midori stood there in the sun of the New York skyline, the whole collection came to her. A study in gold.

She headed into the small alcove of an office and got to work without even bothering to remove her robe. The sketches came to her like lightening. She turned the ruff into a stylized turtleneck in a bright gold, and a high-waisted skirt of a dark copper that would color block a tall, leggy woman. She designed a blouse with a diagonal cut to accentuate the décolletage, and an A-line skirt to downplay the lower half of a curvy girl. She wrapped another blouse of a light gold and paired it with a matching wrap skirt. She sketched a solid gold, off-one-shoulder cocktail dress with a ruched waistline that would work with any figure. She was working on an idea for a textured linen pant with a light gold chiffon blouse when Kimmei came into the room.

"Mama, it's time to meet Mr. Guy."

Midori got in a few more strokes of her pencil before Kimmei pulled her out the door to head to the record company.

She left the hotel feeling great, invigorated and eager to get back to work. She'd pulled on a low cut blouse that brought the eye to her breasts, put a belt around her waist to cinch her curves and further draw the eyes to her breasts. Her skirt showed off the roundness of her ass and the heels she slipped into showed the length of her legs. She applied makeup to accentuate the sharp edges of her eyes, and a shade of lip-gloss that highlighted her full lips.

Dressed to stun, she and Kimmei went down to the ground floor where a car waited for them. It was a short drive to the record company, and when they entered, they were brought to Guy's office by his assistant, Maya.

"Mr. Rumpel tells me you're a fashion designer?" Maya said. "That must be an exciting business. Though, I couldn't stand to be around all of those skinny girls."

"Skinny is in the eye of the beholder," said Midori.

"Says the size six woman."

Midori shook her head. "I'm actually a size ten."

Maya narrowed her eyes at Midori. "Shut up."

Midori stood. "It's the belt. Your eye is drawn to it, which makes my waist look slimmer. Here," she motioned to Maya who wore a colorful scarf around her neck. "If you tie that scarf around your waist it will slim you down a couple of dress sizes." Midori took the scarf and did an artful knot around Maya's waist.

Maya turned and glanced in the window at her reflection. "Oh, my god, you're a genius."

Another stylist might have sent Maya off to do a complete overhaul of her closet or her body. Often times a woman just required a minor tweak in styling. Midori made a mental note to include a myriad of accessories with her line that could be used to enhance certain body types.

"Hello, ladies."

Midori looked up to see Guy leaning against the doorframe to his office.

"Good morning," she said.

"Good morning, Midori." His eyes were on hers. He made no move towards her. He never did. He just seemed to enjoy looking at her, staring at the space around her that showcased her talents.

"You're staring at me." She wondered what shade of gold he saw this morning.

"Because you look stunning." As soon as the words left his mouth, he immediately clamped it shut, as though he hadn't meant to say it.

It had been such a long time since Midori had flirted. A long time since she'd dressed to attract a man's attention, but she couldn't deny that was the intent behind today's outfit.

Kimmei dashed out of her seat and made a beeline toward him. "Hi, Mr. Guy."

Guy tore his eyes away from Midori and beamed down

at her daughter. Midori felt a moment of jealousy at the theft of his attention.

"How's my little star?" He rested his hand on Kimmei's shoulder.

Midori rolled her shoulders to work out a kink that suddenly appeared. She tried to shake off the idea of Guy's hand on her shoulder. She wanted him to look at her again with that beaming grin on his face. She wanted to show him the work she'd done this morning and receive his praise.

"Are you ready to go after your dream?" Guy asked.

Midori opened her mouth to lay claim to something she didn't know she wanted, but before she could, Kimmei answered the question because it had been directed at her.

Kimmei nodded her head enthusiastically, the curls on her head bouncing to their own beat.

"Good," Guy beamed at her. "I want you to meet someone, Kimmei."

They started down the hall with Midori trailing in their wake. They ended at the door to a large office. Behind a large desk sat an older gentleman in a dapper, tailored suit that Midori was sure her father would've coveted during the days of his youth.

"Kimmei, this is JJ Calloway. He's my boss, and the one in charge of the record label."

"How do you do, Mr. Calloway?"

"Manners." Mr. Calloway stood and came forward to take Kimmei's hand. "I like this one already."

"And this is Kimmei's mother, Midori Miller." Guy stepped aside to allow Mr. Calloway to shake Midori's hand.

"A pleasure." Mr. Calloway gave Midori a non-leering smile, but one that took her full measure, and then turned back to Kimmei. "Mr. Guy, here, tells me that you can sing like a little bird. Is that true?"

"Not like a bird," Kimmei frowned. "I'm an alto, like my grandpa. His name was Harvey Miller. Did you know him?"

Mr. Calloway cocked his head to the side. "I knew of him, yes; opera singer?"

Kimmei nodded. "Mama says he gave me his voice. He'd sing to me when I was a baby and then when he went to heaven, mama would play his records to help me sleep. And that's how I learned to sing."

Mr. Calloway and Guy exchanged a grin.

"Mr. Guy said I have to sing for you, so that I can make a record like my grandpa?"

"That's right," said Mr. Calloway. "What are you going to sing for me?"

Without preamble or shyness, Kimmei belted out a perfectly pitched rendition of Gershwin's "Summertime."

Midori watched the older man's eyes narrow in scrutiny of her baby. The warmth she'd felt this morning and a moment ago, under Guy's beaming grin, faded. Midori balled her fingers to coax feeling back into the tips. She fought her instincts to pull her child to her bosom and out of the line of the harsh scrutiny to come. But she knew she couldn't do that. She looked over at Guy and knew she didn't have to.

Guy regarded Kimmei with that same wide-eyed wonder as he did her, only with Kimmei there was no hint of desire in his eyes. Just delight at her talent.

Guy looked up, catching Midori's glance. His eyes danced over and around her. First they caught on her own eyes. Then they pulled back and looked around her, a small smile playing on his lips. And finally, they rested on her lips a moment. She watched him swallow and felt herself do the same.

"That was spectacular, Kimmei."

Both Guy and Midori blinked and looked away at the sound of Kimmei's silence and Mr. Calloway's praise.

"Thank you, Mr. Calloway," Kimmei said. "It's one of the only opera songs I know. My grandpa made me a recording of it because I was born in the summer."

"Well, you did your grandfather proud just now."

"Does that mean I can have my own record?"

Mr. Calloway looked to Guy, an eyebrow raised. Then he turned to Kimmei. "I'd like to see the magic Mr. Guy can make with your voice."

Kimmei squeed and clapped her hands. Midori let out a breath she hadn't known she'd been holding. Kimmei ran into her arms now, burying her face in her mother's bosom out of sheer joy.

"Can you believe it, mama?"

"Of course I can, baby."

Midori smiled up at Guy, the man who was making her daughter's dreams come true. She smiled even brighter when she realized there was no longer any numbness in her fingers, no sweat trickling down her back, because there was nothing to guard herself or Kimmei against, nothing to be afraid of. Guy had kept everything at face value with them. He'd shown his cards from the outset. Midori had no reason to fear his motives, or that he would try to twist, shape, and change her daughter into something that she was not, in order to fit the trend of the day. Guy Rumpel liked her just the way she was.

14

Guy tried to avert his gaze from Midori's backside as she stepped out of JJ's office and headed back to his own office, alongside her daughter. He switched his gaze to the curly headed child who bounced in step alongside her mother. But the top of Kimmei's head was in the same vicinity as Midori's rounded ass.

"I thought you hated working with child talent, Guy."

Guy shut JJ's door and turned back to his boss. "This girl is different."

"I'm looking at the girl's mother. Is that the *difference* in your interest?"

"There's nothing going on between us. She's very focused on her child and her own work, just as I'm focused on my artists and my work."

JJ looked back to the closed door. His jaw moved up and down, chewing the inside of his cheek as Guy had often witnessed him doing when he sized up a potential talent. "I've never heard a voice like that come out of something so tiny."

Guy breathed an internal sigh of relief at the change of topic. He was also thankful that JJ moved to sit behind his desk. Guy moved to one of the chairs before his desk. He needed a moment to calm himself, after watching Midori walk away. These stirrings in his pants were happening more and more these days. Guy was hesitant to get his hopes up that the curse was breaking. His Sight was strengthening—ever since he'd met Midori. And his cock was paying more attention—only to Midori.

"That kid's got something. Don't screw this one up by screwing the mother."

JJ's edict weakened Guy's salute, but only somewhat.

"We could lose Agave if you screw up. Remember Agave? Your girlfriend, and near platinum selling artist."

"There's nothing going on between Midori and me," Guy repeated. "I'm only interested in Kimmei." Guy shifted in his seat to hide any evidence to the contrary.

"The kid's a talent for sure, but how are you going to market her? Kids don't listen to opera and adults don't listen to a kid singing opera. I don't see how you're going to make her a commercial success?"

"She's the first truly talented artist I've been able to work with since Agave. Her voice alone will sell platinum, I know it."

JJ scoffed. "The days of vinyl are over, Guy. The future of music is in branding. You need to figure out how to bring her under the Badd Finger banner so that our customers know she's ours, so that they know what to expect when they hear her sound. Will they be shaking it in the club or slow dancing in the bedroom? By the way, no adult is going to slow dance to a little kid singing."

"Don't worry," Guy headed for the door. "I've got this."

JJ chewed the inside of his lip again. "Fine. I trust you

know what you're doing. One more thing," JJ held up a finger. "I signed Frankie Benjamins."

Guy turned back. "You what? She doesn't have an ounce of talent."

"But she does have a million Twitter followers worldwide."

"Are you telling me that a talentless, washed up stripper who'll screw anything to get fifteen minutes of fame, is the image this company wants to portray?"

"We can take advantage of that fifteen minutes and use it to our advantage. We need the win, Guy."

Guy sighed, thinking about all the work he was about to embark on trying to make magic with Frankie Benjamins.

He walked out of JJ's office and headed down the hall to the two bright spots in his day.

"Can you believe it, mama? I'm going to get my own record, just like Grandpa. My dreams are coming true. I'm going to be like Ella Fitzgerald, like Nina Simone."

Guy cringed at the musical references, but he decided not to worry. At least she wasn't expecting to sing opera. There'd be plenty of time to figure out how to marry Kimmei's soulful voice to the sounds of today and turn it into something commercial. The point was he had real talent on his hands that he didn't have to doctor up. He looked at the two of them: two golden girls. Kimmei shining brighter than anyone he'd ever come across. Midori shone brighter today than the first time he'd met her, dressed in nothing other than a towel, and then again in her underwear with those curves. All those curves.

"Guy?"

Guy tore his eyes away from Midori and turned at the sound of Maya's voice.

"Frankie Benjamins is in the studio and she needs you."

Guy looked down the hall as though he could see the bitter lemon of Frankie. Then he looked back to the sunflower yellow of the girls before him. "Can you put her on my schedule for tomorrow? I'm taking my new client and her manager out to dinner to celebrate."

Midori straightened. "Really, you don't have to do that. You've done enough already. Besides, we have dinner slow cooking back at the hotel."

"Slow cooking?" asked Guy.

"You should come over and join us, Mr. Guy." Kimmei bounced on her toes like a buzzing bumblebee. "I'm making miso soup."

"I've never had that before," he said.

"You'll love it," the child insisted. "Will you come?"

"Sweetie," said her mother. "He's busy."

"I'm not busy," said Guy. "I'd love to come over. It'll be convenient since I'm staying there."

"You're staying at our hotel?" Midori's eyes sat large beneath those sweeping lashes.

"Put that suspicious brow down," he grinned. "My loft is being renovated." His eyes went from her lush lashes down to her full lips. He swallowed. The liquid sparked on the tip of his tongue and left a trail of fire on its way down his throat.

"You're the one who keeps showing up in or near my bedroom," she said.

The fire migrated from his belly and he felt warm in his pants. "My bedroom. Both times."

Beside them, Guy saw Maya raise an eyebrow. Kimmei looked between the two of them with a mix of bemusement and a grimace. He looked back down to JJ's office door, and saw the man standing in the doorway with his eyebrows raised.

"Why don't we get going?" Guy steered the girls towards the elevator, which was away from the studio and the lack-luster talent of Frankie Benjamins, and in the opposite direction of his boss.

15

In the town car, Midori set Kimmei between her and Guy. That didn't stop the electricity from flowing between the two adults. Guy Rumpel had gotten past the barriers she'd erected to steer men in the opposite direction. She uncrossed and then re-crossed her legs so that they faced away from the middle and towards the door, waiting for the car to stop so that she could get out of this confined space, with this man who smelled so good and smiled at her as though stars danced around her head.

For his part, Guy kept Kimmei engaged in a conversation about music. He'd tried to bring Midori into the fold, but when she'd looked over at him their eyes had locked and they'd both stared. Everything slowed down and the colors around them blurred as though they'd fallen into some musical montage.

Kimmei bounced between them, excited about a new sight outside the window, and Midori came to her senses. She did not live in a dream world. She was no princess in need of rescuing. This guy wasn't a prince. A man like Guy

Rumpel had to have a girlfriend, or at least a string of lovers, and she did not want to be another man's side dish. Since their first encounter he'd kept his hands to himself. He'd never made any advances towards her, neither with his hands or his words.

But there was something in his eyes when he looked at her. She didn't know this look. She'd been leered at by some of the most charming, suave men on the planet. Guy didn't leer at her. His glances, like this one, lingered, non-predatory and non-threatening, yet somehow inviting.

His eyes dipped to her lips, then farther south. But then he blinked, as though trying to wipe what he saw from his mind. He didn't peruse and then look directly into her eyes to let her know he was interested. He kept it to himself. Like he was attracted to her, but he didn't *want* to be attracted to her.

It didn't matter. She was not open to a relationship. She didn't have time for one. As a single mother and a small businesswoman, she didn't have time to date. All of her attention went first to her child, then to her business, and then she got about ten minutes to herself every day when she could navel gaze. There was no time to devote to a man who would want to date her, have her attention, and have her body. She just didn't have time for it.

"Are you ready?" he asked.

"Yes," she said, as she locked onto the churning gold flecks in his dark gray eyes.

"Mama, you have to move."

Midori blinked. She looked up to see that they were at the hotel. The driver had opened the door and was waiting for her to get out. Thankful that her cheeks were brown enough to not redden, Midori climbed out of the car.

They made their way up to their floor. She had to get a hold of herself. She'd fallen so easily for Michel and his lies. She had to keep her vigilance around Guy. It wasn't just her life he would mess up if things went left. She also had to worry about Kimmei. Guy had been a man of his word so far, but she knew there would come a time when he would want more.

"Did you get some work done the other day?" he asked.

She nodded. "Oddly enough, I have this idea of gold pieces for my collection."

He grinned.

Midori noticed that there was a slight gap between his two front teeth. The minor imperfection on someone so well-groomed humanized him. Midori didn't need to see Guy as any more accessible than she already did.

"I'm worried that I'll have trouble finding the right hues," she said.

"I have a thing for colors, as you know," he said. "Maybe I can help?"

"Guy, no. You've done enough for us. I have to do this on my own."

"Why? Why is the modern woman so obsessed with doing things all on her own? Men work in packs and tribes, but women have this sense of pride in saying they got each of their battle scars all alone on the battlefield."

"You're a Charmayne. You lot have a hero complex. But I don't need any rescuing."

"It's clear you don't need any rescuing, Midori. You're a strong, capable, and very talented woman."

Midori felt the heat from her fingers and toes rush to the core of her.

"I'm offering aide not a rescue," he said. "People just

take from me. It's nice to have the opportunity to give freely."

"So, this is a purely selfish endeavor on your part?"

He grinned. "I can't wait to see what you create with my meager assistance."

Midori's mouth opened of its own accord. "Do you want to see my sketches?"

"I'd love to."

Now that she was leading him to the small alcove, Midori's palms began to prickle. When she reached for the light switch in the suite's office where she'd left her designs, her fingertips were already cold. The light illuminated the room, but Midori could go no farther. She pointed to the desk. Guy eyed her quizzically and then walked the few steps to the desk where her sketches lay.

Every instinct in Midori told her to turn and bolt. She felt naked standing in the frame of the doorway as Guy picked up her sketches. Her heart sped up as she watched his eyes roam over one, then another, and another drawing. After the sixth sketch, he turned to her, his eyes soft. She knew what his review would be before he spoke it. He would tell her that he loved them, that she was talented, and then the pressure would build up inside of her while she waited for his next review, which could only be negative, just like the photographers and designers. What was she doing, putting herself back on this merry go round?

He opened his mouth to speak and she wanted to shut her ears, shut him out. She wished she hadn't asked him, wished she'd left it alone so that he would look at her in that nonjudgmental way again.

"I made a mistake," he said.

Midori's eyes blinked open and her shoulders jerked back. "I'm sorry, what?"

"I just committed a cardinal sin." Guy's lips spread in a slow grin. "I told a woman I'd give her an opinion on her clothes." He set the sketches down. "I just remembered that I don't have a death wish."

Midori's gaze clouded. "So you didn't like them?"

"Midori?"

He was before her in fewer strides than it took to reach the desk. His fingers tilted her chin up. Midori felt a spark on their impact and she gasped. Guy jerked his fingers back and clenched them into a fist. Had he felt that, too?

After a brief hesitation, he returned his fingers to her chin, his thumb brushing over her cheek.

"I didn't mean to insult you." His voice was gentle, so gentle. "I could tell you that I liked them, but that wouldn't really mean anything to you would it?"

Midori tried to focus on his words, but the heat from his hands and the warmth of his gaze distracted her. In the end, she could only nod. It was very possible that she made that head bobbing choice because it ended with half her face cradled in his big hand.

"I have no credentials in the world of fashion," he continued, rubbing his thumb just below her bottom lip. His pinkie finger rested on the pulse point in her neck.

Instead of saying something trite, she told the truth. "People change their minds. You know the saying; with fashion, one day you're in, and the next day you're out. It's scary being in the eye of the beholder like that. People can say you're not good enough for doing exactly what you did the other day when they loved you."

"I know you're talented," he said. "I can see that with my own eyes."

"Even though I'm not a singer?" She tilted her head up so she saw into his eyes. They were trained on hers, looking deeper into them, past the moisture his initial words caused.

He shrugged, the movement looked helpless on his broad shoulders. "I've never seen a non-performer so clearly…"

They stood staring at each other. His thumb moved rhythmically at her chin. Midori's eyes dipped to his lips. She watched him inhale. His intake stole some of the moisture from her lips. Her tongue darted out and she licked her bottom lip, just missing the tip of his thumb. His eyes dipped to where they narrowly avoided collision.

But then he pulled his hand away and took a step back. "You said something about dinner?"

Midori bit her bottom lip. "Right. Dinner." She preceded him out of the small room and back towards the kitchen where Kimmei had finished setting the table.

Midori went to the sink and splashed cold water on her hands, and then spritzed a couple of drops on her neck. He'd been about to kiss her. Or had she been about to kiss him? Either way, he was the one who'd stopped it. Which was for the best. Right?

Midori watched as Guy cleaned his plate of a third helping of miso soup and udon noodles. The topics of conversation were benign enough for a ten-year-old's active participation. Guy's glances and smiles to Midori were just as benign. He'd completely friend-zoned her, which was as it should be; the only way it could be. So, why was she feeling annoyed?

After dinner, Guy insisted on washing the dishes while

Midori monitored Kimmei's nighttime rituals. For a kid who could hold a long note, Kimmei had a short attention span when it came to chores, and that included showering, brushing her teeth, and all things that came with prepping for bedtime.

With the dishes in the dishwasher, the moon in the sky, and Kimmei tucked tightly under the covers, Midori walked Guy to door.

"Thank you for a delicious meal," he said. "Who knew vegetables could be so filling."

Midori could only offer him a weak smile as she tried to not look at his lips; flushed and full after so many bowls of hot soup. She felt profoundly cheated, having not felt them on her own skin.

"About earlier..." Guy focused on her lips, and then he blinked. And then he blinked again, rapidly. "I just want you to understand—"

"You don't have to explain to me—"

"Getting involved with potential artists is a bad idea that I've done too many times."

"I'm not your artist." Of its own accord, Midori's fingers flipped her hair over her shoulder.

Guy's eyes fixed on her collarbone. "No, you're not." He swallowed, focusing on her eyes. "But it's still a bad idea. I should go."

It had been awhile since Midori had tried to seduce a guy, a long while. Her body flared with each step he took away from her. She was on his heels. He turned abruptly and they bumped into one another.

She wobbled on her feet. Guy reached out his hand and caught her, steadying her by bringing her into his body. Midori felt the unmistakable hump of his erection. His breaths went shallow. He slowly pushed her hips away from him. He offered her a weak smile and then he went out the door of the suite.

On the inside of the suite, Midori's body was heated. A fire that had been out for a long time was lit, as the door closed behind him.

16

Guy pinched the bridge of his nose as nails scratched down the chalkboard. Only he wasn't in a classroom. He was in the studio. And there was no chalkboard. He sat before a black mixing board. Every light jumped up into the red, indicating the sound levels were too high and were distorting.

"How was that take, Guy?"

Frankie Benjamins was dressed like a Catholic schoolgirl on her way to a conjugal visit with the devil. Her pleated skirt barely covered her ass. Her pristine, white shirttails were tied below her breastbone. She wore fire red stilettos to complete the outfit. Frankie gave him a suggestive smile as she toyed indelicately with his four thousand dollar microphone.

Guy sighed.

Frankie dropped her hand from the microphone. "I can do it again."

"No, no." Guy let go of his nose and put his hands up in a halting motion.

Frankie placed her hands on her hips, boosting her

breasts up to her chin, and pouted her plump lips. "Just tell me how you'd like it."

What Guy would like, what would bring him joy, was a session where a voice lit up his mixing board like a Christmas tree instead of flashing police sirens.

Guy looked up at Frankie. The bitter lemon stain still sat on her shoulders. He looked down at the red lights on the board. His eyes went hazy for a split second. But when his vision cleared, he saw exactly how to fix her sound. What tones of Frankie's voice to deaden, which chords to pull forth. If he increased the beats per minute, he could use that off-key note she'd delivered; the one that had nearly drawn blood from his eardrum. He could take her sound from the red and pull it into the green to sound like... every other song playing on the radio today.

Guy took a deep breath and prepared for the work ahead of him. "You can head home for the night. I've got this."

Guy reached for a set of faders. He immediately became lost in the work of rearranging this symphony of errors. That was why the pair of taloned hands on his neck had him leaping out of his seat. He landed with his back against the mixing board. His palms slid up against the faders, sending the notes further out of tune.

"What are you doing?" he asked, as Frankie advanced on him.

"I thought I'd stay and keep you company."

Guy pinched the bridge of his nose again as she pressed her body into his. A year ago, he would've taken her up on the offer of a different type of studio session in the sound-proof vocal booth. But today, there was no reaction to the breasts pressed against his chest, or the palm that overtly brushed the crotch of his pants. He winced when he opened his eyes to her lips coming at him. All he could see was the sour lemon of her aura.

"Listen, Frankie. You have a signed contract with JJ. This isn't part of the deal."

She cocked her head to the side like a confused bird. "I don't get it? Are you saying you don't want to? Because I've heard more than once that that little girlfriend of yours likes the little kitties over the big dogs."

Guy stiffened at her words, but not in the good way. Frankie still had him cornered—he was caught between the board and her breasts unsure which to label the rock and which to label the hard place.

"If you like girls who swing both ways," she continued. "Then I'm down to play. I like to lick up a little spilled milk from time to time."

She licked her top lip slowly, leaning into Guy even more. Guy leaned as far back as he could. And then by the grace of Father Christmas, the door opened.

"I'm sorry. I didn't realize..."

Guy turned to the husky sound of Midori Miller's voice. She stood inside the door. Standing in front of her was a wide-eyed Kimmei. Midori pushed the girl out the door.

"No," Guy said. "Please don't go!"

Midori halted at what could only be the distress in his voice. She turned back and looked from him to Frankie. Frankie shot the mother and daughter daggers.

"We're a little early," Midori apologized.

"It's perfect timing." Guy broke free of Frankie's imprisonment and walked quickly towards Midori and Kimmei.

Midori raised an eyebrow at him. He was certain he looked like he felt: like a caged animal sprung free. He mouthed a thank you to Midori as he reached her. Her lips quirked up in amusement, and then she tugged in her lower lip with her teeth.

Guy nearly tripped over his feet at the sight. He'd woken this morning to the sight of wood. Morning wood was a normal phenomenon for most men. He'd experienced a hard wake- up call most of his life. Except the last year. He'd get twinges off and on, but nothing hard and lasting. He'd felt nothing with five foot six inches of half exposed Catholic demoness pressed against him a moment ago.

Last night he'd come to attention with just the possibility of tasting Midori's lips. He'd stayed that way on the walk to his room before deflating. He'd dreamed of her and his erection had stood straight up in the morning. He'd lain there in the bed as though his body was possessed. He'd been afraid to move, in fear of scaring it away. It had gone away on its own in due time. Now she was standing in front of him, plump lips smirking at his predicament, and he was stirring again.

Guy turned back to Frankie, who watched him from the board. "I'll get to work on your track, Ms. Benjamin, and have my assistant give you a call when it's ready for you to hear."

Frankie took her time collecting her things and sashaying to the door. She paused when she got to him. "You know where I am, if you get thirsty for some milk."

"Thanks, I'm good." Guy shut the door behind her and exhaled. He opened his eyes to the shining brilliance of Midori. His throat was suddenly dry and he needed something to quench his thirst. He looked away from her plump, juicy lips.

He turned his attention to Kimmei. The girl was dressed in a plaid skirt and white blouse this morning. Guy smiled at her innocent and eager expression. "Kimmei, why don't you go into the sound booth and get comfortable."

The little songstress beamed at him and skipped into the room. Guy took a deep breath and turned to her mother. Midori also wore plaid. But her plaid was in the blazer that covered her white blouse. Her white blouse covered her breasts, but the outline still tantalized the eyes. A long pencil skirt that stopped just above her knees encased her lush hips. Guy's fingers itched to hike that skirt up higher.

"Milk?" she asked.

Guy gulped as the reference from her lips made his mouth water and his cock harden. He shook his head. "You don't want to know."

He pulled out a seat for her and she sat. Guy sat too, crossing and then re-crossing his legs. All to no avail. For the first time in a long time, he had wood in his pants and it was unwanted.

"Is everything okay?" Midori asked laying a hand on his bicep. "You look a little traumatized."

Guy stared at the hand on his bicep. His blood supplies were diverting—fast and furious. "I told you, sometimes artists want more than I'm willing to offer."

Midori's fingers jerked and then she pulled her hand away.

Guy wanted to assure her that he didn't mean her. Her touch ignited him. But he couldn't say that either. He couldn't ignite anything with her. Not if he wanted to work with her talented daughter. Not if he wanted to keep up the ruse with his number one artist. Not if he wanted to do his job and get back on the top of the charts. Midori Miller was off-limits. So, he looked away from her fingers and turned to the starlet behind the glass.

"Kimmei, let's start with a vocal warm up."

Guy began a series of vocal warm ups that Kimmei imitated pitch-perfect.

"That's great, Kimmei."

The little girl beamed at him.

"She learned those from her grandfather."

Guy jerked at the sound of Midori's voice beside him. His erection, which had been under control a moment ago, flared to life again. He stared at Midori, caught in the upsweep of her mesmerizing eyes and her proud smile. He desperately wanted to lean in and taste that smile. His cock jumped in his pants.

"Would you mind if we worked alone?" he said.

The delectable smile on Midori's face fell. Guy almost took back the words to get it to return. Instead, he re-crossed his legs.

"I need to build a rapport with Kimmei, and she may be more focused on you than her work." He refused to feel bad for using a little cover for his problems. "You can go back to the hotel and get some work of your own done."

"Oh, okay." Midori stood slowly. "I guess that's fine." She hesitated at the door as though she wanted to say more.

Guy stared at her lips, wanting them to come back closer to his. Instead of beckoning her forward he said, "I'll drop her off when we're done so you don't have to come back."

Midori winced. He may have said the words more harshly than he'd meant to, but he was battling to keep his big head in charge of the conversation that his little head was trying to overthrow.

Midori nodded and went out the door. Guy let out a sigh. With Midori gone, his erection was already beginning to deflate. Good. Back to business.

He turned to Kimmei who stood patiently waiting in the sound booth. "So, who's your favorite singer these days? Taylor Swift?"

"She's okay," Kimmei shrugged.

"Beyonce?"

Kimmei shrugged.

"Okay, you tell me."

Kimmei scrunched her nose. "You've probably never heard of her."

Guy was intrigued. "Try me."

"Audra McDonald."

"The Broadway star?"

She nodded. "I know a lot of kids my age like pop music and rap, but all that music just sounds the same to me."

Guy had to bite his lip to keep from grinning, but also to keep from grimacing. He had a hand in the monotony of today's music, but repetition worked. "Who introduced you to Audra McDonald? Your mother?"

"No, my mom's not really into music. She listens to my grandpa's old albums sometimes. He died when I was little, but I remember him singing songs to me. And then mommy plays his records a lot when she's working."

"I listened to a few of your grandfather's songs." Harvey Miller had a hauntingly powerful voice. Guy tried not to ask the question, but it was out before he could stop himself. "What about your father?"

Kimmei blinked as though she had to wrack her brain to interpret the term father. "I don't know what kind of music he likes? I never asked."

Guy should've let it go. "He's never heard you sing?"

She nodded. "Yeah, he has. Is this the song you wrote for me?" She reached out for the stand with papers on it.

"Yes, it is."

"These lyrics are funny." It was a little ditty about a tween's love of her cell phone and the apps she couldn't do without, notwithstanding that he'd never seen Kimmei with a device in her hands. As her eyes skimmed down the paper, her smile fell and her light dimmed ever so slightly. "Am I gonna have to do pop music on my album?"

Guy looked into her face. He opened his mouth to spin a tale about playing to the audience with the first album, and then having more freedom with the second album. But Agave's face popped into his head. He'd spun that same tale with her and, here, her sophomore album sounded just like her debut, which sounded nothing like Agave's original trip-hoppy, poetry cafe sound. He looked at the board, which still had Frankie's disarray cued up. Then Guy looked into the eyes of his newest little star. Those eyes twinkled up at him, full of trust.

"You know what, Kimmei? Why don't we write something together, like you and Seth did, and see what we create?"

"That sounds like fun."

She instantly brightened. Guy did too. They got down to work, reworking the lyrics into a song about visiting a new place for the first time. They came up with rhymes about tall buildings, crowded streets, the first time on a glass elevator, and lights so bright that night looked like day.

With the song complete, Kimmei returned to the sound booth. At the first note, Guy leaned back in his chair. He removed his fingers from the mixer board and put his hands behind his head. Kimmei's voice flowed out flawlessly. The LED lights bounced up and down in a steady green symphony that reminded him of a Christmas tree.

17

———

*I*t took Midori a few moments to step away from the studio. Before she did, she watched Guy turn to Kimmei. When he did so, the strained look on his face that had been present with the pushy artist evaporated. Guy sat back in his chair, with his hands placed behind his head and a grin on his handsome face. Through the looking glass, Kimmei returned the same huge grin. They looked like two peas in a pod. Midori wished there was room for her in that pod.

Guy was the first man to respect her boundaries. He hadn't made a single pass at her. He hadn't touched her when she was naked in his hotel room, or naked in his bedroom. He'd made a deal with her and kept his end of the bargain without expecting anything more. She'd pushed him away every time he extended his hand to help her. But she'd enjoyed coming to his rescue a moment ago, when fake boobs and manicured claws came after him.

He'd said business and pleasure shouldn't mix. He'd eyed his artist with disdain. But every time Guy's eyes landed on Midori, she saw desire hidden in their depths.

The fact that he wasn't acting on it was starting to drive her insane.

Frustrated in more ways than one, Midori turned from the door with one final glance. Making her way back down the hall, she spied Maya. Guy's assistant hadn't been at her desk when they came in. She stood before her desk now, her hand on the curve of her hip, which was covered in a jersey dress that was cinched at her waist with a belt. A guy whispered something in her ear, then waved and turned the corner.

"You're beaming like a kid who just got into the cookie jar, Maya."

Maya jumped when Midori's voice came from behind her. She turned and beamed. "That's Matt. I've had a crush on him for months. He struck up a conversation with me in the break room. He wants to grab drinks after work."

"Of course he does," said Midori. Maya looked great today, now that she wasn't in a formless dress.

"He's never noticed me before. I have to think it's because of the style makeover you gave me."

Midori opened her mouth to deny it, but the truth was the minor tweaks she gave Maya drew the eye to the woman's best assets. It was why Midori loved fashion. Even if you were feeling blue on the inside, you could dress yourself up in bright, joyful colors on the outside. If a woman was born with short legs, the right cut of a dress could make her legs look miles long. Excess curves could be carved from a pear shape and blown into an hourglass.

Midori's eyes went from Maya's bright, artful curves to the sketches on her desk. "What are these?"

"Oh," Maya returned to her seat. "Those are some style choices for one of Guy's clients, Althea Bentley." Maya held up a picture of the woman. She was plus sized, but she had shapely calves and long legs.

"You might mention to the stylist that she should tailor this jacket to Ms. Bentley's form," Midori said. "Right now it's making her shoulders look bigger than they are."

"Yeah?"

"Absolutely. You never want to hide your curves when you're tall and curvy. Ms. Bentley needs to go for what I call the soft-fit. That's when you hug the curve of the breast or the hip and then let the fabric flow softly down the rest of the body."

Maya cocked her head. "Why don't I send her outfits over to you?"

"Oh, no, Maya. I—" Midori was about to refuse when she remembered the name Althea Bentley. Midori wasn't one for today's popular music, but she remembered the woman's name from decades past. She had to admit, getting clients in the music industry could be a nice side effect of working so closely with Badd Finger Records. She agreed to take a look at the clothing, especially since Althea Bentley was exactly the type of figure Midori loved to dress.

"Oh, before I forget..." Maya reached beneath her desk for a large bag. "Guy wanted me to make sure you got these."

Peering inside, Midori saw an array of fabric. The tones ran from the rich shades of honey, to the brilliant tones of the Tuscan sun. She recalled their conversation last night and his offer of aide, not a rescue. "I can't accept these."

"Why not?"

Midori shook her head even while she marveled at the luster of the fabric. "I've had bad experiences accepting gifts from men in power."

"Guy Rumpel is not a saint by any stretch," said Maya.

"But I don't think there's anything attached to these, Midori. I really think he appreciates your skill and wants to help you shine. He's had a handful of failures over the past year. It looks to me like he believes in you just as much as he believes in Kimmei."

Midori eyed the woman skeptically.

Maya shrugged with a smile. "He saw something in me, too. Gave me a chance when other producers just had me getting coffee and running copies. He actually listens to my opinions and takes what I say into account. He's a good guy."

Maya handed her the bag. After a moment's hesitation, Midori took it. With that renewed vigor, she returned to the hotel and got to work on her line. It would be something the fashion world hadn't seen before.

Well, that wasn't true. They would've seen it before, but they just wouldn't have paid it much mind. She was designing a line of clothes that would translate to women of every shape and size. Standing before her model-sized mannequin, Midori picked up her shears and thread and got lost in the work.

Before she knew it, a knock sounded at the door. Midori looked up past her newest creation to see that it was dark outside. She made her way to the front door and opened it.

Guy stood on the other side with Kimmei in his arms. He cradled the sleeping child like he was someone's father. "I think I tuckered her out."

Midori let them pass and then led the way to Kimmei's room. "You guys are just finishing?"

"No, we finished two hours ago." Guy laid Kimmei down on her mattress. He removed her socks and shoes without direction as he continued talking. "We went out to grab a bite. I offered pizza, but she wanted rice and vegetables. So, we went to an Asian Fusion restaurant. For the second night in a row, I've eaten more vegetables than I have the whole year. What kind of kid doesn't like pizza?"

"With a Japanese mother, I didn't grow up eating those kinds of foods. So, neither of us have a taste for them."

Guy pulled the covers over the sleeping child and tucked her in. He brushed a loving caress down the side of Kimmei's face and then straightened.

"Do you have children, Guy?"

"No," he said. "I have a niece and nephew; my sister's kids."

"Younger sister?"

"She's actually older, by twenty minutes."

"You're a twin?"

Kimmei stirred at her mother's raised voice, but then quickly resettled. Kimmei was usually a handful to get to bed, the child's eyes would fight to stay open, certain she was going to miss something special, but she rolled over as Guy brushed a stray hair off her brow with a chuckle.

Midori led Guy out of the bedroom. She'd assumed he was an only child, but she'd had nothing to go on to make that belief hold. Every time she thought she had this man pegged, he surprised her.

"Did you get a lot done while we worked?" Guy asked, as she closed Kimmei's bedroom door.

"I did. I got inspired with this new batch of fabric. You really shouldn't have gotten those for me."

"It didn't cost me anything. Someone owed me a favor. He had nothing I wanted. Then I realized he had something a friend of mine wanted."

"So, we're friends?"

He smiled down at her. "Yeah."

He seemed pleased with the pronouncement. Midori

noticed he looked completely relaxed and at ease. He was staring at her again, in that gaze of wonderment that he got in his eyes when he looked her way. But still, he made no move on her. Even now, he stood apart from her at a respectable distance. His feet shuffled as though he were going to increase the distance and head out the door.

"You want to rest for a second?" she blurted.

Guy looked at the couch, then back to her. Midori held her breath until he was seated. Then she sat down beside him. Guy inched his hips away from her until they were half a cushion apart.

They sat quietly for a moment, as awkward as two teenagers on their first date. Then they both turned to each other at the same time. Midori's hand brushed Guy's knee. He hissed and lurched away from her.

He stood abruptly. "I should go."

His crotch was directly in her face and she got a view of his erection. Her head tilted back to see his eyes looking down at hers, eyeing his wayward penis as though it were a stranger separate from his body.

"Because this is a bad idea?" She looked up into his eyes and then down at his erection. "Because you have tons of women chasing you on a daily basis, trying to get something out of you?"

"You're not in that category, Midori."

"What if I wanted to be?" Midori's gaze turned seductive. "I'm not trying to get something out of you that you don't want to give."

He blinked his eyes slowly, as though he were having trouble focusing.

It had been years since Midori had used these flirty skills and she was a bit rusty. She saw his mouth trying to form words. A sense of power, of warm heat, surged through her as her groove came back. She stood, allowing her body to brush over his.

"What if I wanted to share something with you?" she said.

Midori reached for his hand. She traced the lines of his long fingers. She heard his breathing change. She glanced up at him from beneath her eyelids. He might not have any thing up his sleeve when he offered her his hand, but she realized she did want something from him.

"Midori..." Guy breathed.

She moved her lips up to his. It took him totally off guard, and he grabbed onto her body to steady himself. But then his hands were like a vice on her.

He kissed her like a man who hadn't taken a breath in years, and she gave as good as she got, because she hadn't had another's breath in years, herself.

He pulled away, breathing hard. "We should stop."

"I don't want to stop. Do you?" She felt his answer poking at her through his slacks. She reached between them, brushing her fingertips over his erection.

Guy buckled. His big body collapsed onto the couch. Midori was on him before either of his heads could clear.

When she straddled him, his eyes grew as big as saucers. He held his hands up in a stop motion, but his hips rose to meet her hands. Guy was thick, and long. She felt the heat coming off him through his slacks.

"I haven't wanted anyone like this in a long time." His voice was choked. There was still indecision on his face, as though his mind was telling him to go, but his body was demanding that he stay.

With one hand still holding his cock through the fabric, she used the other to pull on the zipper to his pants. His mouth made a sound of protest, but again his hips lurched towards her. She couldn't understand why he'd want to fight her? They were obviously attracted to each other. It had been evident from their first meeting in Phancy's hotel room. He didn't deny his reputation. Woman must come at him like this all of the time. What she was doing was nothing new, but Midori was going into this with a clear head.

She didn't expect anything from Guy but this. She wouldn't be a side dish or a main course. She had no intention of staying on the menu past the appetizer phase. She missed the feel of a warm body between hers. She missed the strong hand of a man on her body, the feel of a thick cock buried deep inside her.

"I'm not after a record deal," she said. "I don't need you to help me in my career. I just want this." Guy made her feel warm and bright. She'd missed those feelings while she'd shut herself away in the shadows.

Midori caught Guy's flesh in her hands and then she captured his lips with her own. Any resistance Guy may have felt, evaporated.

"God, I want you, too. So bad." He pulled her onto his lap. As her hand stroked him, he reached under her skirt and found her warm heat.

They came to each other as equals, wanting only one thing. Hands met legs, met fingers, met wet flesh. He slipped her skirt up past her thighs. Midori writhed down onto him as he thrust up towards her. All the while, their lips and tongues mingled.

"Do you have protection?" she asked when she broke away from his hungry mouth.

"Protection?"

"A condom?"

Guy blinked. His fingers paused in their search for wet

heat. "No, I didn't plan on this happening." His hazy eyes cleared for just a moment. "I'm still not sure it *can* happen."

"Why not?"

Guy groaned as she ground her hips into his erection. "I wasn't trying to seduce you, Midori. I genuinely want..."

"You want what?"

"...to be your friend," he finished lamely.

Midori smiled. She still held his cock in her hand. It throbbed and jerked like a kitten reaching up its head for petting. "I'd like to be your friend too," she smiled. It was more than a friendly smile. It was a smile laced in desire and seduction.

Midori rubbed the head of his cock, spreading the precum around the base. The head on Guy's shoulders collapsed back against the sofa. His thumb found her swollen bud. They stroked at each other, eyes never leaving the others'. There were no more questions, no more reasons. Guy pet Midori's bud until she began to purr. She caressed his head until a deep growl broke from him. They came together, their bodies shaking and heaving in pleasure.

Midori collapsed into his embrace and Guy held onto her, burying his face in the crook of her neck.

"BFFs?" asked Midori.

Guy chuckled in the crook of her neck. The gush of air sent trembles down her spine and warmed her through.

18

Guy's hips thrust into soft, warm wetness. He grabbed a fistful of the bedsheets as a delicious tension coiled in his stomach. His fists clenched. His teeth gritted. The tension unfurled. Guy thrust once more, his toes pressed into the baseboard, his fists moved to grip the headboard for leverage. His entire body, mind, and soul opened along with his release. He saw notes dance before his eyelids, strung up on a gold string. Melodies drummed in his ears as ribbons of thread swirled around his head. When he opened his eyes, he came face to face with... his pillow.

Guy jerked back. Beneath him was a wet spot on his sheets. Instead of feeling embarrassed about his wet dream, Guy burst into hysterical laughter. He couldn't remember the last time he'd even had a wet dream. Nor the last time he'd been hard enough to achieve it.

Actually, no. He did remember the last time he'd been hard. It was last night, with Midori.

Guy rolled onto his back, his limbs splayed across the mattress as he allowed his thoughts to go back in time. The taste of her, the smell of her, and the feel of her was still clear in his mind. He couldn't remember wanting a woman as much as he'd wanted Midori Miller.

The past year had been a numbing experience. He'd lost all interest in women, aside from squinting hard to try to find their talent. He'd stopped checking them out physically, knowing there was nothing he could do if he liked what he saw. With his failing Sight and his failing equipment, he'd felt insufficient in and out of the bedroom.

But at the first glance he'd had of Midori he'd felt a twinge. Then he'd gotten hard when he brushed up against her body. Last night was the first orgasm he'd had in over a year.

It was over, the curse. It had to be. But how?

Could Gale have been right? Was this love—between Midori and him? Guy was so sex-starved he doubted he'd be able to tell the difference between busting a nut and falling in love.

He'd never been in love, never been close to it, but he'd gotten off a hell of a lot in his time. It had never been as toe-curling as when Midori sat on top of him, or even this morning with just the thought of her in his head, and cotton sheets in his hands.

Then again, the last time Guy had gotten off had been a traumatic ordeal. He remembered the young woman clearly. She had been model tall with long legs, golden brown skin, and light eyes. It was the golden color of her skin that had attracted him. He couldn't remember where they'd met. He couldn't even remember her name. He just remembered a wild, animalistic, kinda painful night in a hotel room, much like this one he was waking up in.

In the morning, she sang him an awful rendition of Patti LaBelle's "Lady Marmalade." Both the song and her voice grated against the walls. His attempts to let her down gently failed when she climbed in his lap in an attempt to change his mind. Guy deposited her on her ass and switched from gentle to blunt. Her face transformed from seductress to sinister.

"You can fix my voice in the production studio," she smirked. "Everything's faked nowadays." She flipped her weave over her shoulder.

Guy could agree, looking at her fake breasts that were harder than soft. She'd pulled out her contacts at some point during the night and he now saw the normal brown of her eyes. The only thing real about her was her golden skin, but looking clearly, Guy saw that it had been a trick of the eyes. Her aura was dark, so dark it was nearly absent. He'd never seen anything quite like it.

"You make magic," she continued. "Use your magic on me."

Her cultured accent slipped in that last sentence, and he heard her Southern twang as it peeked out. Guy wondered how much she knew about his family. In Louisiana, it was well known that the Charmaynes had a 'spelled' family history, but he didn't make that known in New York. He wouldn't have had a job, or climbed so high, if the industry thought he was mental.

"You don't have talent," he'd told the woman. Not even the pale yellow of the inside of a banana. Everyone had at least the pale meat of a banana on the inside. Not her. "There's nothing I can do for you."

"You can't fuck me and then fuck me over." She stood, crooking two fingers at him that reminded him of Celie in *The Color Purple*. "Until you do right by me, Guillaume Rumpel, and make me a fucking star, I'll be the last woman you fuck."

Guy had stared at her fingers. A chill had gone up his spine. A cloud had passed over the rising sun. A bird flew by the window, then crashed into the glass. By the time Guy turned back, the woman was gone. He'd met a lot of crazies in his line of work, but that girl had topped the cake.

It had been the last he'd seen of her. It had also been the last he'd seen of his erections. After a few months of embarrassment in the bedroom, Guy had begun looking for the little witch. Only problem was, he didn't know who she was. He'd kept a look out in the clubs, he'd asked around, but no one in the music industry knew who she was.

Guy stood looking out the hotel window at the bright light of day. His aunt had told him that love could break any curse. He'd seen the power of love work its magic in his family, time and time again. He'd always hoped for that type of love to make an appearance in his heart.

Midori was so full of light, but it had been clouded. Since he'd been around her, encouraging her to live her dreams, she was shining brighter each day. And now her light was shining on him and breaking him out of his darkness. He didn't know if it was love, but he wanted her to stick around, whatever this was.

Guy looked down again at the wet spot on his boxers. A huge grin spread across his face at the mess. He stripped the bedsheets for the maid service, and hopped into the shower singing the songs that had come into his head during his wet dream.

On his way down the hall, he was tempted to knock on Midori's hotel room door, but he talked himself out of it. He had another appointment and he wanted to be able to share the good news when he saw Kimmei and Midori a little later today. With great difficulty, Guy backed away from their door and headed out.

Inside the record station, Guy sat back as he watched the expressions cross over DJ Bree-Zee's face.

"Wow, G," Bree-Zee said when the track ended. "That's some find."

"Can you believe she's only ten?" said Guy.

"No, I can't believe that. That kid must have an old soul."

"So, you'll play the song during a block?"

"Which block?" Bree-Zee said. "It's too slow for morning drive time. And it's a kid singing. What adult wants to hear that during their workday? Plus this is a pop station. That little girl is singing jazz, damned near opera."

"The Fugees took an old jazz song and struck gold with *Killing Me Softly*," Guy countered.

"While interspersing the track with rap," Bree-Zee said. "Guy, I'd like to help you out. You've obviously found a talent here. But she won't fit with my audience."

Guy hung his head. He knew Bree-Zee was right. It was what JJ had warned him about. He had to figure out where to place Kimmei's brilliance so it could shine. He had to. He couldn't afford another failure, especially not one with actual talent.

He left the radio station and headed back to the office. Along the way, he grabbed three cronuts from a vendor. The cronut was a cross between a croissant and a donut. The little treats were all the rage these days in New York, so much so that most vendors would only allow you to purchase two at a time. But an extra Benjamin got Guy an additional treat.

He went into the studio and placed the box of treats on the mixing board. He pulled up Kimmei's track. The little star's voice lit up the mixing board. He wasn't giving up. He'd find a place for Kimmei in the world of music.

Guy checked his watch. They should be here by now. He

finished off his cronut and got up to check. He *saw* them before he saw them. Today, Midori's brilliance rivaled her daughter's. Midori looked up and spotted Guy. Her face transformed to clear desire. Guy felt himself stir just at the sight of her, until he felt something crash into his midsection.

"Good morning, Mr. Guy." Kimmei wrapped her arms around his waist.

Guy reached down and stroked her curly hair. "There's my little star. You ready to get to work?"

She bobbed her head in excitement and then dashed past him into the studio. Midori sauntered over to Guy. It was a catwalk, a show for him. Guy leaned against the door-post to enjoy it.

"Good morning, Mr. Rumpel."

"Good morning, Ms. Miller."

"Did you sleep well?"

"I did, so friendly of you to ask."

"Well, we are friends," she smiled.

"Best friends," he agreed.

They grinned at each other like schoolchildren. Guy leaned forward, eager to taste her lips. His erection was straining. Her lips were just an inch from his. He leaned in closer and—

"Excuse me, Mr. Rumpel—Oh, hey, Midori."

Midori jerked away from him at the sound of Maya's voice. "Good morning, Maya. I was just heading into the studio to be with Kimmei."

The words were mumbled to the ground as Midori slipped past Guy and into the studio.

Maya raised an eyebrow at Guy. His assistant his relationship with Agave was a farce having procured concert tickets for Caroline, and ushered her backstage, and made travel arrangements for both women. She'd also been with Guy for two years now, so she'd seen the change in his playboy ways. Guy hadn't shown an interest in a woman in a long time. But unlike Agave, Maya kept out of his personal life. She handed him a few documents to sign, and then returned to her desk. Guy turned and made his way into the studio.

"Mr. Guy, can we play Mama my song."

He sat down at the mixing board and played the track for Midori. She beamed from ear to ear as she listened to her daughter's voice sail across the track.

"This sounds amazing," she said. "It reminds me of my father."

Guy hid his grimace and the reference to the opera singer. That kind of music wasn't played on any radio station. It was played in the dens of old folks' homes or on stages. Worry creased his brow.

"You okay?" Midori reached for his forehead and then pulled back at the last minute.

Guy watched her retreat, aching for the connection.

Kimmei popped up between them. "I need to use the bathroom."

"You remember where it is?" Midori asked. "Down the hall—"

"I know, I know." Kimmei hopped out of the room.

As soon as the door closed, Guy turned to Midori. His cock stirred in his pants as he regarded the golden halo around her. He couldn't bear to have any distance between them. "Come here."

Midori looked up at him, then at the door. She gave a shake of her head. "Someone might see. We're just friends, remember"

"What if I want more?"

She looked up at him. Her eyes lowered seductively. "You're welcome to have more. Come over tonight."

That wasn't what he meant, but there would be time to explain it later. Guy knew Midori was skittish. His cock strained against his pants as the blood rushed from his big head and down to his smaller one. He reached for her, but she wheeled backward into the mixing board. A box fell to the floor, sending the two remaining cronuts spilling to the floor.

"Damn," he cursed. "I bought those for you guys."

"It's okay," she said. "Neither of us are a fan of donuts."

"It's a cronut."

"Looks like bread and sugar. Not my cup of tea."

"And what is your cup of tea?" He maneuvered until she was trapped between his arms. She didn't protest. He crashed his lips to hers. Midori tasted sweeter than the powdered sugar he'd had only moments ago. But as he sipped from her, his erection began to soften.

Guy jerked back.

"What's the matter?" Midori reached for him.

"Nothing, I just..."

She reached for him. Kissing the side of his neck. Her cool lips felt amazing against his neck, but they did not register anywhere below his neck.

Her hands slipped down his chest and rested on his belt buckle. Guy shoved her hand away before they went any farther.

She looked up at him, puzzled. Then a wall went up. "Sorry," she slumped back into her chair. "You don't want anyone to see, right?"

"Kimmei will be back any second." It was the second time he'd used the child to cover his failings.

Midori looked to the door, her wall slowly coming back down. "So, you're coming over tonight?"

More than anything, he wanted to fall into her and get lost. He wanted to get inside her body and feel her warmth.

She reached for him again. Guy scooted back and crossed his arms over his chest. "Yeah," he reached for the mixing board and began setting the faders aright. "I just need to get some work done on your daughter's dream first."

"Of course. I mean, if you have time." Her face shuttered halfway closed.

Guy hated the distance that sprang up between them. But he couldn't breach it. The softness between his thighs wouldn't allow him to stand firm. He darted his glance away from Midori and towards the door, turning his torso away from her.

idori pulled through the last stitch of the garment and sat back on her heels. She shook her head slowly to the left and back to the right. It was a masterpiece, some of her best work. Pride filled her heart. Hope swirled around in her brain. She itched to show it to Lorne Gunston right now, but he wouldn't be over to see her work for a couple of days. She waited for that thought to bring fear to her heart, numbness to her extremities, a trickle of sweat down her spine. None of those telltale signs of stress came.

She felt light. She felt energetic. She was ready to work on another garment for the collection. Instead, she glanced over at her phone.

Guy should be calling any second now. She pressed her thighs together in anticipation. Last night had been amazing. She couldn't remember ever feeling so fulfilled just from a man's touch. His kisses and his fingers had left her sated. He'd held her for a long time afterwards, dozing with her in the cradle of his arms. They'd both awakened a few hours before dawn and he'd slipped out before Kimmei could awaken.

It was dark out again now. Midori checked the clock on the wall. It was past normal business hours, but what did she know of the music business?

He said he'd call. She didn't have a reason to distrust him. He'd kept every word he'd made to her, and then gone above and beyond when he hadn't needed to. She wasn't crazy enough to think they were in some relationship; that they were on the road to true love or anything. She wasn't even sure if that was something she ever wanted to put stock in again. She was content to have Guy in her bed. She was willing to let down her guard enough to let him lie close to her. She hadn't done that with a man in years.

She should be afraid. Her heart should be pounding in fear. But it wasn't. She felt... excited. He'd pulled her to him in the studio where anyone could've seen. If he didn't care that anyone could see, that meant he had nothing to hide. He wasn't hiding her. And he'd said that he wanted more. That single word, *more*, made her heart pound even harder. Did she want more? Did she have more to give?

She leaped up as the phone rang. But the name on the caller ID had her jerking her hand back. Her chest deflated at the sight of Michel's name. The phone stopped ringing. Then it started again. She knew he'd keep calling until she picked up. If she didn't pick up, she might miss Guy's call.

"What do you want, Michel?"

"Where are you?" he said. "I've been calling your home phone."

"We're out of town for a few weeks."

"And you didn't think to call me? You have my daughter."

"Whom you take the time to see maybe once a year, if at all."

Michel sighed. "That doesn't mean I can't worry about you," his voice softened, but Midori wasn't fooled. "Where are you?" He repeated.

She decided to placate him to get him off the phone. "We're in New York. There's a talent agent that's interested in Kimmei's singing. She's cutting a demo."

"Really? That's interesting. I have some business in New York. Maybe I could come and see you..." His voice lowered as he said the last sentence.

"Where are you, Michel? Are you at home? Is your wife nearby?"

"Dor—"

"If you want to come for your daughter, fine. Don't come for me. I'm seeing someone."

"Seeing someone?" His voice rose. In the background, Midori heard the faint sound of a feminine voice. Then she heard loud steps and a door slam.

"Are you leaving the room, Michel? Because of your wife? And you expect to leave the country?"

"You know how I feel about you, Dor," he whispered.

"Yes," she shouted. "I do know, which is why you need to stay over there with your wife, instead of trying to sneak around with me. I won't be your whispered little secret, ever again."

"Who is this man you have around my daughter?"

"It's none of your business. Your daughter is fine. We'll be home before school starts. End of conversation."

Midori hung up the phone. But as she did, it rang again. It was just like Michel to ignore her wants and needs.

She hit talk, her fingers gripping the receiver. "I said end of conversation."

"Midori?" Guy's deep baritone rang clear through the line.

"Oh, Guy! No, I'm sorry. I thought you were someone else."

"I'd hate to be that girl... or guy?"

"It was Kimmei's dad. We don't have the best relationship." Midori hesitated, wanting to tell him more, but not wanting another person to look at her with judgment.

"It's okay," he said. "You don't have to explain."

Midori curled into the arm of the sofa with the phone tucked into her cheek. It was the same sofa where he'd held her last night. "How did the rest of your sessions go?"

"Lousy, actually. I haven't gotten a thing done since finishing up with Kimmei."

"She's sleeping now. So... are you headed over?"

The silence that followed was brief, but it tied Midori's gut in a knot. There was an off-key note in his voice when he spoke. "There're still a few things I have to finish up here. It's going to be really late by the time I finish."

"Oh, okay." Was it her imagination or did Guy's voice lower. She pressed her ear to the phone, her fingertips felt cold against the plastic. She strained to see if she could hear another woman's voice in the background.

"It's just going to be really late, and I don't want to creep into your place—"

"No, no, it's fine. I understand." This silence between she and Guy felt even heavier.

"I've been thinking about you all day," he said. "In fact, I can't stop thinking about you, which is probably why I haven't gotten the work done that I need to get done. I just... can't... tonight. I'm tired, and a little stressed out. I wouldn't... be the best company right now."

Midori took a deep breath, willing her heart to slow

down, but it wouldn't. Something was off, but she didn't know what. "It's fine, really."

"Okay?"

"Okay."

"Sleep well, Midori."

The click that ended the call was loud. Midori tried to talk her hands out of sweating. Just because he wasn't able to meet her tonight didn't mean there was someone else.

20

When Guy opened his eyes the next morning, clouds fogged up his window. The sun was nowhere to be found in the early morning light. It had been a rough night. He'd gotten plenty of sleep, but it was anything but restful. He was haunted by dreams of a voluptuous woman with eyes in the shape of a grin, caramel skin, and a lopsided smile. Every sense in his body had been engaged in the dream. His nose smelled her fresh linen scent. His mouth tasted her sweet musk. His hands felt the elasticity of her flesh. Now, in the absence of the dark of night, there was numbness in his fingertips and his head throbbed.

Guy's grumbling stomach forced him out of the bed. The cold floor stung his bare feet on the way to the kitchen. In the fridge, he found leftover takeout boxes. These were likely from days ago, since he'd eaten with Midori and Kimmei the past two nights. He popped open a can of soda and downed it, then chased it with a second can. In the back of the fridge was a donut that may have been reaching a week old. Guy chanced it and devoured the sugary treat in two bites.

Neither the drinks nor the food satisfied the throb in his head, as he prepared for the day ahead.

His feet slowed as he neared her door. He knew he should stay away from her, but his body had a mind of its own. Guy knocked on her hotel room door. Though the weather outside was rainy and full of clouds, he felt her warm yellow moving closer. His cock twitched, standing up to greet Midori as she opened the door.

She looked surprised to see him standing there. "Hey," she said, "I thought you had another long day."

"I do," he said, taking her in. She wore low hanging sweat pants and a crop top. "But I wanted to see you."

She pulled her lip into her mouth. Guy felt parched and hungry again.

"I'm sorry about last night," he said.

"You said you had things to take care of." She didn't meet his eye. She held the door between them like a physical barrier.

"Is that Mr. Guy?"

Midori opened the door wider to reveal Kimmei. The little girl bounced and then bounded into him. "We just made breakfast. You want some?"

He didn't get the chance to decide. Kimmei tugged him into the room and into a chair at the table.

The food was amazing; fruit salad and egg whites with zucchini fritters. With his belly properly fed, his head cleared. In a blink, his eyes shifted focus, seeing more clearly than before. He glanced across the table at the ray of light that was Midori. He reached out his hand to her. She hesitated before placing her fingers in his palm. An electric shock zipped through his fingers. He decided to stop ignoring the signs that were staring at him as clear as day, and twined his fingers with hers.

His phone rang in his pocket. He looked at the caller ID. "Maya," he answered. "Clear my day, something just came up." He curled his fingers tightly around Midori's. "How about we take in a matinee on Broadway?"

"A musical?" asked Kimmei with excitement in her voice.

"Guy." The objection was clear in Midori's voice. "You can't just take the day off to spend with us. I know you have work to do. *I* have work to do."

"Let's call it research," he said. "Kimmei gets to hear new sounds. You get to look at the costumes."

"And you?" Midori raised an eyebrow.

Guy had every urge to lean over the table and kiss the arch in her eyebrow. "My job is to keep my star happy."

She lowered the arch. The shutters that had been up the day before and this morning, opened for him.

They left the hotel and headed to Broadway. Kimmei walked between them, but at some point, she stepped a little ahead of them and Guy's hand wrapped around Midori's again. She looked up at him in surprise, and then she looked around at the passersby on the street. Guy pulled her in close, reveling in the warmth and smell of her.

In the theater, he maneuvered himself so that Midori sat between himself and Kimmei. Their legs never lost contact. Their fingers stayed intertwined. The wonder she felt watching the play zipped across her fingertips and into his body, his soul. This had to be it; the thing his mother talked about whenever she spoke about his father. The thing Gale told him to wait for when he was just a kid. The thing he saw in his cousin Manny's eyes, whenever he looked at his wife.

Guy missed the entire musical. His eyes remained trained on Midori, on the golden halo that sang to him and him alone.

After dinner, at the same Asian Fusion restaurant he'd visited with Kimmei, they returned to the hotel. They sat down to watch *America's Got Singers*. Midori curled on one side of the couch, and Guy took the opposite end. Kimmei bounced in the middle, not seeming the least bit tired.

Watching the show, Guy felt like his old self. Each talent in the showcase was clear to him. No one hazed or shifted colors. Only three of the ten contestants showed a healthy golden color. The other seven were muted. With his polishing abilities, he could turn them into something special. But just the thought of the work that would entail, the stress and strain it would put on him, was unappealing. Guy made a mental note of the three bright lights and endeavored to have Maya track them down before the season ended.

Finally, the program ended, and the news came on. It was only then that Kimmei began to nod off. Guy scooped up the little girl in his arms and carried her into her bedroom. Her mother let her sleep in her shorts and t-shirt and pulled the coverlet over her small chest.

Soundlessly, Midori and Guy made their way back out to the living room. While Guy had been spotting the talent on the screen, he'd had another talk with himself. With each day that he spent with this woman, his Sight got clearer and clearer. His body responded to her with more and firmer frequency.

Guy wanted Midori. He knew it for fact in his mind. He stopped denying that fact as it arrowed toward his heart. But he couldn't ignore that, though his heart and soul wanted her, his body wasn't completely on board. He hadn't felt an urge all day.

Guy decided that the two of them were going to sit down and have a talk. He chuckled to himself. Most men would avoid any attempt at talking, but now he was the one prepared to lead the charge into this one.

Midori, it would seem, had a different idea than conversation on her mind.

He turned to face her and she was in his arms. Her lips locked to his, her arms around his neck, her body pressed against his from breast to groin. Guy opened to her, allowing her tongue to gain access to his. He cradled her head in his palm and angled her face until their noses crossed at the best angle to allow him to sip deeply from the well of her. The words he'd planned to say to her left him, as blood rushed to his groin. It wasn't until Midori's hands ventured south that an ounce of blood diverted to his brain and Guy came to his senses.

"Midori." He gulped in a lungful of air and got a head full of her scent. "We don't have to do anything. I'd be content to just sit with you on the couch, or watch you sew."

"I don't want a needle in my hands right now."

Her fingers brushed over his erection, his firm, throbbing erection. The last ounce of blood remaining in his head retreated and threw up a flag. He allowed himself to be guided to her bedroom. His dick stayed firm as Midori shut the door behind him.

He could do this. They could touch each other like they'd done the other night. He could bring her to pleasure. He was happy to use his hands, his tongue. He clenched and unclenched his fingers to prepare them as he watched her undress. His hands hovered over the front of his pants, trembling at the cold feel of his zipper.

Midori pulled the straps of her bra over her arms, freeing her ample breasts. Guy's mouth watered. His hands went limp at his sides.

She stepped up to him. Her nimble fingers unbuttoned his shirt. His arms felt like heavy weights when she nudged him to lift them so she could remove his shirt. Then her hands went to his fly.

His brain told him to stop her, tried to remind him of his past failures with women. But his eyes couldn't see past her bright smile, as she looked up at him with desire in her eyes. He swore that if his dick went limp, he'd bury his face between her thighs until she sang for him.

"I want to feel you inside of me," she said.

The sound of the zipper unfastening its teeth cracked like thunder between them. His pants pooled at his ankles in a loud thud.

Guy gulped. But he was firm in her hands, throbbing in fact.

She reached over to her dresser and pulled out an unopened box of condoms. He gritted his teeth as she rolled one on him, willing his erection to stay in spite of the constraining plastic.

"It's been awhile for me," she said.

"Me too," Guy grimaced.

"Please. Women are always falling over you."

"They are," he agreed. "Because they want something from me, not because they want me."

"I want something from you."

She reached down and grabbed his encased penis. It pointed at her as she backed up to the bed and scooted on board. Guy followed her like she was a beacon to safety, to harbor, to home.

His lips crashed into hers. His arms anchored around

her back. He held onto her like a lifeboat as the waves of desire drowned everything around them out.

Midori opened her thighs and he seated his hips between her. He reached for himself, hands trembling, but his dick remained firm, aching, as though the warm, wet core of Midori was the only place it would find any relief.

He guided himself into her, slowly, carefully. Even through the thin casing of the condom, the heat of her nearly knocked Guy back.

"Please don't tease me, Guy. Don't make me wait."

He looked down at the writhing woman beneath him. Gold shone so bright he nearly had to look away. Instead, he slipped into her body and knew he was home.

He was hypersensitive. He felt every nook and cranny of her walls. Every move of her hips. Every squeeze of her channel.

Everywhere around him, he saw gold. When he closed his eyes, he was bathed in light. Her fingertips digging into his back were bright rays of sun searing his skin. Her lips against his neck burned, leaving a mark he knew he'd feel for days. He felt possessed. He searched inside himself, seeking more to give her.

She begged him to speed up. Faster, harder, she cried. But he couldn't. It was too good. His thrusts were slow and shallow. He wanted it to last forever. He tried to go even slower, amidst her protests. Couldn't she see that they were on a collision course towards forever?

His voice failed him even as his cock swelled inside of her, preparing to burst with everything he felt inside. Guy stared into Midori's eyes, trying to communicate with her the depth of his feelings.

He thrust into her body, holding her close to him. Midori clutched him, her body trembling beneath him. She looked into his eyes, her guard disbanded. Guy stole on board like a pirate preparing to loot his greatest treasure. He fused his lips with hers, as he cradled her hips in his hands and rocked them both to orgasm.

Only after they both came down from the trembling and shaking did Guy's penis soften. Not even then did he let Midori go. As far as he was concerned, he was never letting this woman go.

21

———

𝒲aking was a cradle of ease. Midori's head was supported by a strong arm. Her back rested against a warm chest. There was a cushion at Guy's abdomen, which surprised her. He looked like a man who would be fit and not have a dad bod. But his soft abs didn't matter to her. Last night, Guy made her feel like a treasure.

She'd allowed him to stare into her eyes as he slowly pierced her core. She'd never been taken to bed in such a slow and deliberate manner. He hadn't allowed her to hide in the cradle of his neck. When his eyes bored into hers, she couldn't look away from him. He'd opened her up for the taking, but left her whole.

She watched him now, as he slept. He was peaceful. She was peaceful. She lay in the cocoon of him and allowed him to support her.

Michel had never stayed until the morning. He always had to get back to the offices he'd say. She'd believed him, when what he'd been running back to was his wife.

Here Guy lay, with the rays of the sun coming in through the window. He'd canceled his appointments and spent the day with them, holding her hand in public. He'd slept peacefully through the night, in no rush to leave her bed in the morning. His arms tightened around her now. She felt something stiff against her belly.

She reached down and ran her fingers against his erection. It was more soft than hard, but she knew she could fix that. She craved to have him inside of her again, eager to allow that slow penetration to delve deeper inside of her.

With the first stroke of her fingers, Guy's eyes sprang open. He inhaled as the sleepy haze cleared from his eyes. He smiled at her and captured her lips. She opened for him, allowing him access to the northern part of her while her southern hemisphere waited impatiently for its attention.

Midori continued to stroke his erection to make it firmer. She threw a leg over him. Guy cradled her thighs as she balanced herself over top of him. She leaned down to kiss him again, but before her lips could connect, he grabbed the skin at the base of her neck and held her still.

He stared up at her, his eyes owl-wide. "Damn, you're the brightest thing I've ever seen in my life."

Somehow, Midori knew he wasn't talking about her brain. He brought her head down and met her lips. She got lost in the kiss and let go of his penis. As the kiss continued, her core met something soft and fleshy lying between them.

Guy jerked away.

"What's wrong?" she asked when her lips met the air between them.

"I..." Guy grimaced, frustration etched on his face.

Midori moved her hips over his. Again, she was met with fleshy softness. She looked down to see that they'd lost his erection. She grinned up at him, pulling her lip into her mouth with her teeth. "Let me fix that." She inched down his body.

Guy rolled out from under her before she could reach for him. "No," he said tersely. "I... I have to get going."

He got up and went for his clothes. He began shoving them on.

Midori pulled the sheets around herself, a chill running up her spine. "Did I do something wrong."

He gulped, not quite meeting her eyes. "It's not you. It's me."

Midori knew those words. They were never true. She pulled the sheets even tighter, trying to trap the escaping warmth that was now in retreat since he'd left her.

Guy was before her again. His hands on either side of her face, forcing her to look at him. "Don't do that. Don't dim your light. You didn't do anything wrong."

"Then why are you running off?"

He sighed, kneeling down and bowing his head. His forehead rested in the valley of her breasts. She heard him gulp, and he raised his head, his jaw set. "These feelings that I have for you are unexpected."

"What feelings, exactly?"

He paused, dark gray eyes set on her. "Are you sure you want to hear this?"

"Yes." But Midori's tone lacked any enthusiasm. She curled her toes into the mattress seeking its warmth.

"You know the... stories that surround my family?" he began.

She assumed he meant the stories of seeing gold and finding true love.

"A lot of it's true," he confirmed. "Most of it's true."

"You mean golden auras and... soulmates." Midori fumbled over the last word.

Guy traced his hands just beyond her hair. Midori's

heart kicked up its pace, as though she felt the unseeable light his fingers touched.

"I don't *see* like Manny and the rest of that side of my family does. But ever since I met you... I *feel* differently. I *see* clearly. There's something about you, Midori. I can't deny it, anymore."

Midori shivered as the sun shone in through the window.

"I *see* you, Midori. I shouldn't. You're not the kind of talent that I normally see. But I see the brightest gold around you." He hesitated, his fingers trembled as they closed in on her cheek. "You know what that means don't you?"

Midori gulped. She shuddered, but not from a chill or any numbness. Heat washed through her, so hot she thought she might pass out from its onslaught.

"It scares me, too." Guy caressed her chin. "I never thought something like this would happen to me. I'm... overwhelmed."

Midori felt overwhelmed herself. She hadn't dared to hope for something like this in her life either. She'd thought she had the fairytale once before and it turned into a nightmare. She'd packed away any dreams of being a princess or a true love. Now, the fairytale was knocking at her door, forcing her to meet its eyes.

"Let's make a deal," Guy said.

Her heart beat so loudly in her chest she thought she was having a heart attack. Guy reached his lips towards hers. He kissed her lightly, and then the kiss deepened. The emotions swirling around between them forced her onto her back and she pulled him down with her. Her emotions were a swirling hurricane. The physical, she could manage. But as her hands trailed down to unzip his pants he pulled away again. Confusion settled on Midori's brow.

Guy sat up and looked down at her, indecision warring on his face. "Let's go slow."

"Slow?"

"Yeah," he grinned pulling her up to sitting. "I just told you I think you're my soulmate, and I haven't even taken you out on a proper date."

"You want to date me, even though what you see tells you that I'm a sure thing?"

Guy shrugged, giving her a lopsided grin, through which she glimpsed the imperfectly charming gap in his teeth. "Are you sure, Midori?"

Midori swallowed again, not answering.

"I want this to work," he said. "I don't have the best track record with women, and I want to do this—you and me—right. Please, let's go slow. Let's make sure that we're both sure."

Midori hugged her knees into her chest and wiggled her warm toes. "Okay, slow sounds good. A date sounds great."

His grin was full of triumph. His gray eyes glowed. Midori felt the beginnings of a fall in the center of her chest. She dug her fingers into the bed sheets to keep herself steady.

"Just know that I'm going to order the lobster," she said aiming for saucy but sounding uncertain.

"I'll buy you five lobsters. You're worth it." He reached up and placed a gentle, chaste kiss on her lips. Then he rose, straightening his shirt. "I'm gonna have to pay the piper for playing hooky yesterday, which means I'll be stuck in the studio all day today. I'll see you tomorrow?"

"Okay."

"Okay." He lingered at the door. He stared again at the

space around her and then he looked directly into her eyes. He smiled big and boyish. And then was gone.

Midori lay in bed for an hour after Guy left, trying to calm her beating heart. She never thought she'd get another opportunity like this. Her daughter was cared for and achieving her dreams. Midori's fashion dreams were within her grasp. And now someone was making a play for her heart, a good and decent person with nothing to hide. A man who wanted to take her out in the light of day to win her over. A man who believed in her, and made her believe in herself.

Midori had sworn she'd never fall in love again. She let go of the bed sheets and uncurled her toes. This felt nothing like falling. This felt like flying.

22

───────

uy watched the young, lithe and limber dancers writhe to the sultry sound of Althea Bentley's track. The track was a departure from her R&B days. Further, it was a departure from her roots in gospel as a teen. But Guy had been able to take all of those influences from the deep, moving notes of the spiritual realm, to the toe tapping rhythm of R&B, and lay it over a track that made the young and old dance in the clubs.

Guy's job was easy when he had such talent to work with. He watched the dancers move effortlessly through a series of sexy moves interpreting the song about finding someone to love. The set was up. The track was ready. The rehearsal was nearly complete. All they needed was the star to enter into the background.

"Where do you want me, Guy?"

Guy turned to the sound of Althea's voice, and blinked. "What are you wearing?"

Althea pressed her hands to her stomach, which looked flat under the ruched fabric. "You don't like it?"

Standing before him was his star. She glowed the

brightest he'd seen her in months. She was dressed in a jacket that drew the eyes to her ample breasts. The dress hugged her curves instead of hiding them. The garment stopped just below her knees and showed off her shapely calves. Guy never knew that Althea had an hourglass figure, a very comely hourglass figure.

"You look amazing," he said.

Her eyes widened, and if possible, she glowed brighter. "Maya got it from a new designer, Midori Miller, she said her name was."

"Midori? Midori made this for you?"

"I don't think she made it. She just styled me, and tailored the dress. I'm so glad you like it. I do, too. As soon as the shoot is over, I'm going to track her down and hire her to be my personal stylist. You wouldn't happen to have her contact information would you?"

Guy chuckled. "I do indeed."

Althea beamed.

Guy led her to her place, front and center of the dancers, and they began.

After two more wardrobe changes, one look more stunning than the next, they called it a wrap.

It was late in the afternoon when Guy returned to the offices. Before he got to his door, JJ stuck his head out of his office and called him in.

Guy took a seat. "Althea's shoot just wrapped. I think it's gonna be hot."

"I saw some of the publicity photos from the shoot," JJ said. "Great work on the styling. It's a picture perfect image for her."

"That wasn't me, it was Midori Miller. Kimmei's mother. Did I mention she's a fashion designer?"

JJ eyed Guy with a knowing smile. JJ knew Guy well. He

had been a second father to him since they'd met. JJ had never put any stock in Guy's Sight, and Guy never pushed the idea on the man, but he realized that he'd have to explain the reality of his family's magic, now that he'd seen for himself how important Midori was to him. But JJ took the discussion in a different direction.

"The stations love Frankie's new track," JJ said.

Guy frowned scooting closer to JJ's desk. "I didn't send it out yet." Guy had spent all night working on the track to get it polished. And by polished he meant hiding Frankie's voice beneath a myriad of base.

"No, *I* sent it to the stations. We have to strike while the iron is hot with that one. Her fifteen minutes of fame are nearly up, and we don't want to miss out."

Guy looked up at the pictures on the wall of JJ in his heyday. Even from the still photographs, he saw the bright talent the man had been. "Don't you miss working with real artists?" Guy asked. "Working with true musicians and true talent, instead of making everything up and using false talent?"

"The game has changed, Guy. Everything's faked nowadays."

The comment hit Guy in the chest. It was the same thing the woman who had cursed him had said.

"We either change with it," JJ continued. "Or we stop playing. I'm not ready to stop playing. I've got too many notes left in me."

Guy looked over at the man he'd admired since he was a kid listening to his music. JJ looked as weary as Guy had a few days ago, before he'd tasted the sweet light of Midori, before he'd started working with Kimmei. "That's what I'm saying, JJ. We should use those notes for the real talent and not waste our time on these flash in the pan hacks."

"Real talent? Like your little jazz singer? I heard that track too, apparently so did a number of the DJ's. But no one's playing it. We can't sell what people don't want to buy, Guy. You know it's about image. No one wants a little girl singing jazz on the radio. Use her voice and sell the image that people want to see and hear. If you can't figure out a way to sell her, you'll need to cut her loose."

"I can make it work with Kimmei," Guy insisted. "I just need more time."

"You don't have much. Frankie is going to need a full album. You still have Agave's second album to drop. And we have a full slate before awards season."

The stress crept up Guy's back.

"You know this," JJ admonished. "It makes me wonder if this has to do with the little starlet's mother? I don't usually get into your personal life, but it's about to interfere with business. We can't afford to lose Agave."

"We won't lose Agave." Guy knew it was now or never. He had to come clean about his relationship with Agave. "There's nothing going on between her and me. It's all for her image. Agave's a lesbian."

JJ pinched the bridge at his nose. "You had the right instinct to cover that up. I can't sell a lesbian pop star to the masses. I'm surprised you didn't tell me sooner."

"I'm surprised you didn't figure it out."

"I wanted to believe it; that she was a sex kitten that was into men, just like every one of her fans. But let me guess, now you have something going on with the fashion momager."

"I think it's the real thing with Midori."

"Then you've got a lot on your plate. You have to keep men believing their sexy pop princess would screw them. Figure out how to make a little jazz singer into a pop princess that everyone want to listen to. Take advantage of Frankie's temporary star power. And now, you're tossing a real relationship on top of that? Good luck, buddy."

Guy left JJ's office with even more weight on his shoulders. With night setting in, he decided to call it quits. He needed to escape and relieve some of the pressure. The contractors were putting the finishing touches on his loft, but he hadn't yet checked out of the hotel. He didn't head back to his room, he headed straight for Midori's.

When she opened the door with a huge smile, Guy felt a wave of relief and got a burst of energy.

"I thought we weren't seeing you until tomorrow," she said.

"I couldn't stay away."

"You're just in time for dinner." Midori lead him inside, took his coat.

Kimmei ran up to him and gave him a hug. Guy was ushered to the table in the midst of two conversations going on at the same time. He answered each of their questions without missing a beat, smiling the whole way.

This was life. This was the life he wanted, seated between two shining people he cared about. He just had to figure out how to make it all work, how to marry the two worlds.

"How was your day?" Midori asked.

"It was great, thanks to you. The styling you did for Althea made her look stunning."

Midori beamed. "I was happy to help. All you needed to do was highlight her assets and cover her unflattering bits."

Guy nodded. "Exactly." He turned to Kimmei. "I think that's what we need to do with your track Kimmei. We need to highlight the power of your voice, but we need to cover some other aspects."

"Okay," she shrugged and dug into her rice.

"Is there a problem with her track?" Midori asked.

Guy hated the worry crease on her lovely face. "Not a problem. I'm just having a hard time finding a station where her voice fits. So, maybe we need to change tactics, offer a compromise so the radio stations see how things fit."

"Cool," Kimmei said around a mouthful of sautéed vegetables.

Guy reached up and soothed the crease between Midori's brows with his finger and she let him. "Trust me?"

After a brief hesitation, she nodded.

Guy knew he should've left after dinner. But he also knew he had no intention of leaving. Midori handled the dishes while Guy did Kimmei's bedtime duty. The two of them sang until she began to doze.

With her eyes shut, he closed the little girl's bedroom door and went in search of Midori. She was in her bedroom, undressed down to her underwear. Guy's temperature rose. But that was all.

She came towards him, taking his lips. Guy kissed her, willing an erection to come up. Midori reached for his belt buckle. Guy pulled away.

"What?" asked Midori. "What's wrong?"

"I... I'm a little tired." The lie felt wrong on his tongue. He sighed, closing his eyes. "That's not true. I'm not tired. I was tired when I came here, but seeing you always gives me a jolt of energy."

"Then what is it?" she asked.

"There are some things that I haven't told you about me, things you might find hard to believe."

Midori backed away from him, grabbing her t-shirt. Even though Guy wasn't up for it, he didn't want her to cover herself. He decided to just come out with it.

"I was cursed," he blurted.

Midori had been in the process of pulling the shirt-sleeves on. Now the garment hung loose on her arms.

"I used to be a bit of a... ho is the only word to describe it; different girl every night. Making promises I didn't always keep. I'm not proud of any of that. I was just able to get away with it. Then one day I met this woman, her aura was muddy brown, nearly black. The darkest aura I've ever seen, still haven't seen anything like it again. I made the mistake of misleading her, and she cursed me. She said, unless I made her a star, she'd be the last woman I'd sleep with. I didn't believe it at first, until things stopped working properly."

Midori looked down at his crotch area. Nothing looked back.

"Are you freaking out?" he asked.

"No," she said but her head bobbed slightly. "Are you telling me you're impotent?"

Guy winced at such a technical word. "I know this all sounds crazy, but it's true. I haven't been with a woman in over a year. No one's gotten a rise out of me until you."

Midori took a step back.

"Things are just starting to work again for me," he continued. "But it's not all back to normal."

She halted her retreat. "Is that what happened this morning?"

Guy nodded.

"So, it really wasn't me?"

"You? No, I told you. It's me. You..." he chuckled. "You saved me."

"Because I'm..."

"The One," he supplied for her. "Gale said all curses can be broken by one thing."

Midori looked a little green around the gills at those two words. "Why me?"

Guy looked at the obvious, but then realized she couldn't see what he saw. Not just the gold around her. He saw the weariness in her eyes that he wanted kiss away. He saw the calluses on her hands that he wanted to hold. "Maybe it's because you're the first woman who hasn't tried to get something out of me. It's made me want to give you anything that's within my reach."

She took a hesitant step towards him. "This is really scary for me, all this trust that I'm giving you. I trusted Kimmei's father, and he hurt me badly."

As soon as she was just within his reach, Guy reached out and grabbed her. He held her firmly to him. The only thing that rose between them was the beating of both their hearts. "I'm not going to hurt you, Midori. I just want to hold you."

"I want that, too."

"I can't promise much more." He peered down between them.

"That's okay with me." Her lips shut him up before he could make any more excuses.

She stripped him down to his boxers. They crawled into bed kissing and exploring each other. Guy stroked her with his fingers until she came for him once, then twice, and because he loved the expression of abandonment that came over her face, he coaxed a third orgasm out of her. An erection did not come to Guy that night, but he felt more satisfied than any night with a woman before.

Midori spooned her lush ass in the cradle of his crotch and fell asleep in his arms. Sometime later as the sun began to rise, so did Guy.

23
____

"These are exquisite, Midori." Gunston said, as he ran his hands over Midori's cocktail dress. "You've created a new silhouette. This is exciting."

Midori felt her chest swell with pride. She also felt a little sore after all the attention she'd received from Guy last night and then again this morning. His words still swirled in her head. He believed she was his One, that she'd broken some curse, even. It was a fairytale and she was a real live heroine. She kept telling herself to keep her feet on the ground, but that voice had grown smaller and smaller with each beat of her heart.

And now that her heart and her body were sated, she was getting her spirit validated. Gunston beamed at her designs.

"These colors are fashion forward." He moved down the line. "What made you think of gold?"

Midori pulled her lip into her mouth as a vision of Guy popped into her head. Her body heated at the memories of his, moving over hers last night, inside hers this morning.

He'd said that he'd been impotent for a year. It had

been too much to believe at first. But then she'd thought back to their first night, when she'd been dressed in a towel and she hadn't gotten a rise out of him. The next night at Charmayne House, he'd never made a pass at her, even though she'd been practically naked in his bed. The way he'd kept distance between them, then held her so close their first time together as he'd taken her so slowly, so carefully.

He hadn't been afraid of hurting her, he'd been afraid of losing his erection. He'd wanted to savor every minute of the experience inside of her before it was gone. He'd made love to her the same way this morning, just as slowly, just as carefully.

He'd left, with Kimmei in tow, after sneaking back to his room for a shower and change of clothes. Midori worried about Kimmei seeing how close she and Guy were becoming. But the worry had stopped, now that she understood the depths of Guy's feelings for her. This wasn't a temporary thing for him. He wanted her by his side, likely forever. Midori waited for the panic to come. It didn't.

She turned to Gunston who appeared to be waiting for her to speak. He'd asked her a question. It had been about her color scheme. "The city in general was my inspiration, and how it's changed from the time I was last here ten years ago. I tried to mix the old with the new."

The city wasn't the only thing that had changed. Midori could've been talking about herself. Ten years ago she'd let this city—this industry—tear her down. She'd had no one by her side, no one who had her back. That was different now. Guy had been standing beside her for such a short time, and in that short span of time he'd seen through her and helped her see herself clearly. She was who she'd always been, but with the small changes in her confidence, she was a better version of herself. It was as though she'd had an internal makeover.

He'd said she'd saved him from this curse, but he'd saved her too.

"These are going to sell like hotcakes in our stores," said Gunston.

Midori turned her full attention to the man. Today he was dressed in a mash-up of Chinese and hippie culture. He had on a Mandarin collared shirt with flaring bell-bottoms.

"You're going to put them in the stores?" she asked.

"Absolutely," Gunston said, as he rounded the mannequin, his belled pants legs swishing the fabric as he walked. "Next season, everyone will be wearing Midori Miller."

Midori's hands balled into fist. She didn't feel air between her fingers. She felt the callused pads of her own fingers pressing into her palms. Those calluses were from her hard work. She'd reached up, grabbed the tendrils of her dreams, and brought them down to make them a reality. And she'd done it on her own.

Well, not entirely on her own. Sure, it was all her talent and her hard work, but if it hadn't been for Guy, she wouldn't be here in New York with this fabric, with this confidence.

"But we will have to do something about these side panels," said Gunston. "They make the hips look larger."

Midori blinked. The pattern didn't make hips look larger. The pattern was for women with large hips, to accentuate those curves. She decided to use diplomacy. "Well, asses are in this season."

"No, honey, that was last season, as in right now. Asses will be out next season. Waifs are back in. Flat will be all the rage."

Midori balled her fists. How could they expect women to be curvy for a few months and then flat the next? "But you do know that the average woman is a size twelve. She has curves that stick around month after month, season after season."

Gunston let go of the fabric in his hand. "Who cares about the average woman? The average woman doesn't walk the runway. It's called a catwalk for a reason. Have you ever seen a fat cat? We are in a business of fantasies. The average woman doesn't want to be average, she wants to be modelesque. There's a reason the diet industry is booming, honey. You don't put reality on the runway. You put the dream up there. Now, you'll have to get rid of these panels. And you'll need to alter this top. Flatten the chest area out on this one too. Think twelve year old girl, not Marilyn Monroe. Kay-kay?"

She'd been *in* just a moment ago. Now all of her hard work, her vision, was being ousted. Midori felt panic rising in her chest. From the sides of her eyes she saw the walls closing in on her. Then Gunston filled her vision.

"You are extremely talented, Midori. Your designs are going to be the talk of the season. You just want the right people saying the right things about them."

Gunston leaned in to kiss her on both cheeks, and then he was out the door.

Midori slumped onto the couch and stared at her designs. She balled and unballed her fists. The calluses remained. The dream was still within reach. She eyed her scissors. All it would take would be a few snips and she'd be back in.

She thought of Guy, who saw her as a brilliant talent. She'd come out of her shadows because of Guy and his belief in her. Gunston believed in her, but he wanted to polish her. Wasn't that what Guy did? He took someone who was already talented and then polished them into a shine. Maybe that's what Gunston was trying to do for her, polish her designs off a bit, not push her out.

Midori picked up the scissors and snipped. She expected a weight to lift off her shoulders. Instead her stomach sank as the fabric fell to the floor.

24

—————

The base in the beat bounced off the walls in the studio. The sound kicked up the beating of Guy's heart, causing his toe to tap against the floor. Everything seemed to be moving in fast motion today, but he saw it all so clearly.

Lying with Midori last night, Guy had known peace, true peace as he brought her to the highest heights of pleasure. There had been no anxiety about his performance, no fear of failure. Though he hadn't stirred that night, Guy conducted Midori's pleasure like a perfect symphony. Using his fingers, he took her through movements that struck a chord at her core. When she decrescendoed, he'd held her to him until he could flip her over and play the B side in the morning.

His body hummed with the knowledge that he'd found the woman he was destined to spend his life with. His eyes were opened wide, seeing shades he'd never seen before. His ears heard the pauses between quarter notes. The notes lined themselves up and fell in perfect tune. The bass didn't skip a beat.

Guy saw it all clearly now. He saw how he would extend Frankie Benjamins fifteen minutes of fame into an hour-long movement. He knew exactly what was missing from Agave's sophomore album, saw the spark that would skyrocket her next album to platinum status in record time. He knew exactly how he needed to brand Kimmei to gain her entry into any radio station's airtime.

Guy saw it all clearly, and it made his head throb. Sitting at his mixing board with one of the best beats of his career thrumming through the speakers, he pulled up the faders and nodded at the sound booth.

The voice couldn't catch the beat. It tripped and landed flat. For the first time since they'd been working together, Kimmei ended a song on a sour note.

"I'm sorry, Mr. Guy." Kimmei hung her head, her bright eyes glistening. "It's just so fast."

Guy had taken the demo song they'd cut together and added a club beat to it, which sped the song up. From his place seated behind the mixer, he looked up at the little girl's downcast face.

Her face was so like her mother's. The same grinning tilt at the corner of her eyes. The same soulful iris. The girl even pulled the corner of her lip into her mouth when she was nervous. She was dressed in a long flowing skirt and a loose t-shirt with a flower spread across her chest.

The thrumming in Guy's head increased as he looked away from that flower, shutting his eyes to the clarity of his vision. He knew that Midori was his One, because he'd never seen everything so clearly in his life before. He knew he had to take her cherubic ten-year-old and turn her into a wanton sexpot. He needed to make her alto voice more nasally and shorten her skirts.

"It's not you, it's me," he said.

In real time, he watched as clouds descended around the girl's shoulders. It confirmed that it didn't matter what age you were, everyone knew what those words truly meant. Everyone knew that to whomever those words were directed, it meant that they didn't live up to the expectations of the person aiming the words.

"I've been trying to get your song on the radio," Guy began.

"But the radio people don't like it?" Kimmei said.

"They like it…"

Kimmei waited patiently for Guy to drop the other ball.

"It just doesn't fit," he tried to explain.

Kimmei shrugged, loosening the clouds threatening her. "That's okay," she offered a small smile. "I don't mind if I'm not on the radio. I just want a record, like my grandpa."

Guy opened his mouth to explain that people didn't buy records anymore. But he felt a pain in his chest. He reached up, but his fingers were numb. "I was hoping that other people would want to listen to your songs."

All traces of clouds fled at the suggestion. "Can I go on stage and sing my songs?"

Guy opened his mouth again, preparing to explain the way the music industry worked, but then he paused. The pain cleared from his chest and again he saw everything. He tapped his fingers on the mixing board and then hit the reset button, clearing the previous track. "I have another idea."

Kimmei leaned forward, eager and trusting. She'd placed her life, her dream in his hands, and Guy had been about to mangle it up into something she would never recognize.

"How about we don't change a thing and instead—"

"Knock, knock!"

Guy turned to look over at the studio door. The bright ray of sunshine in the frame nearly knocked him on his back.

"Agave," he rose. "You're back early"

Agave came into the room and gave Guy a hug. She was dressed in a pastel sundress and stylish riding boots. Her face was devoid of any make up, but her smile lit up her pretty face casting a rosy halo on her cheekbones. Trailing behind her was her girlfriend, Caroline. Caroline didn't have any discernible talent that Guy could spot, but her face glowed one thousand watts as she looked into Agave's face.

"Looks like you girls had a good vacation," he said.

"Yes, we did," Caroline answered. "Thank you for giving her some time before this next album comes out."

Guy and Caroline had a cool relationship. Caroline was a social worker and an LGBTQ youth advocate. She lived her life out of the closet. Guy could only imagine how difficult it was for her to be in love with a woman who kept her feelings a secret.

"Who's this little star?" Agave peered behind Guy at Kimmei.

"This is my newest find. Kimmei, I want you to meet another artist I represent. Her name is Agave."

"It's nice to meet you Ms. Agave." Kimmei held out her hand for Agave to shake.

"What lovely manners you have."

"Thank you," grinned Kimmei at Agave, and then turned to offer her hand to Caroline. "What's your girl-friend's name?"

Agave's smile froze. Not one single adult moved. "Oh, you mean my friend," Agave laughed a little too forcefully.

Kimmei shook her head, no. "My friend Natalie has two moms. You guys remind me of them."

Panic crossed Agave's face. She turned to Guy.

Behind Agave, Guy saw Caroline's face stone over.

"Mr. Guy, I have to use the bathroom." Kimmei hopped from one foot to the other. "I've been in there for an hour."

"I'll take her," said Caroline. "I understand what it's like being stuffed into dark spaces and needing to get out." Caroline looked pointedly at Agave before she took Kimmei's hand and left the room.

Agave looked like she was about to have an apoplectic fit. "I knew I shouldn't have brought her here. She wanted to see where I worked. Now everybody knows."

"Agave, just take a breath," he said.

"If a ten-year-old can see it, an adult will know for sure. My career is over."

Guy had seen it clearly back when he first met Agave. Even with his faulty vision, he'd known that Agave had no interest in anything below the head on his shoulders. But he'd constructed this image standing before him. He'd taken Agave out of her sundresses and cowboy boots and put her in sequined catsuits. He'd wiped off her pastel makeup and put her in neon-glitter. Now she looked like a lost little girl in her sundress and boots.

Guy opened his mouth, prepared to speak the words that would bring his star back on track—the track that would lead her to platinum status and an even bigger celebrity than he'd achieved with any other artist.

"Maybe you should come out," he said.

Her eyes opened as wide as saucers as she looked at him, horrified.

"People love your voice, your talent," he continued. "If a ten-year-old doesn't have a problem with who you love, then other people probably won't either."

"Probably? I can't risk my career on a probably, Guy. I've worked too hard for this."

"You love her?" asked Guy.

"Of course, I love her."

"She deserves everything you have to give. She deserves a whole you."

Agave shook her head, looking at him as though she didn't know who or what he was. "Where is this coming from? You were the one who told me to hide it."

"Well, now I'm telling you I was wrong. I was wrong about a lot of things. You should come out. You have real talent, pure talent."

Agave stared at him. He could see her weighing his words.

"Agave," Caroline stood in the doorway as Kimmei came back in. "I'm just letting you know that I'm leaving."

The look on Caroline's face told them both that she was leaving more than the building.

Agave stood there frozen. Standing next to her, Guy couldn't hear her breathing any longer. Looking down at her chest, it appeared as though her heart had stopped as well.

For her part, Caroline stood with the same stillness. A plea clearly visible behind the hurt and anger in her eyes. "If you have to think about this..."

"Caro, please," Agave whispered.

Caroline shook her head. She closed her eyelids to catch the tears that spilled. She turned to leave, but bumped into another ray of sunshine.

"I'm so sorry," said the ray blocking Caroline's escape.

Caroline didn't spare Midori a glance. She dashed around her and headed down the hall.

Midori looked after her, then turned back to the adults in the room. Her eyes found Guy's. "Hey?"

Guy offered her a smile that told her he'd explain later. But then he frowned. She looked dimmer than when he'd left her this morning. He knew she'd had a meeting with Gunston. Had the meeting not gone well? He wanted to clear the room so that he could find out.

"I'm a little early," Midori apologized. "I didn't mean to interrupt."

"Hey, mama," Kimmei bounded into her mother's middle. "Mr. Guy and I just finished. Ms. Caroline had taken me to the bathroom."

Midori looked up at Agave and reached out her hand. "Caroline?"

"That isn't Ms. Caroline," corrected Kimmei. "This is Ms. Agave."

Agave straightened her shoulders. She clenched and then unclenched her shaking hands before reaching one out to Midori. "Your daughter is very talented." Her voice was dead despite trying to regain her composure.

Guy wanted to tell Agave to stop making niceties, to go and chase after the woman she loved. He knew it was real between the two of them. A little fame wasn't worth losing true love. He knew he couldn't let this facade he'd help to create tear the two of them apart.

"Thank you," Midori was saying. "How do you say your name again?"

Agave cleared her throat, appearing to rally from the events of just a moment ago. "It's Agave. I'm Guy's girlfriend."

In real time, Guy saw the light that shimmered off Midori's skin cloud over and then disappear.

25

———————

idori stood in the doorway and stared, transfixed, at the hand on Guy's arm. The first time she'd seen Michel's wife, she'd had her hand on his arm in the same way. It had been a light touch, not possessive. Her arm hadn't been looped under his elbow. Her fingers hadn't been curled and dug into his bicep. Her fingertips had dusted his shirtsleeve.

When Midori had been out with Guy on their tour of Broadway, they'd held hands. He'd pressed his palm against hers, seeking a firm connection. He'd curled his fingers until the webbing between each of his digits made contact with each of hers. It'd been firm, possessive.

This morning, he'd held her lightly, brushing his fingertips softly down her back. When she'd awakened, she'd burrowed into his chest and spanned her hands across the planes of his shoulder blades until she felt safe and secure, like nothing in the world could touch her. She should've known better.

Guy frowned at her. In the frown, she saw his confusion. Midori almost laughed out loud. Of course, he wouldn't understand why she would have a problem with him having a girlfriend. She was just a sidepiece. Again.

As though he read her mind, his eyes went wide and his hands went up in a lame attempt to stop her thoughts. "Midori, it's not what you think."

Why did they all say that? As though she didn't know how to think for herself. As though there was something wrong with her eyes.

Guy looked back at his girlfriend. "Agave," Guy pleaded. "Tell her."

Agave swallowed. Midori saw the woman's hands tremble before they clenched into fists and then came to wrap around her middle.

Guy's face crumbled. "Agave, please."

For a second there was hope in Midori's heart. Maybe this was a misunderstanding. Maybe she had gotten it all wrong.

"I can't..." Agave looked up at Guy, her eyes imploring. "You promised. Don't do this to me. Please."

Guy looked between Agave and Midori. Midori saw a decision being made in those dark gray eyes and he came to her. She was so shocked that he came to her instead of the other woman that she allowed him to take her hands in his. "Midori..." he began and then paused.

He opened his mouth again. Midori stared into the depths. She sensed that a tidal wave of words and explanations and pleas were about to break forth. But then he shut his mouth. He closed his eyes. A pained expression crossed his handsome features. His hand came up to the right side of his chest and he squeezed, his face contorting in discomfort.

For a moment, Midori panicked, wondering if he was in

pain. He opened his eyes and his mouth again. Resolve set in the strong line of his jaw.

Midori decided to cut him off at the pass. "This is your girlfriend?"

Guy's hands came up and cupped either side of her face, and she let him. His forehead came to rest against hers, a warm spot in the otherwise cold room, and she let him. Then he released his hold on her. She almost snatched him back to her, but she let him go.

"Let me explain."

That wasn't a no. She had to swallow, blink, shake her head, and blink again.

Midori looked over at Agave. The woman wasn't paying any attention to either of them. Her eyes were fixed on the door. Her skinny body tensed, as though caught between fleeing and staying. Though Midori's heart and her spirit were splintering, her mind knew something was not right about this situation.

"It's not that simple," Guy was saying.

A part of Midori believed him. A part of her wanted to stay and hear him out. The only problem was that his voice sounded farther and farther away.

"I love you..." Is what she thought he said, but she couldn't be certain. He sounded as though his mouth were full of marbles. Beyond that, she didn't trust her own ears. He sounded so far away. It was as though someone was actively turning down the volume in her ears and turning up the cold in the room. Her whole body felt chilled and hollow.

"Please... chance... mess..." Guy's lips moved but he made less and less sense. He scratched at his heart. His face looked pained. Something wasn't right.

Midori was losing it. She had to get out of here. She

caught sight of Kimmei watching the spectacle with wide eyes. "We have some place else to be." She grabbed Kimmei's hands.

"Midori," Guy reached for her, but she eluded his grasp easily.

He hadn't tried too hard. He'd barely left the spot where he'd been standing. In fact, he was now bent over the mixing board. His work obviously meant more to him than she did.

"We'll leave you two alone," she said.

"It's not real," he said. "Please just stop, and let me explain."

As Midori turned and walked out of the door his voice became farther and farther away until she didn't hear him at all. He didn't chase after her. Why would he, when he'd been caught red-handed, or Agave-handed. Why hadn't the other woman launched a protest at his words denying their relationship?

It didn't matter. Midori wanted to get as far away from him and this place as possible. She felt eyes on her as she headed down the hall. Who else had known? Likely, everyone in the building. Probably people all over the world. Agave was his artist. He'd said he'd dated his artists in the past. Everyone would know he was in a relationship and everyone would know Midori had been duped, again.

Coming around the corner, Midori saw Maya taking her seat behind her desk. The woman looked up and smiled at Midori's approach. Then she frowned.

"Midori?" Maya rose from her seat. "What's wrong?"

"I just met Agave," Midori accused.

Maya nodded, appearing to wait for a larger bomb to drop.

"I thought you and I were becoming friends?"

"We are friends." The concern on Maya's face looked all too real. Her hazel eyes held no mischief. Her glossed lips didn't smirk.

"Friends don't let friends date other woman's boyfriends."

"Whaa... oh." Realization dawned on Maya's face. Realization, but not guilt. Maya's face contorted into something that looked like compassion. "Did you talk to Guy about Agave?"

"I *saw* them together."

Maya tilted her head confusion. "What do you mean *together*?"

"Just now in the studio. She said she was his girlfriend."

Maya nodded calmly. "You need to talk to Guy."

Midori had had enough. She didn't need Guy to talk her out of what her eyes had seen. She re-gripped Kimmei's hand, and headed towards the elevator.

Once out the glass doors of the record company, Midori haled a cab and she and Kimmei hopped in. The cab ride was a blur. Neither she, nor Kimmei spoke until they were stepping out of the cab at the curb of their hotel.

"You okay, mama?"

"I'm sorry, baby," Midori sniffled. "That was probably all very confusing to you."

"Yeah, it was" Kimmei nodded. "I know a man and a woman can get married. And a man and a man can get married. And a woman and a woman can get married. But can more than two people marry the same person?"

"Kimmei what are you talking about?"

"Ms. Agave and her girlfriend, Ms. Caroline. They're just like Ms. Lucy and Ms. Julia, Natalie's moms. But I don't understand how both Ms. Agave and Ms. Caroline can marry Mr. Guy, too?"

Midori stopped just inside the hotel's glass doors and stared at her child.

"There you are."

Midori glanced up at the sound of that high-pitched, nasally voice. Phancy Jennings or now Phancy Jennings-Mason or was it just Phancy Mason now, strode towards them in six inch stilettos and a designer skirt.

"I've been waiting here for over ten minutes," Phancy said.

"What are you doing here?" Midori said.

"Gunston sent me. He said you needed help making the line 'commercial.' And we worked so well together on my wedding dress."

"So, he sent you." Midori's head felt fuzzy as Phancy smiled in her face. Her lavender eyes twinkled as if they knew the joke. Phancy probably did. Midori wouldn't be surprised if Phancy had known about Guy's relationship with Agave, and apparently Caroline, too. And now it seemed the humiliation would once again extend from Midori's personal life to her professional world.

26

Guy bent over the mixing board. The board, which had moments ago mixed a symphony, let out a distorted screech when his palm slid the faders up. With his left hand, he hit the mute button. His right hand clenched at his chest.

Watching the sun fade from Midori's eyes had been like walking to the beat of a death march. The sound thudded in his ears. His heart felt ready to burst out of his chest. He wanted to run after Midori, but his body refused to move. He slammed down into his chair. His body collapsed in a heap. The springs on the chair groaned a tune of protest.

The sound of an animal in pain caught his attention. As though moving through molasses, Guy turned to look over his shoulder.

Agave stood rooted to the same spot as when Caroline had walked out the door. Streams of tears soiled her cheeks. "I just fucked up the best thing I ever had," she sobbed. "Didn't I?"

She had, and Guy had done the same. For a year, he'd kept up this facade with Agave, this facade with everyone.

He hadn't wanted his boss to know he'd lost his touch, and worked himself ragged turning brass into gold. He'd kept his family at a distance, pretending he didn't mind being alone, that he liked his solitude. He'd crafted this false image around himself, just like he'd done with Agave and a number of his other artists. And now, it was all crumbling down before him, just like lies often did.

"We both did," he said. The thought of losing Midori was sending all feeling from his body. Guy looked down at his hands as, one by one, sensation drained from his fingertips, like lights blacking out across the city. "You have to go after her."

He'd meant the words for himself, for motivation to get his sluggish body in gear to chase after Midori. But the numbness was now creeping down his legs. He couldn't feel his toes.

Agave nodded at his words, her head bobbing like a puppet on a string. "I'll take her away again. We can go back to the island. I can make this right."

Guy shook his head. Agave's voice sounded farther and farther away. "You can't hide any more. It's not enough to tell her how you feel. You have to show her. Literally and figuratively; you have to *show her.*"

Just like he'd do with Midori, as soon as he got out of this chair. He would race down the halls and tell her everything; that what was between him and Agave was fake, but what he felt for her was real. That he'd almost pulled a curtain of fakeness around her brilliant daughter. That his whole life had been taking fake diamonds, polishing them off, and presenting them as real. Until he met her, and remembered what a real gem looked like.

But he couldn't move. The lights were blacking out up his torso now. He was losing feeling all up his left arm.

"Guy, you're not making any sense."

Guy turned to Agave. It was a slow, wearisome process. She looked blurry, even though she stood a few feet away from him.

He opened his mouth to assure her that everything would be okay. But the truth was that he didn't know. Sure, the world was a more open place than it had been a decade ago. He might be able to spin her sexuality if she came out. Weave her sexuality and talent together. He wasn't sure. He couldn't see it clearly. He couldn't see anything clearly, anymore.

He wanted to tell her that her talent would shine through. He could see it, even now. There, in her gut. Agave was pure gold and he'd covered her up with rhinestones and costume jewelry. He felt the white hot of shame burn through the numbness. It tingled in his chest.

Agave was a full blur to him now. He knew she was near him. He knew she reached out to him, but he couldn't feel her hands on him. Everything had gone numb.

"Guy? Guy, are you okay?"

"I think I'm having a heart attack…"

"Guy? What are you saying? Your words aren't making any sense."

Guy slumped down in the chair. And then everything went black.

27

*M*idori stared vacantly at the clock on the side table. She blinked once, twice. Its angry red numbers glared back at her, the same numbers as yesterday. It was eleven in the morning. The last time she'd looked at the clock, it was eleven in the evening. Midori hadn't moved during the in-between time.

She remembered the saying that a broken clock was right twice a day. Midori felt broken. The gears in her body immobile. Like a broken clock, her position hadn't changed in the last twelve hours. But instead of being right twice a day, she'd gotten it wrong twice in her lifetime and had wound up in the same position.

The clock struck 11:01. A new cycle had begun. This time would pass just like the last twelve hours. Midori hung in the balance, barely moving, hardly thinking.

Her stomach grumbled, but she ignored its protests of neglect. Her throat ached, but she had no energy to fetch water. Her fingertips were frozen to her palms even though the sun poked its way through the pulled curtains. Midori shut her eyes and let the oblivion take over.

On the bedside table, her cell phone buzzed. Midori's eyes snapped open. She balled her fingers into a fist to get the blood pumping. She swallowed to saturate her throat. Her stomach stilled as though it knew it was about to receive the sustenance it craved from the other end of the line. But then her eyes landed on the face of the device and she sank back down into the oblivion.

The phone continued to call out to her unanswered. Five minutes later, silence rang through the room, as it had done for the last twelve hours and six minutes. Michel had given up his quest of her today.

When she'd run away from Paris with his baby in her belly, he hadn't chased after her. He had called, repeatedly. He'd begged her to come back, to return to him, to give him another chance. Midori had never done so. Her pride had never let her.

When she'd walked away from Guy the other day, he had not run after her. He had not come to see her. He had not called. Her anticipation at her phone ringing a moment ago led her to wonder if she would have run back to him, believed anything he had to say, given him another chance. Her pride was nowhere to be found at the moment. Instead her heart was breaking, her body was numb, and she knew that Guy's arms around her, his kisses against her lips, his words of praise were the only things she wanted.

Midori turned away from the phone, away from the clock, away from the light. She'd been embarrassed when she learned about Michel's marriage. She'd been destroyed to know that Guy had hidden an attachment.

Her phone rang out again. Midori couldn't help but turn to it. She reached cold hands out.

"Hey, girl!" Pumpkin's voice brought the sun back into

the room. "Wanted to see how everything is going up there?"

"Did you know?"

"Did I know?" Pumpkin repeated. "Did I know what?"

"That he had a girlfriend?"

The silence on the other end of the phone didn't sound guilty, it sounded confused. "Are we talking about Guy?"

"So, you did know he had a girlfriend." Midori sat up in the bed, anger at being betrayed by yet another woman who professed to be her friend heating her through.

"If he does have someone in his life," Pumpkin said, "he's never brought her around."

"Probably because he's been hiding her."

"That's not how this family works, Midori. When they fall, they don't hide it. His sister and I are pretty close, and she's never mentioned anyone. In fact, Manny thought there was something going on between the two of you. Gale even hinted at as much. I was calling trying to see if I could sniff something out."

"Well, he has a girlfriend, and it's not me."

Again, the silence was telling. It was the silent pity she'd endured as she walked back stage before a runway, before she found out about Michel. There was no whispering or the huffing laughs of someone trying to keep a joke quiet on the other end of the phone line.

"Midori, I'm sorry if he's lied to you. I don't know Guy very well, but I never thought he'd be *that* guy."

All the heat of anger drained from Midori as the warmth of Pumpkin's words assailed her. She could almost see the other woman and the concern in her eyes. Maya had looked at her with the same concern that rang true in Pumpkin's voice. Something was off, but Midori was too exhausted to puzzle it all out. Her body, having gone from the heat of Guy's embraces, to the cold of his absence, only to return with the warmth of Pumpkin's words, felt as if she were recovering from the aches of the flu.

"Is there anything I can do?" Pumpkin asked, her voice as soothing as Midori's mother had been when she had a bellyache as a child. "Do you want to talk? We can call room service and order up some ice cream and a whole New York style cheesecake. I won't judge."

A small smile wrestled up the edge of Midori's lips, but then she lost her grip. "I can't. I have to get to work."

"You'll call me if you need me. Anytime, okay? I'm here."

Midori got off the line without making a commitment. She dressed in layers, her body still alternating between hot and cold. By the time she pulled a thin sweater over her head the front door buzzed.

"I'll get it," Kimmei called as Midori left her bedroom.

No doubt, the child expected it to be Guy. They had an appointment today. For the past couple of sessions Guy had gotten into the habit of picking Kimmei up himself, and taking her in so that Midori could work.

Kimmei reached for the door, eyes glowing in anticipation. Midori stood frozen on the threshold of her bedroom. Her heart pounded as the door creaked open. Her fingertips pulled the edges of the sweater down past her wrists until her hands drowned in the warm fabric.

She hadn't needed to seek the protection of the fabric. It wasn't Guy who stood on the other side of the door.

Kimmei's face fell at the sight of Phancy, who was dressed in a purple, princess-cut dress. Her severe makeup wiped away any trace of innocence or naiveté of young royalty.

"Are you going to a Halloween party?" Kimmei asked, with wide eyes and a scrunched nose.

"Why, do I look like one of your Barbies?" Phancy struck a pose emphasizing her small waist.

"You look like the evil queen from that Disney movie."

Phancy looked down at Kimmei as though she were an insignificant mouse. "I'll turn you into a toad if you don't get out of my way."

"Phancy," Midori interrupted. "We're in here." She directed Phancy to the little alcove with her line of fabrics. The last thing Midori wanted to do was work with this woman, but the sooner she delivered the line to Gunston, the sooner she could go home. Not five minutes later, Midori was already wishing the day was over.

"That effect has to go." Phancy stomped around the room in her heels, as though the office nook were a catwalk.

The scissors shook in Midori's hands as she held the fabric. She'd worked so hard to make the panels on the skirt, playing around with the measurements to ensure that the fit would stretch to accommodate any dress size. "I did this to cinch a woman's waist and show off her curves."

"Yeah, but curves were, like, two seasons ago. We have to be fashion forward. Didn't Gunston tell you? Waifs are back in."

Phancy eyed herself in the reflection of the window. The sun was setting outside and the glass cut her shape in half, making her look even skinnier.

Midori looked around the room at her line. Each piece had been touched by either Gunston or Phancy to make it more fashion forward. Midori hadn't known she was so fashion backwards. She kept hearing the term 'make it pop.' Or it's missing 'that spark.' Fashion forward wasn't very specific.

She didn't care anymore. She wanted to hand over this line and get herself and her daughter back home to their life in Saint Anne's. Guy had never shown up to take Kimmei into the studio. He hadn't even called to cancel. It was all well and truly over; the dream of an inclusive line of clothing, the fantasy of a real relationship. And now even her daughter was having her hopes dashed. The sooner she got them out of this wretched city the better.

Midori let go of her dream and grabbed the fabric. She steadied her hand and snipped. "How's your husband?"

"Who?" Phancy turned from her reflection. Then she shrugged. "He has a weeklong conference in Vegas. Cut our honeymoon short for business." Phancy ground her teeth as she straightened the unwrinkled hem of her skirt. "Gives me the free time to do what I need. I'm so thankful he's not one of those men who's on my heel every minute."

"You don't worry about him being around all that temptation?"

Phancy smirked. "Not at all. I made sure he can't get it up without me."

Midori looked up from her work, certain she'd misheard Phancy. But then Phancy turned from the glass and aimed her venom at Midori.

"What ever happened with you and that guy?" asked Phancy. "You know, the married one?"

The end of the fabric clung stubbornly to the garment. "I broke things off with Michel once I learned he was married." Midori set down the scissors and ripped the last piece off with her bare hands.

"But not after you had a—"

"Mommy!"

"—kid." Phancy turned with a wrinkled nose as Kimmei entered the room.

"Mommy, I'm supposed to be meeting with Mr. Guy."

Midori picked up the scissors again. "Well, he's not here."

"Did he call?" Kimmei asked.

"No, he hasn't called." The panel fell gracelessly to the ground.

"Maybe something's wrong? He's never not come for me." Kimmei turned and went out of the room.

Midori turned to look at her child. Kimmei had never once said such about her father. Guy had been in their lives for less than a month. She shouldn't have taken this deal. She should've kept Kimmei locked away safe. She should've kept herself locked away safe, instead of facing all this scrutiny and criticism.

"New boyfriend?" asked Phancy.

"No... he's... it's not important."

Just as she'd never been important to him. The scissors slipped from her numb fingers. Midori clenched and unclenched her fist, then reached down for them. Once they were in her grasp again, she began hacking away at the other side of the skirt.

28

———

Guy opened his eyes to stark white walls. No, they weren't actually white. The fluorescent light bulbs above, cast a harsh yellow glow that hurt his eyes, and he closed them again. With his eyes closed, his other senses came alive.

His body ached in every crevice. He felt cold, as though he were in the winter without a coat. He knew he was lying down on something soft. A bed? It had to be. It wasn't the hard floor he remembered crashing onto, before everything went dark.

He felt his toes. They tingled as though they rested on a guitar string strummed hard. His fingers felt the same. But his fingers came in contact with something warm.

Guy chanced his eyes open again, looking down instead of up. He was in a bed, covered in a wool blanket. He pulled the blanket up higher on his body, but the coldness, the numbness remained.

Needing a break from the light and the cold, he shut his eyes, and his brain allowed his ears to take over. There was a beeping sound. A steady pulse like a metronome, only this was electronic instead of mechanical. Guy opened his eyes again and looked around for the source.

His eyes landed on a mixer. The dark box tracked the greens, reds, and blues; much like his mixing board. It measured degrees and rates and a host of other initials that Guy couldn't make out. But he saw no measure for decibels. The beeping had no melody, just a steady rhythm. It reminded him of a pulse.

Guy moved his arm and found that his hand was restricted. There were wires attached to him. He heard his heart pounding in his skull, and realized the beeping sound was in time to it. A face came into view.

"You're back." Agave peered over him, tears staining her cheeks. "I thought I'd lost you."

Guy opened his mouth to talk, only to find his mouth dry. What the hell had happened to him? The last thing he remembered, before everything went dark, was a crushing pain in his heart as he watched Midori walk out the door. He'd wanted to chase after her, to take her in his arms, to spin her around, and make her listen. He wanted to shout out and proclaim his love for her. But he hadn't been able to shout. He hadn't been able to move. All he'd felt was pain. Had he had a heart attack?

A woman came into the room dressed in colorful scrubs, and a friendly smile. The sight of the nurse confirmed that he was in a hospital. "Take it easy," she said offering him a glass of water with a straw.

Guy leaned forward and sipped the proffered drink. The cool water felt like spring rain to his deserted vocal chords. Guy sipped until he heard the sucking sound of the cup drained dry.

"Wha..." He cleared his ravaged throat and tried again. "What happened?"

"You had a stroke," said Agave.

Guy blinked. The light glared in his eyes, causing him to squint. His fingers felt cold and numb, even where Agave held his hands. The predominate sound in his ears was still the pulsing beep of the machines he was plugged into. He couldn't have heard her correctly. Guy turned to the nurse who nodded at Agave, as though she were cosigning her words.

"Your friend here saved your life," said the nurse.

"My grandmother had a stroke when I was a teenager," Agave said. "My mother had one a few years ago. Heart disease runs in my family. I know the signs."

"She said one minute you were speaking clearly," said the nurse. "And then in the next you were slurring your words and your face drooped."

Had his face drooped? Had he slurred his words? He didn't remember.

"But I don't understand how he could have a stroke?" Agave addressed the nurse. "He's in his early thirties and I don't remember him ever telling me about a history of heart disease. How could this happen to him?"

The nurse looked between them, her kind face full of empathy. But she didn't answer. Instead, she turned behind her as a woman dressed in a white coat entered with an official looking clipboard in her hands.

"Mr. Rumpel?" she said without a smile, her expression haggard, business-like. When she spoke, it was to the clipboard and not anyone in the room.

"Doctor?" Guy assumed. "They're saying I had a stroke?"

The doctor looked up, sparing him a glance. "Oh, good, your speech is recovered." The doctor made a motion, appearing to check something off on a list. "Yes, you had a mild ischemic stroke. Your blood vessels became blocked by fatty deposits. The obstruction is what blocked the oxygen to your brain for a short time, which in turn caused the stroke."

The doctor flipped a page, made a few notes, and then looked up at Guy expectantly.

All the water Guy had swallowed evaporated and his throat became dryer than a desert again. The ice in his fingers and toes went to his heart. The beeping in his ears turned to ringing.

Blocked vessels? His brain deprived of blood? A stroke?

"Am I gonna die?" he asked.

Agave squeezed his hand, tears stinging her eyes.

The nurse came to his other side, resting her hand on his shoulder, compassion shining through her eyes.

"Not today," the doctor looked down and flipped another page on her clipboard. "We ran some tests and it looks like you have diabetes."

"Diabetes?" asked Agave. "Isn't that something obese people suffer from?"

"It's often hereditary, or develops with age. It's growing more and more common in men your age." She spoke to the monitors reading Guy's vitals, instead of towards Guy himself. "Have you experienced fatigue, insatiable thirst, a feeling of numbness in your extremities, weight gain..."

Guy mentally nodded to each. He was tired all the time, increasingly so over the last year since the curse. He'd given up alcohol after that night with the little succubus who'd zapped his mojo. He'd thought swapping out sodas for beer wouldn't lead him to a beer belly, but he rested his cold fingers on his soft belly and continued to listen to the doctor rattle off symptoms.

"...blurred vision, erectile dysfunction?"

Agave released his hand. The nurse removed her fingers

from his shoulder. Guy cleared his throat and moved his hips until he sat up straighter.

"These are all indicators of delayed onset Type II Diabetes. It's becoming an increasingly regular diagnosis in young men with stress-filled, sedentary lifestyles and poor diets."

"You're telling me I have diabetes?" he said.

"Yes." The doctor slid the cap on her pen.

"So, I'm not cursed?"

The doctor set the clipboard down and finally looked him in the eye. "I don't have a diagnosis for magic, but I can read the signs in blood. You have Type II Diabetes, which is reversible if you make different lifestyle and diet choices."

The doctor nodded to the nurse, turned on her heel, and headed out the door. The nurse patted Guy on the shoulder with the same kind smile. "I'll bring you some pamphlets and set up an appointment with your regular doctor so that you can learn to manage this. Don't worry; this isn't a death sentence. You're going to be fine, if you make some changes."

When both medical practitioners were gone, the beeping of the machines was the only sound that remained. Guy pulled the sheets around his middle.

"Erectile dysfunction?" Agave said.

He shut his eyes instead of facing her.

"Is that why you..."

Guy sighed. He opened his mouth to come clean with Agave.

"Mr. Guy!" Kimmei bounded into the room and onto the bed.

Guy's heart warmed to see the little ball of light, but his pulse raced as he looked around for a glimpse of her mother. Midori was nowhere to be found.

Kimmei climbed onto the bed and peered into his face. "Are you okay?"

Guy had shielded his eyes from the overhead lights, but he basked in Kimmei's warm concern. "I'm fine sweetie. Where's your mother?"

"She's at the hotel."

"How did you get here?"

"We were supposed to meet today. When you didn't come, I called your office and they sent a car to pick me up. When I got to your office, Ms. Maya said you were at the hospital, so I got the car service to bring me here."

"Does your mother know you're here?"

"No, I think she's still mad at you because you're going to marry two women and not her."

"What?" Guy and Agave said at the same time.

"Aren't you marrying Ms. Agave and Ms. Caroline?"

The beeping on the machine picked up its tune. Guy took a deep breath. How was he going to sort all of this out?

29

———

*M*idori rushed out of the elevators as soon as they opened. Stark white walls greeted her, nearly blinding her as she moved with quick steps towards the receptionist. She hadn't spent much time in hospitals, but she saw that the dreary walls could do with a pop of color to set the families who waited in the dull beige chairs at ease. Everything was too bright, too stimulating.

"I'm looking for Guy Rumpel's room," she told the receptionist.

The woman, dressed in pink scrubs and a red cardigan, barely spared her a glance. "Are you family?"

Midori grit her teeth. It was the second time today that someone demanded to know her relationship status with Guy. She didn't know what she meant to him. She didn't know what he meant to her. She was only here to retrieve her child who was in big trouble for sneaking out.

Kimmei had called twenty minutes earlier. "I'm at the hospital with Mr. Guy," she'd said.

Those words had sent Midori on a tailspin. She hadn't even realized Kimmei had snuck out. She'd been so overloaded with Phancy and the line. Was her baby hurt? How did it happen? She never should've trusted Guy. But then Kimmei's next words sent Midori spinning in the opposite direction.

"He's sick," she'd said.

Midori had dashed out of the hotel, leaving Phancy, and her criticisms, and the tattered collection behind.

Her body continued to vacillate from hot, to cold, on the cab ride to the hospital. Her mind raced as the street numbers ticked up. Sick could mean any number of things. Perhaps he was suffering from a bout of carpal tunnel after pushing all those buttons on his mixing board. Or he could've pulled a muscle from having acrobatic sex with his hot, young girlfriend.

All those thoughts came to a halt, standing in front of the receptionist, mulling over her ties to Guy. Visitation at hospitals was usually restricted to family members only when the condition was serious.

Midori rocked back on her heels. Her fingers clutched at her heart. Tears pricked the edges of her eyes.

"Actually, no." The receptionist tapped a few keys on her computer. "He's been moved out of Intensive Care. He's just down the hall." She pointed, and gave Midori the room number.

It took a minute for Midori's legs to move. When she did turn around, she came face to face with a hot, young woman.

Agave was model thin, with tear-stained and puffy eyes that didn't detract from her beauty. Instead, it looked artfully tragic. "Midori, right?"

Agave, Guy's girlfriend, moved towards Midori. The young woman's fingers worried each other as they pressed into her flat belly. Midori stared, transfixed, at the cutouts in

Agave's sundress that exposed her stomach.. All six packs of those abs moved steadily towards Midori, without any discernible limp or injury from excessive bed sport.

"You're looking for Kimmei?" she asked.

Midori's eyes snapped up to Agave's face at the mention of her child. Looking more closely at the other woman.

"She's fine," Agave continued. "She's with Guy."

Midori's heart slowed at the confirmation that her daughter was okay. Now she was able to spare a moment to think about Guy. "Is he okay? What happened?"

"He's going to be okay. I should let him tell you... what's up with him. Or down rather." Agave grimaced. "Listen, I want to apologize for all the confusion. It's just that Guy's been taking care of me for so long and—"

Midori shut her eyes and held up her hands. She did not want any of the details of their sordid relationship.

"No, no. You misunderstand me. There's nothing—" Agave looked around the crowded reception area and lowered her voice. "There's nothing going on sexually between us. It's fake." She motioned with her hand up and down her body, as though to encompass her whole persona. "It's all fake. He was trying to protect me. Guy's a really great man, and I know he cares about you."

Midori opened her mouth to protest, but her lower lip trembled. Her eyes shot to the exit door. She had to blink rapidly to keep the bright red sign in focus.

"You should give him a chance to explain," Agave said. "If you'll excuse me, I have to go and beg someone else for another chance." She gave Midori's shoulder a squeeze, then stepped around her and headed towards the exit.

Midori turned back in the direction of Guy's room. Her feet made slow progress as her mind tried, and failed, to slough through all of the new information it had to weigh.

The top of the list was Kimmei. Now that she knew her daughter was safe, the child needed to be punished.

Second was Guy's sickness. She still had no idea what had happened to him, or what state he was in.

Midori decided to halt the list at two. Her weary heart and aching hands couldn't hold any more than that, at the moment. She took a deep breath and poked her head into the room the receptionist indicated. Kimmei sat next to Guy, who was propped up on pillows. They looked snug as bugs in a rug.

"Hey, mommy!"

Guy's eyes connected with Midori's. They brightened, lighting up in that incandescent awe that switched on every time he looked at her. Midori felt pulled in by them. His gaze warmed her through, erasing all the cold, darkness she'd felt the night before.

The sound of the door clicking shut behind her broke her from her trance. Midori blinked and refocused on priority number one. "You're in big trouble, missy."

"But why? What did I do?" Kimmei whined.

"You left without my permission."

"I came to see Mr. Guy. He's family."

Kimmei's simple statement took the bite out of Midori's anger. Midori's eyes went back to Guy. He looked pale lying in the dull sheets. There were dark circles under his eyes. His lips had a glistening layer of moisture, but Midori saw the cracks beneath. Priority number two was creeping its way to the forefront. What had happened to him?

"Your mother's right, Kimmei," said Guy, his voice reedy and thin. "What you did was dangerous. You always have to let her know where you are, and get her permission before you go. Understood?"

Kimmei looked properly sullen as she nodded.

"Can you step outside for a moment so I can talk to your mother?" he said.

Kimmei slid down off the hospital bed. Walking by her mother, she gave Midori a squeeze before going out and closing the door.

"Are you okay?" Midori held herself back from launching herself onto the bed.

Guy looked weary and tired. He tried for a smile, but it resembled a wince. "Too much sugar."

"I don't understand?" she said.

"I collapsed after you left the other day."

Now she did rush to his side. She took Kimmei's spot and reached for his hand.

Guy laced his fingers through hers all the way down to the webbing. "I tried to run after you, but I couldn't move. I couldn't speak. I started having chest pains. It turned out to be a minor stroke."

Midori gripped his fingers tightly and used her free hand to place it on his face. His lips turned and sought her palm. He closed his eyes and breathed in at its center.

"I'm okay," he whispered, placing a kiss on each of her fingertips. "Or at least, I will be. It turns out I have Type II Diabetes. I didn't know it and I've been doing everything to send my health down the drain." He opened his eyes and stared at her, leaning his face into her palm. "I thought I was having a heart attack because I'd screwed things up with you."

Midori brought his upper body into her arms. She buried her face in the dark curls atop his head and inhaled that earthy scent of him. She drank from it greedily. She curled her fingers around his neck, allowing his warm flesh to bring feeling back to her fingertips.

"My relationship with Agave is all for show," he said. "There's nothing sexual between us."

"Because of Caroline?" Midori had known it, but she'd been too scared to believe. She'd seen the way Agave looked at the retreating woman, Caroline, with utter devastation. She'd heard Kimmei's childish assessment that Agave and Caroline would marry Guy. A few minutes ago, she'd stepped aside as Agave rushed to repair whatever damage she'd done to that relationship.

"Oh, great," he sighed. "You saw through it, too?"

Midori didn't bother to explain how she'd connected the dots.

He pulled away from, bringing her eyes level with his. "I thought I was cursed. For a year, I haven't been able to see properly. I've been tired and miserable all the time, and now I know why. I've been waiting for you."

Midori had the sensation that she was weightless and flying. She gripped Guys fingers. He held onto her even tighter.

"I was lost in darkness until I saw you," he said. "Sick until you fed me. Cursed until I kissed you." He planted a feather light kiss on her lips.

Hot tears spilled down Midori's cheek.

Guy brought her close and kissed each droplet away. "Kimmei called me family. I've been running from mine, because I didn't want them to see me like this, to see the lie I was living. I know it's too soon. It's too fast, but I'm a Charmayne. I've told you what I see when I look at you, Midori. It's never going away."

Every word Guy uttered rang true deep inside Midori's core, and that scared her to death. Every time he was presented with the opportunity to let her down, he rose to the occasion.

"I want you to be my family," he said. "I promise it will be the best deal you ever make. I'll keep the clouds away from you. I'll make it so you shine every day for the rest of our lives."

Even though he lay in a bed, she looked up at him on high. It was the highest she'd ever climbed. The fall from this height would kill her if ever he let her down. She sat on the bed, keeping her feet firmly on the ground.

30

———

"It's not you, it's me."

Guy cracked a smile as he watched the quiver in Agave's lips. It was the first time he'd ever known those words to ring true.

Agave stood before Caroline. She reached out a shaking hand towards the woman. Caroline folded her arms around herself and looked down at the floor. She held her posture stiff. She took a deep breath and held it.

Agave placed her empty hand over her heart. Her eyes stayed fixed on Caroline. "You brought light into my world, and I hid you in the shadows. You fed my soul, and I left you starved for attention. You gave me your trust, and I returned it with lies."

Guy watched as Caroline took in a shivering breath. She peeked up at Agave from beneath heavy lashes. Her grip loosened around her middle.

"I screwed up, Caro. It's all my fault. I don't know if you'll ever forgive me. I don't know that I'll ever deserve you. But I promise you, from this day forward, I will not hide any longer."

Agave reached towards Caroline, and this time Caroline did take her hand. Caroline came into Agave's embrace, resting her head against her heart.

Agave planted a kiss on her forehead. "I'm doing this for you. But I'm mostly doing it for me."

Agave released Caroline. She turned and caught Guy's encouraging gaze. Guy reached out his hand to her. With shaking fingers that belied her brave face, Agave stepped into him.

"Ready?" he asked.

Agave nodded. Her face was pale, but her gold was blinding.

He slid the curtains back. An even brighter light blinded them. These lights flared and flashed at them both. Agave stumbled back a step at the onslaught of reporters. But a second anchor came up beside her.

Caroline threaded her fingers through Agave's. Agave stared at that hand.

A flash of despair flickered across Caroline's face. Guy saw her inhale and hold another breath, as though fearful she'd gone a step too far. Her free hand crept up to her belly in a fist.

But then Agave leaned over and placed her lips against Caroline's. The camera flashes went crazy.

Agave pulled away with a huge grin on her face and a visible weight lifted from her slender shoulders. Caroline stared at her, dazed, and then a goofy grin spread across her face.

Guy released Agave's hand and let Caroline and her stride forward. Agave took the microphone in her hand. He'd never heard her voice ring truer than when she told her story.

The press ate it up. Intrigued by the deception. Charmed by the love story.

Off in the back of the room, standing with a look of displeasure, stood JJ. Guy made his way past the media frenzy to his boss.

"A head's up would've been nice," said JJ.

"You would've shut it down and this needed to... come out," Guy said.

"You think I would've shut this down?" JJ looked around the room with eyes as big as silver dollars. "Look at them. They're eating it up. We're going to milk this lesbian angle for all we can. It opens up a whole new audience in the LGBT—"

"I can't."

JJ blinked, eyes returning to normal size. "You can't what?"

"I can't milk, I can't shine, I can't polish anymore. It's bad for my health."

JJ stopped and gave Guy a good look over. His boss had been there for him, in his own way, while Guy recovered in the hospital. But it was clear that JJ hadn't learned the lessons that Guy's illness had brought on.

"On your desk is my letter of resignation," Guy said.

JJ's brown face turned a shade paler. His fist clenched, rising to his belt buckle. He took in a breath and didn't let it go.

"I understand that this business has changed, is changing," Guy continued. "Anyone can be a star today with enough polishing and synthesizing. But I can't do it anymore. I'm not going to run myself ragged to make them into something they are not. I'm only working with people who have actual talent."

JJ's jaw tensed "So now you're going to leave me? You're

going to take everything I taught you, including my top artists, to start your own company?"

"No," Guy blanched that JJ could even consider such a betrayal. "This is the best place for Agave, the only place. The same with Althea and a number of my artists."

"Your artists?"

Guy took a deep breath. "I'm going to continue to produce for a number of the artists on my roster. We're going to make the type of music that they want to sing. We'll give you the first listen, but if you decide it's not the right fit for Badd Finger, then we'll look somewhere else."

It was Guy's turn to hold his breath while he waited for JJ to speak.

JJ's chin rose high into the air. His fingers clenched and flexed.

"You've given so much to me," Guy said. "But this business nearly took my life. There has to be another way. I can't keep chasing after these trends with you. If I keep going down this path, it'll kill me."

JJ released his breath slowly. His hand relaxed at his side. He hung his head a moment before fastening his eyes back onto Guy. The two men stared at each other, years of history flooded between them. Guy knew when JJ's eyes went to the bags under his eyes that still remained, even though he was sleeping better. He rubbed the pads of his finger together absently, feeling the scabbed skin from testing his blood sugar daily.

Guy watched the argument rage through JJ's eyes. Saw the moment JJ knew he couldn't win, that to win would be to lose his protégée, his friend.

Finally, JJ reached his hand up and laid it heavily on Guy's shoulder. "I take it Frankie Benjamin's isn't on your roster."

"Hell, no," Guy measured each word. "She is not."

JJ chuckled. The tension released from Guy's hands and he laughed too.

"What are you going to do about that little jazz singer?" said JJ. "The one with the pretty mama? She's not trendy material."

Guy nodded. "I think I've figured out exactly where Kimmei belongs."

The sun was setting that evening, as Guy left his loft and made his way over to the Waldorf Astoria. Midori had told Guy she needed time to think over his proposal, because it was that. He was asking for more than casual dating. He was asking for forever, and they both knew it. He'd given her these last few days as he'd recovered. He'd kept his distance, focusing on his health, while she focused on finishing her line. But time was up.

He felt stronger every day, with his change in diet and medications. Aside from culling his roster of clients, he'd cleared out many other stressors in his life. And now he was approaching the woman he loved, with a curse lifted off his head and a cure in his veins.

He was finally taking her on the date he'd promised her weeks ago. He had every plan to use his natural born talents to make her the deal of a lifetime.

"Hey, Mr. Guy!" Kimmei bounded into him as she opened the door. "Mommy's in the office with Queen Phancy Pants." Kimmei scrunched her nose in disgust as she said the name.

Guy didn't have time to ask the little girl who this cringe-worthy Queen Phancy Pants was. He spotted Midori leaning against the doorframe of the makeshift sewing room where she housed her designs. The sight of her took him aback, but for all the wrong reasons.

She wore a ragged t-shirt with the collar torn along one side. Loose fitting sweats hung low on her hips. He'd never seen her so casually—okay, slovenly—dressed. Her thick hair was piled haphazardly on her head. Her arms were crossed over her middle, each limb ended in clenched fists. Her jaw was tense and her eyes vacant. There were clouds resting heavily on her shoulders.

There was another woman with her. This must be the nose-crinkling Ms. Phancy. Was she the reason Midori slumped against the door in a worn down state?

Guy knew his first order of business would be to lift those clouds from Midori. He would relieve her of her ill-fitting clothing. He'd wipe away every worry from her brow. He hadn't had occasion to test his stamina since his hospitalization. It didn't matter. He would please her with his fingers, with his tongue, with his mouth, anyway and anything, to make her smile, make her shine. She was the one person for whom he would run himself ragged.

Guy opened his mouth to call her name, when he choked.

The other woman inside the doorway moved into his view. The blood drained from Guy's entire body, and was replaced with ice. Standing in front of Midori was the woman who'd cursed him.

31

Midori pinched the space between her brow. It was less out of annoyance and more to try to keep herself awake. She felt bone weary at the end of this long day. All around her, her vision lay in tattered pieces of fabric.

"That ruff can stay, but the high-waisted skirt has to go. We need to make it a low-hanging mini skirt instead."

Midori's hands rose to the cloth automatically, at Phancy's critique. At the end of her finger, the pads were a deep, bruised red from all of the cutting and restitching she'd done over the past few days.

Gunston had stopped by the other day and was thrilled at her progress with the alterations. Midori had watched the excitement on his face but had not been able to join in. He'd praised her, told her it was exactly what he'd wanted, that she'd achieved his vision perfectly.

She snipped the fabric of the skirt she'd intended to fit tall, curvy girls. The strip of cloth meant to cover that woman's midriff fell away.

"Perfect," clapped Phancy.

The silent impact of the piece of cloth rang through Midori's person like a gong. Midori stared down at the ragged edge. The floor was littered with a ton of pieces. Discarded pieces of her vision had been replaced with someone else's. She reached for the cloth that had been the top of the skirt. The sound of the gong rang through her fingers as she held the scrap of material.

"All right, the last thing we have to do is change the fabric of this cocktail dress." Phancy picked up the garment from the rack. It was the only thing that hadn't been touched in Gunston's assault. "This fabric is all wrong. It needs to be made of a stretch material to get rid of all that ruching."

"Phancy, if we get rid of the ruching, it will throw the whole design off. Plus women with large breasts won't be able to hold up the bustiere."

Phancy waved the comment away. "They can just go braless."

"Women with anything above a B cup can't go braless—legally." Midori clenched her fingers around the fabric. She looked down again at all the discarded pieces on the floor. Had they all somehow come closer to her, as though seeking her protection? She looked up at the skirt. It was wrong, all wrong. Maybe she could reattach it? "It's unrealistic. Everything you've asked me to do is unrealistic."

"Gunston was crazy to give you this chance. You've never been able to handle the spotlight."

Midori looked up at Phancy, who stood backlit by the setting sunlight coming in from the window. There was darkness around Phancy, like she sucked the light out of a space. Midori felt the light seeping out of her as Phancy stood in front of her.

"It's always been so easy to step in front of you," Phancy

sneered.

Not in front of her. Step *over* her. That's what Phancy had done with the friendship Midori had extended to her when they were young models on the runway. Phancy had encouraged her pursuit of Michel, and then told everyone about the affair once Midori's back was turned. The humiliation had knocked Midori down, and Phancy had stepped right over her and taken her place on the runway.

Midori looked at her collection. The reams of golden fabric on hangers all seemed muted now, like the bitterness of a lemon instead of the array of gold that Guy had procured for her. Her fingers ached from all the pin pricks of the needle and adjustments.

"Well?" Phancy stood in front of her expectantly. "Are you going to get to work?"

It wasn't work. It was destruction. The way they'd changed the sleeves on her ruff blouse would cut off a woman's circulation, leaving her fingers numb. Many women couldn't wear the diagonal cut blouse anymore, because it would show their belly bulge. Women would have to contort themselves just to get into the mini skirt. These clothes were everything that was wrong with fashion. She'd spent the last ten years showing women how to celebrate their bodies. How to step up into the spotlight, not down and away from it. If this line got out with her name on it, she'd be a part of the problem she'd escaped.

Midori stood in the doorway; one foot out, one foot in. She took a deep breath and stepped back into the office that she'd made into a workroom. She stepped past Phancy and gathered up all of the ruined garments.

"I'm done," Midori said.

"No, you're not. We still have to fix the cocktail dress."

Midori shook her head as she ripped the untouched

garment off the hangar and clutched it to her breasts. "This is not my vision. It's completely unrecognizable. I won't put my name on any of these."

"Like your name was going to go on any of these," said Phancy. "This is my line. I had to redesign everything."

Midori's blood boiled at the audacity of the woman. She dropped the garments to the ground, all except the mini skirt she'd just hacked away at. "Then that works out perfectly." She grabbed her shears and began to cut. "Since you designed them, you'll have no problems recreating them."

Phancy gasped, stretching her hand out as though she would try to stop Midori. But then she jerked back. "Are you mental? Gunston will never work with you again, after he hears about this little episode."

"Fine with me," said Midori. "I'm not putting anything in his store. My clients don't shop there anyway."

"If you snub Gunston, no one else will work with you."

It didn't matter. She could never work with Gunston, or anyone who would take her vision and turn it into a nightmare. She'd just go home and continue to work with one client at a time. Or maybe she'd create an online shop. She did want to help more than one woman at a time. But not like this. This line would only be a part of the problem. She'd go it alone if she had to.

"She has my full support."

That voice washed over Midori and erased any remaining cold or numbness. It was the first time she'd heard his voice in days. He hadn't called. But he hadn't left her entirely alone, either. He'd sent her texts every night since she'd left him at the hospital. He wished her good morning every day via text message. He sent bright yellow flowers with lyrics on the attached card.

He launched a quiet, aggressive assault to show her his feelings. And they weren't kept in the dark. Midori knew there was no other person in this world who had her back the way Guy did, no one who believed in her more, who would never let her down.

She'd agreed to see him tonight. At the time, she hadn't known what she'd say to him. But, turning around and looking at him now, it seemed so obvious. She couldn't remember the second before, when he wasn't here. He'd been standing there in quiet solidarity while she'd taken her stand against Phancy. He was here now, and she knew she didn't have to spend another moment without him. She knew he'd never let her down. Never keep her in the dark.

"Well, well, well," Phancy purred. "It's been a long time, hasn't it lover?"

Midori lowered the scissors; the garment fell from her hands. She looked between the two of them, certain she'd misheard.

"I have been looking for you for the last year," Guy said quietly.

Somehow, Midori stood on wobbly legs as she stared at Guy, replaying those words in her head. Lover? He'd been looking for her? There was something going on between him and Phancy?

"You ready to make that deal," smiled Phancy, her wedding band looked dull in the setting sunlight.

"What deal?" asked Midori.

"A year ago, she wanted me to make her a star," Guy said. "Problem was she didn't have an ounce of talent."

Guy came over to Midori and placed his hand at the small of her back. At first, she jerked from the shock of his support. But she allowed his palm to mold into the curve of her back. Hadn't she just proclaimed that he'd stand with her? Had he ever let her down? He pulled her to his side and she felt strong.

"Didn't stop you from sleeping with me," said Phancy.

"And for my bad judgment, you cursed me," he said.

Phancy tsked. "There's no such thing as curses."

The way she said it made Midori know, for a fact, that Phancy wasn't telling the truth.

Phancy smirked. "So, this is your new plaything?" She turned and indicated Midori, pointing crooked fingers at her.

Guy stepped in front of Midori as though to shield her. But from what? She was through paying any heed to Phancy's venom. "No, she's my main thing," said Guy. "My only thing, my everything. I've stopped thinking with my dick. I spent the last year thinking I'd been wrong to not take you on, and make something out of nothing."

"Still not too late. Especially if you're still having... problems." Phancy looked down at Guy's fly.

Midori looked at the trajectory of Phancy's gaze. A year ago? The curse. It was all true. Midori didn't realize that she doubted Guy's words about the curse, until she stood between him and Phancy. "What are you?" Midori said. "Some kind of witch?"

Phancy smiled that evil smile again, but she kept her lips sealed.

"It doesn't matter," Guy pulled Midori even tighter into his side. "I already found the cure."

Guy looked down at Midori. His gray eyes looked directly into hers. He showed her everything he felt for her in that gaze. She saw both the depth of his love and his patience. He wouldn't deny his feelings for her, not to anyone. But he would wait as long as she needed to return those feelings to him.

"Yes," she said. She wanted that one word to convey everything. Yes, he had her. Yes, she would have him. Yes, he'd found her and she was his cure for all his ailments. Yes, she'd found him and he was the cure to all her hurts and disappointments.

Phancy's cackle broke the private moment between them. "What the hell is this? Some Disney crap?"

"Yeah," Midori didn't spare her a glance. "Yeah, it is, and unless you want me to throw water or a house on you, I would suggest you get the hell out of here."

Midori didn't bother to look up to see if Phancy left. She reached up to Guy and pulled his head down for a kiss. It was a kiss that told him thank you for having her back. It was a kiss that told him she'd have his for the rest of their lives.

"Mommy? You know that Disney didn't make the *The Wizard of Oz*?"

Midori broke away from Guy and blinked at Kimmei, who stood in the office doorway.

"You compared Ms. Phancy to the Wicked Witch of the West, that wasn't Disney. You should've compared her to the witch from *Sleeping Beauty*, her name was Maleficent. The one that cursed Sleeping Beauty with a needle."

Midori grinned. "I'm sorry, baby. I'll be sure and consult you the next time I'm faced with a real live witch."

Kimmei smiled between the two of them. "Does this mean Mr. Guy is going to marry you, too?"

"No, Kimmei," said Midori. Her warm fingers wrapped around Guy's neck. She stood on nimble tiptoes to capture his lips. Heat rushed down her spine and certainty filled her heart when he met her kiss openly. "It means he's going to marry *only* me."

EPILOGUE

Midori's fingers raced across the fabric of the garment. Her back was against the wall, and she faced a staunch deadline, but she chose to hand-stitch the garment, instead of use the sewing machine. The material was once again way over budget, but it was a lovely thing to behold. She knew she'd have an argument with the manufacturer about getting the costs down, but that was a bridge she'd cross later.

Her very own line of casual wear for women of every shape and size was going to be a hit. She'd salvaged many of the designs from the tattered Gunston line, after backing out of their deal. But instead of slinking back to Saint Anne's in defeat, she'd gone the next week to another retailer. They'd immediately seen the appeal of a line that catered to the everyday woman and they weren't the only ones. In the corner, Midori also had a huge list of private clients: from small town women, to divas at the top of the charts. She was going to be busy for a long time.

The door rattled, breaking her attention from her

creation. A tall, dark figure loomed in the doorway. Midori reached for her shears. "Get out of my room."

"Technically, it's still my room." Guy came in and closed the door behind him. He relieved her of the scissors and pulled her into his embrace for a kiss.

Midori and Kimmei were spending the rest of the summer in Guy's newly renovated loft. It was a spacious three bedrooms, and he'd given her one of the guest bedrooms for a makeshift studio. Guy had set Kimmei up on auditions for a number of musicals. She'd nailed the first audition and they'd signed her on immediately. Rehearsals began at the end of the summer, which left Midori with a decision to make.

She expected Guy to launch into a carnal attack at the end of this toe-curling kiss. But he pulled away, not with a serious face, but with a smirk. "What are you grinning about?"

"Have you seen the morning papers?" He unfolded the newsprint and held up the headline.

Midori scanned the headline, and then the first few sentences, her eyes growing wide with shock and then glee. "I knew it wouldn't last, but an annulment?"

Guy nodded. "Mason claims Phancy mislead him, and that he wasn't in his right mind when he made his vows. He's making claims that she drugged him. She's firing back, claiming that he's impotent and the marriage was never consummated. It's a media circus."

Midori tossed the paper aside, as though the ink would contaminate her. "Serves them both right. I've never seen two people who deserve each other more."

"Speaking of deserving each other," Guy gathered her into his arms once more. "Have you thought any more about my proposal?"

"It's still a lot to think about, Guy. Leaving everything we know in Saint Anne's to move here."

"We both have ties to Saint Anne's. We'd be down there a good deal. You could even hire someone to run your shop there."

Every point he made made sense, like always. Midori had to admit she was pulling at threads. She still had some fear that this was a dream and she'd wake up.

Every morning she did wake up, wrapped tightly in his arms. He'd take her out nearly every night, introducing her to every one they met, whether he knew them or not, as his fiancé. He'd even said it in a television interview for an entertainment show when they asked why he'd stepped down from Badd Finger Records. He'd told them he wanted to spend more time with his new family, and said her name on the airwaves. Guy made sure that everyone in the world knew they were together.

"It doesn't matter to me where we live full time, Midori. I'll set up camp wherever you are." He brushed a hair out of her face. "Once we're married it'll be a lifelong sentence. No Charmayne has ever gotten a divorce. It's always been 'til death do us part."

Midori liked the sound of that, a lifelong sentence with this man by her side. There was nothing holding her back, except the fear of the unknown. But she knew Guy. And more than anything, she knew she could always count on him. The last vestiges of doubt shook loose from her shoulders. She opened her mouth to proclaim it, but Guy's phone rang.

He glanced down at it with his finger aimed at the mute button, but then he grinned. "It's my sister."

Midori hadn't been formally introduced to his sister, yet,

but she was looking forward to spending time with the woman Guy clearly adored.

"Hey, Beau Beau." Guy toyed with Midori's fingers as he spoke into the phone. Slowly his fingers tightened on hers and his smile turned into a frown.

"Guy?" Midori said. "What's wrong?"

"It's my sister. She's getting a divorce."

---

*T*urn the page for a sneak peek at the next book in the series, *Beau: a Cindermama Story*!

BEAU SNEAK PEEK!

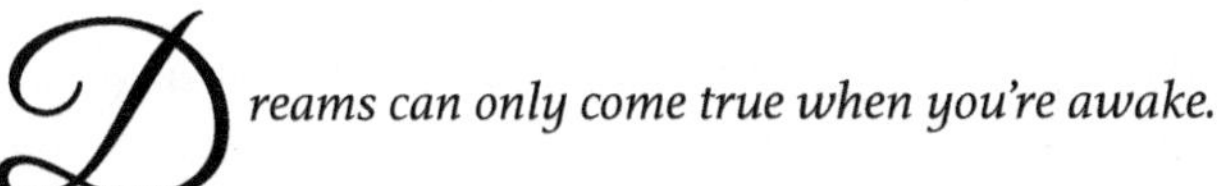

*B*eau Rosen has the perfect life—mostly. Thanks to her family's magic, she saw her "One and Only" love in a dream. So why does she go to bed next to him every night and wake up from nightmares? Exhausted, overworked, and under-appreciated, Beau seeks relief from her insomnia in the healing hands of chiropractor, Darrell Walker. Darrell brings her sweet dreams and a glimpse at a different life. For the first time Beau questions if her gift has really led her to a happily ever after.

*D*r. Darrell Walker doesn't believe in the "One." But his logical and scientific plan to find a life partner is going all wrong. So, when one of his patients with a penchant for matchmaking claims she saw his perfect match in her dream, he decides to hear her out. As Darrell and Beau work together to find his dream woman, Darrell falls under the spell of a very off-limits Beau. He can only hope that she wakes up to the fact they're perfect together, before it's too late.

Chapter One

Beau wrenched herself awake and out from the dark tendrils of sleep. Her eyes slammed open to the glaring twilight. Her arms flew out to ward off the cloying shadows. Her chest heaved in shallow pants and her fingers curled around the empty air. Her eyes took long to adjust to the darkness that shone bright in the room.

Bile on her tongue mixed with the metallic tint of iron. She reached her cold, shaking fingers to her lip. They came away wet. She eyed the contrast of the dark blood on her pale fingertips, and then glanced up at her surroundings.

Nothing looked familiar.

Where was she?

She took a deep breath, but her tight chest protested, only allowing one tiny puff of air at a time through its constricted channels. It left her dizzy as the four walls crushed in on her with the ever-growing darkness.

This was wrong, her mind whispered. Her restless legs tingled; eager to get up and run. Her churning stomach insisted she wasn't supposed to be here in this place; this cold, dark place.

A hand snaked out to grab at her. She wrenched away from it, skittering to the far side of the bed.

Bed? She was in a bed?

"Beau?" A deep voice, muffled with sleep, called out into the night. "Baby, it's me."

Who?

The voice sounded irritated, annoyed. Beau wasn't certain she wanted to get any closer to the owner of the voice. She peered down into the darkness until the face attached to the voice came into view. She couldn't make out the man's features. His face was shrouded in the shadows that surrounded them both. But there was something familiar about him.

He reached out again. This time he caught her. His fingertips left cold spots on the underside of her wrist, causing her pulse to jump. She stared down at the cold spots as her pulse kicked at his thumb.

She balled her hand into a fist, meeting another cold shock. It was a piece of metal. A band; a thin golden band. Her thumb snaked between her middle and fourth finger and met the sharp point of a stone.

"It's okay, baby." The words came as though from a record player that had worn out this particular song. "You had the nightmare again."

Nightmare? Had she had a nightmare? She didn't remember any pictures in her mind, only darkness. She'd been lost inside of darkness. Darkness from all around her; in her head, and now in reality.

She'd been looking for something? Or maybe for someone? She wasn't sure? It had been so dark. She shivered at the memory of it. Opening her eyes, she shivered again at the reality of it.

"You're home, baby," he said.

Beau looked around the dark room. This was her room, in her home. But why would she have a room so dark if she hated the darkness? Even with her eyes open, she felt the dense shadows crushing her still.

"You're with me," he said.

That sounded right. She moved closer to the voice, to him.

She knew this man, had known him for much of her life. She'd known him back during the time when sleep came quietly and peacefully to her. When dreams had whispered secrets to her. When waking had been a delight. Before nightmares of darkness kept her from her dreams and stole a little piece of her soul every time she closed her eyes.

"Everything's fine." The man with the familiar voice sighed heavily. The bed creaked as he turned over onto his other side. "Go back to sleep." He settled into the sheets. Within a minute, he was softly snoring.

Beau took another deep breath. Her chest now calm enough to allow clear passage for enough air to fill her lungs. Her heart slowed. Her stomach settled.

She closed her eyes, but the darkness waiting beneath her lashes crawled over her eyelids. It taunted her like a schoolyard bully, goading her to try and escape its wrath. She opened her eyes, but the shadows rang loud from their place in the corners of the room. She swore she heard them mocking her.

She slid closer to the man on the far side of the bed, seeking out his warmth. She ran her hands over his strong bicep.

He jerked away from her. "Babe, I've got a busy day tomorrow."

He turned to her, and gave her a quick kiss at the corner of her mouth. Then he turned away, scooting to the edge of his side of the bed. He gave her his back again.

Beau scooted away from him, back to her side of the mattress, which was colder, darker. She shoved the fear down. She pushed away thoughts of being in the wrong place. This was exactly where she was supposed to be. Lying beside the man of her dreams, in the house of her dreams, with the life of her dreams.

She had everything she'd ever dreamed of, and when she woke in the morning it would all be here to greet her. She pulled the covers up to her chin, then over her eyes.

She willed herself to sleep. But the darkness hovered, waiting to make its next attack.

Beau decided to stop fighting. She tossed off the covers and got up to greet the day, even though it was still the dead of the night.

hapter Two
      "Green means go, Mommy."

Beau blinked her eyes awake. She jerked in the driver's seat at the blare of the horn behind her telling her to move forward. She'd closed her eyes for a split second while being stopped at a stoplight on a residential street. At least, she hoped it had only been for a split second.

"Are we gonna be late again, Mommy?" In the mommy-mirror Beau's five-year old daughter, Flora, clutched at her pink, Disney princess backpack. Blue-gray eyes blinked back, moistened from anxious tears. The precious girl pulled a lock of jet-black hair into her mouth.

"No, sweetie," Beau soothed, flicking her own light-gray eyes up to the car's rear mirror. She pushed a lock of her own jet black hair behind her ear. "We're almost there."

Beau pulled her lower lip into her mouth at the small

fib. They were almost to the children's school, relative to where they were five minutes ago. She took her foot off the brake and tapped the gas. Turning one-handed into the next lane, she took the opportunity to take a healthy gulp of her second cup of coffee.

The dark roast sent a liquid shot of adrenalin into her blood stream. Unfortunately, the caffeine from her first cup still lingered in her veins and the newest sip from her second cup fizzled on impact. The insomnia was killing her. She had to keep alert. If not for herself, then for the precious cargo she carried in the backseat.

"Mommy, I said I wanted a strawberry cereal bar." A face identical to Flora's, but with cropped curls, filled the mommy-mirror. Her son, Faun, screwed his face at the blueberry cereal bar.

The children were having backseat breakfast again, because Beau missed her alarm clock. After waking in the middle of the night, she'd putzed around the house, finally venturing into her home office, which was a floor away from her bedroom. She'd picked up a file from work and had begun making notes. She didn't remember exactly when she'd closed her eyes.

The next time she opened them was to the slam of the front door, which had been her husband, Philip, leaving for the gym. He couldn't start his day without a good workout. Back in the home office, Beau had taken one look at the computer's clock and realized she and the children would be late starting their own day, which meant she didn't have time to make them a healthy breakfast from scratch.

"Faunie, you already ate yours."

"But Flo has one now," Faun kicked the back of the driver's seat.

Beau glanced at Flora. The little girl took the lock of

hair out of her mouth and pulled it over her shut eyes. The unopened cereal bar lay on her lap.

"I want another one," whined Faun.

"Here," Flora handed hers to her brother. "You can have mine. I don't want it."

Faun smacked the food away. "I don't want yours. I want my own."

Flora tried again to hand the unopened bar to her brother, but he pitched an even bigger fit, kicking up a storm that Beau felt along her spine.

"Flo, if he doesn't want it then stop teasing him," Beau admonished. The last thing she needed this morning was her son to have one of his meltdowns. When he got riled up it was almost impossible to calm him down.

Everyone told her that having twins was a full time job in and of itself. Not only did Beau have two children whom she loved, she also had a full-time job that was her life's passion. A job she would be late for, if she didn't get it into gear and get the kids to school on time.

Finally, she rounded the corner to Parish Academy with a moment to spare before the first bell. It was a straight path to the front of the school, as the drop off lane was empty of cars. The majority of parents had already kissed their kids and ridden off to make it to work on time. Only the moms of the shame-squad lingered, chatting in their Lulelemons and designer jeans. Since Beau couldn't escape the late-walk-of-shame, she pasted on a bright smile as she put the car in park and hopped out to unload her children.

"Hi, ladies," she sing-songed.

"Hi, Isabeau," rang a chorus of falsettos.

"What I wouldn't give to have the luxury of sleeping in on a school day," one voice broke off from the pack.

It was Chantelle, the leader of the pack. The dark-skinned woman wore a size zero yoga pants with a matching crop top that hinted at a flat, stretch-mark-less belly. Her artfully messy ponytail swished across her shoulder blades and her smoky-shadowed eyes cast shade at Beau.

Beau couldn't pass her puffy, encircled eyes off as a new makeup craze. She would love the luxury of sleeping in herself. She couldn't remember the last time she'd slept longer than a stolen nap during the day.

"Traffic was a nightmare," Beau offered as an excuse.

They all knew she only lived a couple of miles from the elite private school. They all lived in the same neighborhood. Most of them jogged here with their tricked-out jogging strollers, with designer tennis skirts hugging their perky asses. Beau didn't have time for jogging. She also didn't have time for small talk in the kiss-and-ride lane.

She unbuckled the twins and they hopped out of the car. Faun barely spared his mother a glance as she leaned down to kiss him goodbye. He ducked and sprinted for his teacher, Mrs. Knighting, giving the older woman a hug.

Mrs. Knighting straightened and gave Beau an enthusiastic wave. Beau had known Mrs. Knighting when her gray hair was still a lush brown and her name was Ms. Clark. Twenty years ago, the night after her first day of Kindergarten, Beau had seen Ms. Clark in a dream. She hadn't understood what it meant that her teacher and the school crossing guard were holding hands as they walked in a meadow. Mr. Knighting had held Beau's hand that morning when she'd crossed the street to school. The next morning Beau told Ms. Clark about the dream. That afternoon Beau saw the two adults talking. Within the year they were married.

Flora waited patiently for her mother to lean down and

kiss her forehead. "Love you, Mommy," she said, before skipping off to join her brother.

Beau took a moment she didn't have to watch the two children disappear into the school with their teacher. They were the last two children to do so. Then she turned to head back to her car, but she knew better. The Mom Squad swarmed on her.

"We've been looking for some parents to come and talk with the children next week for Career Day." Chantelle's ponytail swished hypnotically as she sized up Beau.

"Oh, I..." Beau fell under the spell of the dark mane and didn't get an excuse out in time.

"We have a lot of fathers coming in, but not many women work outside of the home. You're one of the few." Lindsey stood at Chantelle's side, coordinated from her jean belt to her earrings, to her nail polish. Beau wondered what time the woman got up in the morning to affect such a look?

"We were hoping you'd get more involved this year, like you promised." Kathryn pulled up on Beau's other side. They'd effectively boxed her in. There was no way to escape.

They'd not only boxed her in physically, they also cut her at her Achilles' heel. Beau came from money; lots of money. She never wanted to be accused of being entitled — even though just about every woman whose kids were enrolled in this prestigious and expensive private school was connected to money and rarely worked a day in their lives.

Three pairs of eyes regarded her, looking down on her even though she had a couple of inches, and a few more zeros in a trust fund, on each of them. Chantelle's ponytail swished back and forth in anticipation of Beau squirming out of yet another school function, as she'd done in the past.

It wasn't that Beau didn't want to help out. She just didn't have the time to. Her philanthropic enterprise, aimed at educating girls in the Middle East so they'd have options other than arranged marriages, and rescuing boys taken to soldier wars in Africa, always interfered with the involvement in this high-priced, exclusive, private, primary school.

Chantelle's gaze broke from Beau's. She cocked her head, ponytail swishing like a lion scenting easy prey. "Uh oh, look out. Charity case incoming."

Beau turned to see an old-school Chevy pull up. The muffler grunted as the car pulled to a stop. A woman Beau didn't recognize hopped out of the car. She wore loose-fitting jeans and a sweatshirt with a stain at the collar.

The woman opened the car door with a squeak of metal and three kids paraded out. It was a Benneton of Color ad. One child was Asian, another black, and a third... Beau couldn't quite distinguish the third child's ethnicity, but he had pale-skin and European features.

"They're here on scholarship." Chantelle crossed her brown arms beneath her perky breasts. "The board is trying to get into Affirmative Action."

"I heard her husband left her after the second child came out Asian," said Lindsey.

The woman in question had skin the color of milk with a teaspoon tipped with chocolate, and bright orange-red hair. The combination of her skin and hair was stunning. Beau wondered if the woman was an albino.

The mom opened her arms and each child came will-ingly into her embrace before heading into the building. When the red-head straightened and turned, her face did not read excitement at the prospect of a face-off with the Mom Squad. In fact, she tried to side step them altogether.

Beau let out a small sigh for the woman. That move never worked, she wanted to tell the newcomer. Best to just face the pack head on and soldier through.

"Duchess," Chantelle sing-songed across the lot. She leaned into Beau and whispered, "Can you believe that name?"

Duchess didn't venture too close. "Hello, everyone. It's good to see you all."

Chantelle stepped in front of her, cutting off Duchess' exit. "You know that part of enrollment in Parish Academy is that every family has to do community service hours. We were hoping you could come in next week for Career Day. You're one of the only working moms in the school. And we want to show the little girls that there are a few other options than an MRS degree."

Duchess cocked her head like a bird, unsure if the landing was safe. "I don't know. I work during school hours." Duchess took another step towards her car.

"Oh, it won't take much time at all. You'd be speaking along with Isabeau, here."

Duchess took one look at Beau in her pressed suit and pumps and winced. For all of her wealth and popularity Beau had never been a mean girl. She broke off from the herd and extended her hand to Duchess.

"I'm pleased to meet you," Beau said. "I think it would be fun to speak with the kids, and I'd love if we did it together."

Duchess blinked at Beau's genuine smile. Then she took her hand. Duchess' grip wasn't firm, but it was warm.

"You headed in to work?" Beau asked.

Duchess nodded.

"Me, too." Beau commandeered them towards their cars and out of the way of the Mom Squad.

"Thanks," said Duchess.

"No, thank you. I really do have a meeting to get to. They would've kept me there all day. I'm Beau, by the way."

Duchess cocked her head to the other side in the same bird-like motion. "Yes, I know."

Right, Chantelle had said her name. "Well, Duchess, maybe we could get together sometime on a weekend to get to know each other?"

"You want to hang out?" she said. "With me?" She pointed her thumb to her chest. It landed at the stain on her shirt.

"Sure," said Beau. "Maybe make a play date out of it with the kids?"

"Yeah... okay." Duchess' smile was wobbly with uncertainty, but it wasn't fake.

They exchanged numbers and then the two women hopped into their cars and left the school, and the Mom Squad, behind.

Twenty minutes later, and with truly horrific rush hour traffic, Beau pulled up to her office. The Rosen Foundation was a small non-profit, only three years old. Unlike the Charmayne Foundation run by Beau's family, which focused on the sick and the needy, the Rosen Foundation focused its efforts specifically on children.

The office occupied what used to be a flower shop in the market district of Saint Anne's parish. The shop had belonged to Mr. Matthews. Mr. Matthews had been a widower when he bought the shop. One night in high school, Beau had seen him arranging black and white flowers for her brother's music teacher.

By this time Beau had come to understand her gift, and

was sure to tell the music teacher about the flower shop. The flowers at the wedding were beautiful. Beau's brother, Guy, never forgave her for butting into the life of his favorite teacher, who became pregnant within a year and never went back to teaching after the first, then second, and third child was born.

The converted flower shop was mainly one large room with a small office in the back, next to the bathroom. Beau could have run the organization from the Charmayne offices free rent, but Philip had insisted they have their own space and their own identity.

The business didn't take up too much space, as most of the work was done on the phone, calling up potential donors; and at social events, networking with wealthy socialites and philanthropic business professionals whose consciences were eager to give back. Beau and Philip shared the small back office, but Beau spent most of her time in the main room with her small staff. The staff consisted of college interns; mainly poli-sci majors. Interns worked for free in exchange for college credit. Unfortunately, Beau's interns had the bad habit of acing the internship class and then moving on, leaving her with the task of training a new batch every few months.

The office was empty at eight in the morning, when most of the interns were hitting their snooze buttons. Beau set her bag down on one of the empty cubicles and walked back to the office. Philip stood at the window of his office in a tailored suit.

Beau halted in her stride. The sight of him standing there in that particular pose, in a suit... it called to mind a dream she'd had of him when she was in college. That dream had changed her life.

Magic ran in Beau's family. Her mother had seen her

father coming a mile away, when he'd glowed bright, before her eyes. Beau and her brother didn't get the Charmayne gift of seeing golden auras around their true love. Their gifts were different. Her brother Guy saw gold around people with talent. Beau didn't see any gold. In fact, she didn't see anything at all any more. Her gift had been short-lived. But it didn't matter. It had served its purpose and brought her the man of her dreams.

Beau allowed herself a moment to admire the man she'd pledged to spend her life with. She got her feet moving again, eager to feel the warm, reality of him with her hands.

"There you are," he turned with an exasperated look when he saw her. "You're late. I had to entertain Stefan Paulson for the last twenty minutes."

The office they shared also doubled as a conference room. Meeting Mr. Paulson was the first thing on her long to-do list today, and she was thankful to her husband for taking care of that task.

"Thank you for doing that. How much is he in for?" she asked, leaning against the solid oak desk that Philip insisted they needed to impress big donors.

"How should I know?" Philip coordinated a shrug and a frown. "That's your job, to work with the small businessmen."

Stefan Paulson was a local dentist. His mother was origi-nally from Sudan, but had married an American man when she relocated to the States. Dr. Paulson had no ties to his mother's homeland, but he felt pulled to do something about the violence occuring in that land, especially the theft of bright, young boys who were then turned into killing machines to feed an endless war.

"He came with his checkbook," she said. "All you had to

do was offer him a pen. What did you talk about for twenty minutes?"

"Sports." Philip barely spared her a glance as he shoved items into his golf bag. "He'll be back later this afternoon to speak with you."

Beau stifled a sigh. There went her early escape from work to get to the grocery store before she had to pick the kids up from school. The day crowded in on her like the darkness of her dream last night. What she wouldn't give for a day's rest. Instead, she'd be brewing a third cup of coffee in less than two hours.

"You also need to look over some documents from the IRS about our non-profit status," Philip grabbed his cell phone and tapped a few keys. "Something about new guide-lines with phone calls. I don't know? You take a look."

Beau looked down at the IRS documents she had to view. Besides that, she had a mountain of paperwork to go through on her desk. Then she had a ton of calls to make. Not to mention she'd have to spare some time to think about what she'd say for Career Day next week. Which reminded her about her empty fridge. It looked like it would be another take-out night for the Rosen family.

"Anyway, your tardiness is going to make me late," he said.

"Late for what? What's on your agenda today?" she asked as Philip struggled with his briefcase. There were very few documents in the case's belly.

"I'm headed to the golf course. I have that meeting with a new consultant."

"Consultant?"

"Yeah. Yohance Stanley. I told you about him. He's perfected this new technique to help fundraise; it saves tons of money."

Philip poked at the latch on the case, it refused to close. He smacked at it, then huffed when it still refused to close. Beau reached for the case and took it from his grasp. The last thing she needed this morning was her husband to have one of his meltdowns. When he got riled up it was almost impossible to calm him down.

Beau lined the latch up and it snapped closed. Philip sighed. He pulled her close and kissed her temple. Beau relaxed into his arms.

"Listen baby, I know how hard you work to get the money in. But we should be thinking of working smarter and not harder. I'm going to hear Mr. Stanley out, see if we can use any of his techniques to lighten the load around here."

He kissed her temple again, and then released her. She knew she should ask Philip to schedule a meeting so they could both hear this consultant out, but the thought of another thing added to her list made her bones weary. Instead, she waved to Philip as he hefted his golf bag over his shoulder and headed out the door.

She'd just sat down at the expensive desk and begun mentally organizing her to-do list, when she realized he'd left his brief case behind. It was too late to go after him. She knew he'd call her if he needed anything. She pushed the light case aside and got down to work.

Chapter Three

. . .

"Are you enjoying your meal?" Darrell asked, as the smell of butter and sea filled the air.

His date's lobster was almost as big as her head. She held a tiny fork in one hand and a steak knife in the other. She dug in, but the crustacean fought back, slipping first to one side of the buttery dish then to the other as she tried to reel it in with her utensils.

"I've never had lobster before," she said.

Darrell sat back and watched the show. It looked like he would get lucky tonight. He'd read up online about dating and dishes. A psychologist compiled a study that gave the personality traits of individuals based on what they ordered on a date. Ordering meat and potatoes meant that a person was steady, dependable, and enjoyed the comforts of home. Looking down at his plate, Darrell could confirm the diagnosis.

When a woman ordered an expensive dish like a lobster, which was the most expensive dish on the menu, it meant they were wild, adventurous, and up for taking chances. Darrell didn't want to take any chances tonight. He'd rather the chance be taken a few nights from now. He'd be open to rolling the dice in a couple of weeks, even. The thought of another one-night stand, or a temporary bed-buddy pact did not interest him. He was looking for something more.

Darrell focused on the woman seated across from him. Carla was her name. He'd repeated it to himself exactly twenty-one times. It was scientifically proven that doing something twenty-one times would cause it to become a habit. That would've been the worst thing —to forget someone's name on the first date.

"So Harold—"

"It's Darrell."

"What? Oh, right, Darrell."

Carla shoved her fork up the lobster's tail and plopped the extracted white meat into her mouth. Then she made a face and spit the hunk of meat out. The white blob settled on his plate, right on top of his steak.

Darrell put a hand to his stomach to stop it from roiling.

"Gawb." Carla dabbed her tongue with the linen napkin. Her face screwed up like a toddler who'd just tried baby peas for the first time. "Oh, woub bay por dat cwab."

Darrell picked the mangled bite of lobster off his steak using his napkin. He could admit that lobster was an acquired taste. He called the waiter over.

The mountain of a man made his way over to their table. The waiter's movements were like the parting of the sea. With each step he took, women turned to look behind him at his backside.

Darrell knew that women were biologically predetermined to favor large men. Their lizard brains understood that a large male could protect them best. That a well-filled chest meant he got the best portions of food and she would too. That big men would likely breed big children who would continue their line.

Times had changed since the Mesozoic Era. Changed even further from the hunter-gatherer societies. Nerds now ruled the world. If that waiter's cell phone wouldn't turn on, if his computer caught a virus, if his surround-sound stereo went on the fritz, he would have to call someone from Darrell's tribe.

Darrell shoved his glasses up his nose and tilted his head back. He opened his mouth to speak for his date, only to find she'd been caught up in the parting of the seas along with the rest of the women.

"My current dish isn't to my liking." Carla waved her

hand above her dismembered lobster. Her fingers waggled in the general direction of Darrell.

"I'm not surprised," said the waiter, his wide back to Darrell. "I didn't think you were the kind of girl who liked bottom feeders."

"Lobster's a little rich for my tastes." Carla flipped her hair over her shoulder and batted her eyelashes. "What do you suggest I try?" Carla ran her tongue over her bottom lip. The waiter followed the movement and his own lips curled.

"Maybe you're the type of girl who needs an aphrodisiac. Try the oysters."

"Oysters are high in zinc, which is great for fertility," said Darrell.

Both Carla and the waiter blinked and frowned down at him.

"I'm on the pill, the patch, and a cervical cap. Nothing is getting fertilized any time soon." Carla turned her attention back to the waiter and winked. "But I'll try the oysters."

The man was absolutely not getting a tip for this shoddy service. Darrell's water glass was empty. He'd asked for a steak knife ten minutes ago. And to top it off, the man was hitting on his date. But what did he expect?

Darrell had been to a number of speed dating events in the past couple of months. To his shock, he learned that a lot of women were out looking for short-term hookups, not a lasting relationship. Apparently, today's workingwoman didn't have time to forge relationships. He'd heard a number of women say so, on more than one occasion.

Today's woman had needs and went out to bars and clubs and speed dating events to get those needs met. Darrell had learned the hard way that there was no requirement for breakfast in the morning, or even cuddling at night. Today's meat market was no longer full of female lambs meant for slaughter. Male lambs were often on the block as just a side dish.

He'd met Carla the other day at one such event. He'd read her dating profile on the lock-shaped card that hung around her neck. His profile data was listed on a key-shaped card. He admitted the whole scenario was a bit phallic, but it saved time. Their cards had told him they had a lot in common. Commonality, he believed, was the foundation of any good relationship.

"So, Carla," he began. "I remember from your profile that you're a nursing student."

Carla shook her head. "That was, like, forever ago. I dropped out two years ago."

"Oh?" Darrell rubbed at his chin. "Well, what do you do now?"

"I work for the cable company."

"You're in communications?" He worked with people too, both as a profession and in his spare time.

Carla shook her head. "Debt collection."

They were silent for a moment. Both glancing around the restaurant. Carla had suggested they go out for an early dinner. At the time, Darrell had thought she was being cautious to not be out late with a man she didn't know. Now he wondered if he was just the warm up act and the main show would later take the stage. Carla looked at the curtain where the wait staff passed through. Darrell looked at the exit sign in the corner.

"You're a doctor, right?" Carla's eyes held a spark of interest when they turned back to him.

One thing Darrell knew he had going for him was his credentials. Just as jocks grew up to be in the service of nerds, women grew out of their infatuations with high school quarterbacks and later aimed for the men whose careers didn't have them bashing into one another and running in circles. "I am. I'm a chiropractor."

Her eyebrows drew together. "Is that a real doctor?"

Darrell kept his grimace at bay as he nodded. "I specialize in the spine. You can't get by without a back."

Darrell grinned but Carla looked at him confused. He'd tried that joke out on a number of women at the speed-dating event. Not one of them had laughed. He'd have to retire it from his repertoire.

"So, Carla, what is it you're looking for in a man?"

She parted her lips in a smile that read cynical. "Are we talking in his head or in his pants?"

Darrell choked on his sip of water.

Carla narrowed her eyes at him. "Don't tell me you're one of those romantics? What? You believe in love at first sight?"

Unfortunately, Darrell didn't have the luxury of denying it. He'd seen love at first sight happen. It just so happened that the woman whose attention he had been trying to catch had looked right past him and fallen in love with the friend who had stood beside him.

Darrell cleared his throat. "It's statistically improbable to determine that you'll marry a person based on the first time you see them."

Carla scratched at her eyelid as she frowned at him.

"But it is possible," he conceded. "By a very small margin. I think it's more sound to get to know someone first. To look for things you have in common with each other, before you decide if you'll spend the rest of your life with them."

He waved a hand between the two of them, but Carla wasn't looking at him any longer. She was looking over her shoulder. Darrell saw the approaching waiter with her oyster dish.

"I don't believe in marriage," she said as the waiter placed her new dish before her. "I'm just looking to get laid."

Beside them a child began a tantrum. Darrell looked over to see the neighboring table's empty plates. The mother held up her hand, trying to get the waiter's attention. The waiter had his full attention on Carla's breasts instead.

Darrell had been raised by a single mother. He understood the need for a mother to get out of the house and not cook a meal. When he was a kid, he tried to have dinner ready for his mother as often as he could. Normal gender roles were non-existent in his house. He'd do laundry when necessary. His mother would do the plumbing. They worked together. She had to take on the role of nurturer and father since Darrell's father had chosen to make another family when he was young; a family that didn't include him.

He handed the breadbasket on his table over to the young mom. She made to make a motion to refuse, but when the child's eyes lit, and his crying stopped, she mouthed a 'thank you' at him.

Darrell considered switching tables. But he caught the sparkle of a diamond on the mom's left hand when she reached for the basket. Darrell sighed and turned back to the woman across from him. Unlike the mom, Carla was up for grabs, in more ways than one.

Darrell wanted to find someone. Single life was not for him, though he'd been single most of his thirty years. He'd had a girlfriend here and there. He'd had a few one-night stands and brief trysts over the past year that left him feeling nothing but lonely. Sitting across from Carla, who was busy watching the waiter walk away from their table, Darrell felt that loneliness crush into him. He wanted to be the one chosen for once in his life. Instead of sitting by and bearing it, he did something he was not too proud of.

He reached in his pocket and pulled out his cell phone. He gave Carla an apologetic wince—not that she was paying any attention to him as she dug into her oysters. Darrell turned his attention to the dark screen of his phone. He tapped the blank screen and placed the phone to his ear.

"Hello... Oh, no... Really? Well, of course, I'll be right over." He sighed as he placed the phone back in his pocket. "I'm sorry, Carla but I've got to go. Chiropractic emergency."

"I didn't know there was such a thing," she said, around the food in her mouth.

Darrell pulled out enough cash to cover the bill. Unfortunately, his conscious wouldn't let him exclude the tip. But he only gave ten percent. "It was nice meeting you..."

He hesitated to tack on the customary 'We should do this again' or 'I'll call you.' They both knew this was the last time they'd ever see each other.

No sooner had Darrell stepped out of the restaurant did he spy, through the window, Carla leave the table and make her way up to the waiter. The two pulled out their phones, smiling carnally at each other.

Love at first sight? The One? True Love?

Those were all pipe dreams. That wasn't love between those two, it was lust. They'd slake each other's needs later tonight and likely be on to the next dish by tomorrow evening.

Darrell wasn't into that. He wanted a partner, someone to share his life with. A woman who was kind, smart, and loyal. Most of all loyal.

One thing he would concede was that Carla and her waiter had it right. The way to find companionship nowadays was through technology. Darrell was a man of science and he would go about finding a woman to share his life with in a scientific manner. No more speed dates where he'd try to gauge a woman's interest in five minutes.

The sun was starting to set as he pulled open his phone and walked to his car. He wasn't going to give up. He was just going to go about this smarter. He tapped a few keys and the dating app downloaded.

The app was like applying for a job. He had to put in his qualifications, accomplishments, and interests. It promised to show him his perfect matches based on algorithms. This was a much simpler, foolproof way to date. And within ten minutes, he already had his first match.

Chapter Four

Beau reached for her fifth cup of coffee. She smiled as she brought the cup to her lips. The coffee mug was a Wonder Woman cup; starry blue with a red handle. Her mother gave it to her when she was a child.

Gabrielle Charmayne-Rumpel had been a devotee of the Amazonian warrior princess. Growing up during an era when the feminine archetype was under attack by burning bras, Gabrielle had found her ideal in the 70's television show. There was no situation Wonder Woman couldn't handle. No villain she couldn't outwit. No brute she couldn't lasso into submission. Gabrielle had seen the woman she wanted to be in the liberated, strong, unconventional, yet still feminine, woman that Lynda Carter portrayed, and she'd passed these ideals on to her only daughter.

Beau was Amazonian tall with dark tresses and light eyes. She'd been raised to be a strong and liberated, yet still feminine, woman. She was all these things. But try as she might, she never seemed in command of her days.

Two of her interns called in to say they would be late. One never showed up at all. A huge donor fell through her hands because she hadn't had the time to call and schmooze him before another charity did. She'd never even made it to the new stack of papers Philip had laid on her desk. And then there was her other full-time job waiting to be picked up from the afterschool program, all the way on the other side of town.

Motherhood was harder than the job she spent her days at. She had thirty minutes to make it to the grocery store and then across town to pick up the kids. She had more balls up in the air than she had hands to juggle. If she wasn't careful, everything would come crashing down around her.

"Mrs. Rosen?"

Beau looked up at Judy, her longest and most dependable intern who would, unfortunately, be graduating soon.

"Mr. Paulson is back."

Beau moved one stack of papers over and pulled forth another. A second look at the clock told her that she wouldn't be able to take this meeting with Mr. Paulson, plus get groceries, and get the kids from school on time. Something would have to give.

"Thanks Judy, I'll be out in just a second."

Beau picked up the phone and called for backup.

"Hey, baby." Philip's voice was a rushed whisper. "I can't talk. I'm at the club."

Beau frowned at the phone. "I thought you were golfing with that consultant, what was his name again?"

"Yohance Stanley," said Philip. "I'm with him now. He's interested in taking a look at our organization, but first you're going to need to cut a check for ten thousand."

Beau balked. It wasn't as though they didn't have the money. Well, she had the money. The business didn't.

"Philip, that's incredibly steep."

"It's a steal, Beau. Stanley says 'no' to ninety-percent of the organizations who ask for his services."

"We should at least talk about this more before we cut a check. I haven't had a moment to look up Stanley or his business practices. We should look into this together and meet him together. We are partners, after all."

"Look, they're calling me. I gotta go, babe."

"Wait! Philip?"

"Yeah, babe? What? I'm working here."

"I know, sweetie. But I'm about to meet with Mr. Paulson."

"Okay," he huffed, impatience lacing his voice.

"Which means I won't be able to pick the kids up on time and get dinner on the table. The club is near their school. Can you swing by and get them?"

"Babe, I have no idea how long this meeting is going to last."

"If he's as exclusive as he says, we'll intrigue him by playing hard to get. Besides, these are your children."

The silence on the other end of the phone was crushing. "What's going on here? Are you trying to say I'm a bad father?"

"Philip, I would never say that."

"Because I'm out working, trying to feed my family. If you can't handle all of your responsibilities—"

"Wait a minute. That's not fair."

"Did I call you up asking you to come down here? No, I

didn't. I took it upon myself to seek out someone who could make your life easier."

Philip was getting riled up. He was almost impossible to calm down when he got upset, and she didn't want him to cause a scene in the country club.

"You're the one who wanted to be a working mother," he huffed. "You could've stayed home with the kids."

That had been the plan; for Beau to stop working at Charmayne Foundation and stay home with the twins. Shortly after she and Philip were married, and she was still in her first trimester, Philip had gone to work with his father. Unfortunately, things didn't work out there because, well, Philip and his father were too alike, and two cooks in the kitchen was a recipe for disaster.

So, Philip's father gave him a loan and sent his son off to start his own company. That company never got off the ground because something or other about not filing the right permits by the deadlines. Beau had never gotten a clear explanation out of her demoralized husband. In her final trimester, and large with the twins, she came to learn that he'd spent the majority of those funds on their new home and filling it with entertainment systems and a man cave in preparation for the twins.

By the time the twins were resting on their mother's belly, Philip had depleted the remaining startup funds. His father turned him away for a second loan.

After spending a few weeks at home with newborn twins, Philip was raring to try his hand out in the real world again. This time he enlisted his wife's help instead of being beholden to anyone else. He begrudgingly agreed to use money from her trust fund, with a promise to pay back every cent, and the Rosen Foundation was born.

"It's all right," Beau said. "I'll figure it out."

"Call an Uber to pick them up. They'll be fine."

Beau's chest squeezed at the idea, but she didn't want to fight. She really couldn't blame him. Men didn't understand parenting. Not the way a mother did. "Good luck with your meeting, sweetie."

"You too, babe."

Before Beau could say 'I love you,' the line went dead.

She straightened her skirt. She reapplied her lip-gloss and reached into her desk for her emergency mascara. Rolling her neck, she heard the bones crack as the pressure released.

She stood and prepared herself to greet the potential donor. She excelled at this. She was the daughter of a socialite after all.

"Mr. Paulson," Beau reached out her hand to the tall and lanky dark-skinned man who entered her office. "I'm so excited to finally meet you. Thank you so much for making the time to return and speak with me."

She directed him to the guest chair in her office. Though he sat his form in the chair, he was so tall it looked as though he'd only bent over.

"I've been very fortunate in this community," he began. "My mother immigrated here before I was born, and she wasn't the only one. There's a large number of Sudanese refugees living in our community. I want to do something for the children here."

Beau leaned back in her chair. "The Rosen Foundation typically helps children abroad."

"These children began their lives in Sudan. They are the children who escaped the war torn lands. Many have a tough time adjusting to this new way of life; the girls and the boys alike."

Beau took a breath and leaned forward again. "I'm

embarrassed to say I've never considered extending our services to the children who make it to our shores."

"I've heard horror stories of organizations raising money and then the money never reaches the needy. Or only a small portion reaches them while the rest is pocketed by the organizations. Not that your organization would ever do that."

"Of course not," Beau said. "We're here to help, and the Rosen Foundation will help the refugees living here in Saint Anne's."

When Beau shook his hand to seal the deal, she noted the time. She had ten minutes to make the twenty-minute trek across town to pick up her kids on time.

Walking Mr. Paulson out, with assurances that she would come up with plans to address the refugee children in the parish, Beau dashed to her car the moment his driver's side door closed. Her car's engine roared to life and she took off across town.

She should feel glad. She'd accomplished so much today. But even through all that hard work, she felt it was her family, her children, who suffered.

She went through her mental rolodex of restaurants that were fast and that the kids liked, because there was no way she was going to have the time and energy to cook dinner tonight. She knew that when she got home there was a mound of laundry to do. Not to mention she had to take a look at the household bills. There was just never enough time in the day.

Speaking of time, she glanced at her dashboard clock. She had three minutes to get to the school before the official end to the Afterschool program. She was five minutes away.

She could do it. She wished she could get there on time for once and not be running late, not be ushering her children in or out of the building like they were in a race. She wished she had time to sleep.

She wished so hard that she missed the red light above her. A bright, white beam of light flashed into her eyes. Beau caught sight of snow white sheep jumping over a mattress on the side of the truck before she smashed into its side. Her eyes closed and everything went black.

Chapter Five

The woman before Darrell didn't exactly match her profile. She'd said she was five-nine. She was more like four-nine. Darrell thought maybe that was a typo in the dating app where they'd connected. A woman's height had nothing to do with her kindness.

Janet had mentioned that her body was athletic, but she was more on the curvy side. Which Darrell didn't mind at all. He liked his women with a bit of extra skin. He also liked them thin. He'd never found that the numbers on a scale or a measuring tape made any difference to a woman's intelligence.

Janet had said she was blonde, but her brown roots were showing. That was fine, too. Hair color had nothing to do with a person's loyalty.

Kindness, intelligence, and loyalty; that's all that mattered to Darrell. After a night of filling out survey after poll after questionnaire on the dating app that asked him what he looked for in a woman, he'd narrowed it down to those three items. Sure, he wanted to be attracted to the woman, but looks rated low on the results for his profile.

Getting along with his partner was paramount. Darrell couldn't abide mean-spirited people. His partner would have to have a big heart. He wasn't the most talkative of people, but when he did engage in conversation he also wanted to share his days with someone who would engage his mind. So, intelligence also ranked high on his list. And then there was loyalty. That was the most important thing on Darrell's list.

Even though Janet had fudged a bit on her profile, she was standing up to the first two items on his list. She'd said that she volunteered at a food pantry on weekends as part of her church ministry. And she was smart. She was a programmer at a local tech company. But the best thing about Janet, her eyes hadn't strayed to one of the waiters walking by. A good indication that she might have the loyal trait he was looking for.

"I've had a really good time, Darrell."

And she knew his name to boot. Yes, she was looking like a great candidate.

It was a lunchtime date instead of dinner, like the makers of the dating app suggested for a first date. Darrell and Janet had agreed to meet for a coffee between their busy schedules. He'd had his coffee black. She'd added foam and sugar. There was a study that people who preferred their coffee sweet tended towards kindness.

Janet drained her drink. At the bottom of the cup Darrell saw a lump of crystals gathered at the edge of the Styrofoam. With their drinks finished, they stepped outside of the coffee shop.

"Maybe we could do this again sometime?" Darrell hedged.

Janet looked up at him with a twinkle in her eyes. "I'd like that." She bit her lip and leaned in.

Darrell realized it was his cue for a kiss. He'd never been good at reading those cues, but dating as much as he had over the past few weeks had taught him something.

He leaned down a foot and touched his lips to hers. They were pleasant lips. Thin, but soft. He tasted the sweetness of the sugar at the crease in her lip. He pulled away and she blinked.

"What?" he asked.

"Did you feel it?" she asked.

"Feel what?"

"A spark?"

Darrell frowned.

"You were perfect on paper," Janet sighed. "But no spark."

He blinked again.

"Well..." she sighed. "It was nice meeting you anyway." She turned and trudged down the street.

Darrell stared after her. Could she be serious? They were perfect on paper. And she was going to throw all of that away because there was no static electricity that sparked between their coffee moistened lips?

He threw his hands in the air. He would never understand women.

He made his way back to his office, walking through the market district of the parish. The parish was large enough that he didn't know everyone, but small enough so that faces were familiar. He waved to a few business owners he knew by name or by use of their products.

The walk in the cool air helped to cool him down —a little.

What did women want nowadays? He thought he was

approaching modern women who wanted equality. He'd find women with level heads who still had their heads up in the clouds. They spewed gibberish about love at first sight and true love's kiss and golden auras.

It was all nonsense. Just a way to make an excuse for going after someone you lusted after or letting down someone you didn't. Darrell didn't have time for it. He wanted a life partner, a wife. In his case, he would be making that decision based on science and compatibility, not off some imaginary, chemically imbalanced absurdity.

He came up to a building with his name on the glass door. When he'd first begun practicing, he'd shared an office with five other doctors. It had taken him a few years, but now it was solely his name on the office door.

"You have a new patient, Dr. Walker," said his receptionist.

Darrell heard a squeal from the waiting room. He peered in to see two pint-sized human beings. A little girl in a frilly, princess dress, and a boy in scuffed up jeans with a t-shirt that read "Mother's Little Angel." From the looks of them, they were clearly related; twins perhaps?

The little girl stood before the boy with trembling lips as he held something above her head. It was one of the toys Darrell kept in his office to entertain children.

The little boy frowned indignantly at the girl. "I'm going to play with it first. Then maybe you can have a turn."

The little girl didn't argue. Her little shoulders slumped in defeat as though she expected this outcome.

"Hey, buddy," Darrell stepped in. "A gentleman always let's ladies go first."

The little boy looked at Darrell. His wide, blue-gray eyes were the definition of incredulous. "She's not a lady. She's my sister."

"Then it's your job to make sure that all boys, including you, treat her like a lady."

The boy thought on this. He looked at the toy. He looked at his sister.

The little princess' eyes welled with hope. She looked up at Darrell as if she'd never thought anyone would ever take her side. But then the boy turned on his heel and ran into a corner with the toy clutched in his grasp.

Darrell reached up on a shelf and took down another toy. It was a stretch to call the wooden board with colored marbles a toy. The game was the child version of the adult game, Sudoko. In the child version, the player had to arrange the colored marbles in a unique pattern using logic.

"Here," he said to the little girl. "This game is only for the smartest children with the biggest imaginations."

Her eyes widened in the same incredulous shape as her brother's had. Her brother peered from his hiding place.

"Are you smart?" Darrell asked.

She bobbed her dark curls enthusiastically.

"Do you have an imagination?"

"My mommy says I have my head in the clouds. That's where my imaginary friend, Milly, lives."

Darrell looked down into the little girl's light eyes. Like her brother's eyes, there was gray on the outer rims of her irises and blue in the center. It was a startling combination. He wondered where her parents were.

The child took the game from his hands with the greatest care. "Thank you," she said as if he'd just slain a dragon for her.

"Well done, my dear."

Darrell knew that voice. For a moment his lonely heart swelled with joy as Gale Charmayne came into view. Her gray eyes twinkled at him just like the little girl's had. But then he remembered another pair of gray eyes. Kind, intelligent gray eyes that had promised loyalty, and stabbed him in the back as soon as he turned around.

"Ms. Charmayne," Darrell said coolly.

Gale sighed. "Dear heart, you can't begrudge another for finding their truth. Especially not when yours is just around the corner."

Gale had said those words to him a year ago when he found his friend Manny Charmayne kissing his girlfriend in a closet. Manny had insisted that Pumpkin, Darrell's girlfriend, was *The One* he'd been searching for his whole life; his golden girl. Darrell had always listened to the tales of the Charmayne family in good humor, until the fabrications came to bite him in the ass.

Gale had determined that love was on its way to Darrell. But that had been a year ago. His good humor and patience had gone over six months ago.

"Is there something I can help you with, Ms. Charmayne?" Darrell pulled his professionalism around his shoulders like a heavy cloak.

"No," she smiled sadly. "I'm just helping to watch these rascals while their mother sees you. She was in a car accident the other day. I made sure to bring her to the best doctor in the state."

"I appreciate your business." Darrell grabbed the chart and turned away.

He walked down the hall, and slipped into his office. Pulling on his white coat, he gave his hands a wash, and then headed next door into the exam room.

He opened the door quietly. The woman on the exam table had her eyes closed. She lay back with her dark hair fluffed around her heart-shaped face.

Darrell's heart stuttered in his chest. He'd always told

himself that beauty wasn't important enough to be on his list. But this woman, lying peacefully on his exam table, made him a liar.

She looked the way every fairytale princess would if they stepped out of a storybook. Her complexion was olive-toned. Her eyelashes lay thick on her cheekbones. Her lips were plump and naturally red, with no glossy help. In her repose, her breasts perked up to the sky. He spied long, shapely calves outlined beneath the light fabric of her skirt.

Darrell held still for fear that a step would send him fumbling like a buffoon. He had the urge to go over and kiss her lips to wake her, as in a fairytale. But as soon as he took a step, her eyes opened. He halted immediately as he looked into pale gray eyes.

"Mrs. Charmayne." Darrell's jaw tightened around the surname.

Her brow creased in confusion. "No. My last name is Rosen. Isabeau Rosen."

Darrell blinked. Had he gotten it wrong? Was she not one of Manny's relatives?

"Charmayne was my mother's maiden name," she smiled up at him.

It was the charming Charmayne smile. Darrell looked away and down at his paperwork. His feet unrooted from the spot and he made his way to the small desk beside the exam table. He put the papers down, preparing to sit. Thought better of it, and picked the papers back up. He turned to speak directly to Mrs. Rosen.

That was a mistake.

Isabeau Rosen watched him thoughtfully, expectantly. No interest in her eyes, as there shouldn't have been. He clearly spied the diamond rock on her left hand.

Darrell cleared his throat. "What seems to be the problem, Mrs. Rosen?"

"I was in a car accident the other day."

"I'm sorry to hear that."

"Luckily, it was minor. I was cleared from the hospital with only a few minor bruises, but they recommended seeing a chiropractor to assess if there was any trauma to my spine."

Darrell nodded, slipping fully into professional mode. "That was wise," he agreed. Often times, people in car accidents leave the scene on their own accord only to feel the impact a day or two later when the spine finally registers it.

"My Aunt Gale said you were the best, and my cousin Manny agreed."

Darrell only nodded.

"Do you know my cousin?" she asked.

"We were friends."

"*Were*?"

Darrell ignored the question. "I'll need you to turn over." He indicated the exam table.

She did as she was told and lay on her front.

"I'm going to fold your blouse up a bit so that I can have access to your spine. I apologize if my hands are cold." Darrell reached for the bottom of her shirt. When his fingers made contact with her skin a spark zapped his hand.

He jerked his hand away as she jumped.

"Looks like I've got a bit of static cling there," she smiled apologetically over her shoulder.

Darrell nodded giving his hand a shake. He wiped his hand on his pants and reached for her shirt again. This time there was no spark between them. He placed his hand under her shirt and got down to work.

There was nothing remarkable about her spine. He felt

tons of tension in the tendons. "Were you driving while tired, Mrs. Rosen?"

She sighed in answer.

He'd seen it time after time. Women who ran themselves ragged. His mother had been a prime example. He'd had to wrestle her into retirement. Even today, she still insisted on working part time rather than taking his money to relax on.

Darrell knew that when he was married he'd insist that he and his wife share all duties and he'd be more than willing to up his share when he saw that she was overwhelmed. There was no sense in one of them running themselves ragged and then forcing the other one to take over one hundred percent.

No, he knew that the best working relationships were the ones where everyone worked to their strengths. Not exactly an even distribution, but a distribution where they kept an eye out for the other. Mrs. Rosen obviously didn't have that type of arrangement with her husband.

"It's just been busy at work," she said. "And I was rushing to get the kids and—"

"It's okay." Darrell laid a hand at the center of her back and she instantly quieted. He felt some of the tension seep out of her with just that much of a touch. "I'm going to do some adjustments now. The sound may startle you."

Darrell went about contorting Mrs. Rosen's body into the positions to put her spine back into alignment. She didn't jerk from him or tense up. She closed her eyes and allowed him complete control of her body.

Darrell finished his work, giving Mrs. Rosen a light massage to allow the muscles time to resettle. He knew they would come out of alignment in another day or two, so she'd need to schedule a series of appointments until she was healed and the adjustments held.

Darrell grabbed his charts to record his notes. When he looked up at Mrs. Rosen she hadn't moved. She was resting peacefully. Her eyes closed, her head resting on the exam table. This happened every once in a while with patients. Once the pressure released they were able to find peace and slip into sleep.

Looking closely at her, Darrell saw the dark circles under her eyes. He decided to let her sleep for a few minutes more. Even though he no longer cared for her cousin, it didn't mean he didn't feel for the plight of women who tried to take on the world alone.

Just as there were no fairytale princesses there were no super women. Just every day women who took on too much. Which reminded him, he needed to call his mother today.

He pulled a blanket over Mrs. Rosen. A spark of electricity zapped his fingertips when he lightly brushed her skin. She stirred but did not wake. Darrell shook his fingers and left the room.

The sparks are already starting to fly between these two. Find out what happens when Beau wakes up.
*Grab your copy of **Beau: a Cindermama Story** today!*

ACKNOWLEDGMENTS

I couldn't have done this book without my daddy, Joseph "Badd Finger" Johnson, bass player and music producer extraordinaire. I grew up in a funk band and learned at a young age that music has many layers of story within its notes. I carried this lesson with me through my career in media production and now romance writing.

I also need to thank, as always, my critique partner, Leslye Penelope, who cheered me on during the days this manuscript kept getting pushed further and farther back down the schedule and I began to doubt it would ever see the light of day. Another thank you to Kate Marope at Ribbon Marker Services for her beta reading of the rough manuscript.

I wanted to tell this story for two reasons. The first reason comes from my time in television production, namely when I worked with child talent. That scene when Midori and Kimmei are corralled into the Badd Finger showcase auditions is not far fetched, unfortunately. I've seen parents and children do some *thangs* for fame. The second reason comes from my family's myriad of health issues including heart disease and diabetes. Hopefully, I found a way to bring attention to these health concerns that was thoughtful and not preachy. A small change, whether it be in diet or style, can make a huge difference in the quality of your life!

ABOUT INES JOHNSON

Lover of fairytales, folklore, and mythology, Ines Johnson spends her days reimagining the stories of old in a modern world. She writes books where damsels cause the distress, princesses wield swords, and moms save the world.

You can sign up for her mailing list and receive alerts and free reads at http://bit.ly/InesReaders.

ALSO BY INES JOHNSON
Pumpkin
Rumpeled
Beau